COPYRIGHT

ALSO BY LAUREN BLAKELY

Big Rock Series

Big Rock

Mister O

Well Hung

Full Package

Joy Ride

Hard Wood

One Love Series

The Sexy One

The Only One

The Hot One

The Knocked Up Plan

Come As You Are

The Heartbreakers Series

Once Upon a Real Good Time

Once Upon a Sure Thing

Once Upon a Wild Fling

Sports Romance

Most Valuable Playboy

Most Likely to Score

Lucky In Love Series

Best Laid Plans

The Feel Good Factor

Nobody Does It Better

Unzipped

Always Satisfied Series

Satisfaction Guaranteed

Instant Gratification

Overnight Service

Never Have I Ever

Special Delivery

The Gift Series

The Engagement Gift

The Virgin Gift (coming soon)

The Exclusive Gift (coming soon)

Standalone

Stud Finder

The V Card

Wanderlust

Part-Time Lover

The Real Deal

Unbreak My Heart

The Break-Up Album

21 Stolen Kisses

Out of Bounds

Sweet Sinful Nights

Sinful Desire

Sinful Longing

Sinful Love

The Fighting Fire Series

Burn For Me (Smith and Jamie)

Melt for Him (Megan and Becker)

Consumed By You (Travis and Cara)

The Jewel Series

A two-book sexy contemporary romance series

The Sapphire Affair

The Sapphire Heist

ABOUT

Never have I ever been so infuriated by a man I wanted to kiss.

They say opposites attract, but I beg to differ. Combust is more like it. Because every single time I talk to Zach Nolan, I see red.

The too-good-looking, too-smart, too-effortlessly charming single dad who works down the hall from me has turned getting under my skin into a sport. Call it the battle of wits between the wedding planner and the divorce attorney.

Trouble is, when we're forced into closer quarters planning an engagement party for our best friends, I start to see his other sides.

And I fear I'm falling for the enemy.

***

I'm not out to make friends. My goals are simple -- fight till the end for my clients, and my family.

The last thing I need is a vibrant, outgoing, snarky, and surprisingly big-hearted wedding planner to spend my precious free time with...except, watching Piper bond with my daughter just might break down the cinder block walls I've built around my heart these last few years.

Second chances don't come around for guys like me...or do they?

HIS PROLOGUE

Zach

Present day

Don't believe what you hear about me.

I'm not that much of an asshole.

Well, maybe I am.

But, in my defense, I'm paid to be.

The thing is, beneath the he-has-no-heart exterior, I swear I'm not a bad guy. I'll give up my cab for an old lady, I'll hold the elevator for anyone, and I don't ever complain that my neighbor has four dogs, even though that's against the co-op rules.

Because, hey, I like puppies.

So I must be a good guy, despite what some say.

He has a heart carved from ice.

It's as black as night.

He doesn't have that beating organ in his chest.

Those rumors made me who I am today. No one

comes to my office because they want a soft touch or a shoulder to lean on. I'm not a "there, there" guy. I'm the guy they want beside them when they go into battle.

If being the go-to guy in life's roughest times makes me an asshole, slap the title on my office door. I've been called that and worse too many times for it to bother me.

That's the problem.

Because suddenly—as in out-of-the-blue, what-the-fuck-is-this-feeling?—it drives me absolutely crazy what one person thinks.

I don't even want this particular person in my life.

In fact, I want her out of it. She's the enemy.

But by the time the news about London comes, she's superglued to my world, whether I want her here or not.

And I don't want her here. I don't want anyone. Or anything, ever again.

I swear I don't want her.

No matter how good she looked that night when I started to see her in a whole new way.

HER PROLOGUE

Piper
Ten years ago

I have one of those faces that's easy to forget.

Not ugly. Not beautiful.

Simply . . . *pleasant.*

Works for me.

I call it the Blender Factor. I'm like that fruit you put in a smoothie and no one quite knows if it's strawberry or orange or apple. You take a sip, you try to figure out what that taste is, and it's sort of an *everything* fruit.

That's me. I'm the everything fruit.

It comes in handy in all sorts of situations, kind of like a good party trick. Somehow I just fit in.

Like now, at 4:04 p.m. on a Saturday afternoon at the swankiest hair salon in Manhattan, as Adrien finishes Sasha's hair.

His time-warp-fast hands sweep her platinum-blonde locks into a gorgeous updo that looks absolutely stunning when he adds a jewel-studded comb, one I helped the bride pick out several weeks ago at Katherine's flagship jewelry shop on Fifth Avenue. She only tried on seven types of hair accessories, so all in all, that was easy as pie to find.

"The pièce de résistance," Adrien declares, with all the particular panache a silver-fox hair stylist to the chicest brides in Manhattan possesses. After he secures the comb, he kisses his fingertips then blows the kiss to Sasha's hair.

"Wishing you luck. Though of course you don't need it." He swivels the plush leather chair toward the scalloped mirror, giving the bride a view of her finished hair.

Sasha gasps.

I clasp a hand to my chest. "You look beautiful," I tell her. She tilts her chin up and flashes me a pink-glossed smile. "Do I really?" Nerves are stitched tightly through her tone.

I nod vigorously, squeezing her elbow for emphasis. "One hundred percent. Wait. No. You are one hundred fifty percent beautiful and one hundred fifty percent stunning."

She smiles, sighs contentedly, then looks to Adrien for his reassurance too. "What do you think?"

He parts his lips to speak, but a boisterous redhead from one booth over cuts in. "Sasha-bear, you look so damn perfect they're going to need a new word for beautiful fucking bride."

Tania's still slurring her words a touch too much for my taste. No surprise. Tania required the most babysitting at the bachelorette party last night, I was told.

"Yes. She does look *magnifique*," Adrien adds, sliding into his native French.

Tania slashes a bridesmaid-knows-best hand through the air. "No. She's more than magnificent. Sash, you're the most gorgeous bride I have ever seen."

Oops.

Here's the thing. Sasha looks amazing, but there's a fine line to walk with brides, and Tania blundered right over it. Never tell a bride she's the most beautiful ever. They know that's bullshit.

Sasha senses the exaggeration, rolling her eyes. "You're so sweet, Tania-loo, but that's impossible. I can't be prettier than Beyoncé."

Tania stumbles, trying to walk that back. "But I didn't think we were counting Beyoncé."

Sasha shakes her head. "You can't not count Beyoncé. She was the most stunning bride ever, and likely will be until one of the royal boys marries." Sasha looks to me. "Wouldn't you say?"

I'd say there's nothing I want more than to see a royal wedding. Unless it's to be invited to a royal wedding. Or better yet, be hired for a royal wedding by a royal bride. Well, not true. I want Harry or William to invite me. Better yet—I want whoever their brides are to hire me.

But I'm not going to say that.

Because here's the *other* thing about brides.

You can't say she's the most beautiful bride ever, but you also can't acknowledge a world in which she's not.

I lean in closer to look at Sasha in the mirror. Sasha, who's required nine dress fittings; four bridesmaid tailorings; six cake shop visits, each time with a cake spittoon, lest actual cake calories be consumed (by the bride, that is, since you bet your sweet buttercream ass I swallowed rather than spat when it came to cake); twenty floral shop bids; and five check-ins with the tux shop of the "Please don't let Robert mess up the cummerbunds" variety. I smile at the bride, amazed we've made it to within mere hours of her nuptials without a full breakdown. There's only been a couple of half breakdowns so far, so I'm knocking on wood.

Hers is the biggest wedding I've scored in my three years as a wedding planner, thanks to Jessica, one of my friends from college and one of Sasha's bridesmaids. She knows Sasha through work and referred me to her. This is the most important wedding I've planned by miles, and I want it to go perfectly as much as the bride does.

So it is with complete honesty that I say to Sasha, "All I know is when Robert sees you walking down the aisle, he is going to think you're the most beautiful bride. And you look absolutely stunning."

There. That's how you praise a bride. I should know. I was a bridesmaid six times before I turned twenty.

Like a toddler, Sasha opens her arms wide, inviting me in for a hug. "You're the best wedding planner ever, Piper," she says, wrapping her arms around me.

"That's why I won't let you squeeze so long and risk ruining your makeup."

Sasha beams as I disentangle from her. "That's what I'm talking about. You are the best."

I check my watch. It's 4:11. One hour and forty-nine minutes until showtime. "We should go. Let me gather the girls."

I spin around, ordering—nicely—the quintet of bridesmaids out to the waiting limo. "All right, lovely ladies. Let's hit the road and get this beautiful woman hitched."

They squeal in concert as they gather their purses.

"You're going to look breathtaking walking down the aisle," Tania coos as she heads toward the bride.

The other four chime in too—Madison, Praveen, Dawn, and Jessica all bestow their compliments on the bride, like perfect bridesmaids.

"Thank you. Oh my God, I'm so excited for my wedding," Sasha says as she stands.

"You should be. Look at your perfect hair." Tania lifts a hand as if to touch Sasha's do.

Adrien winces and waves her off. "Do not touch the art, love."

Tania stumbles, pitching forward then covering her mouth.

Mayday, Mayday.

Leaping forward, I grab the redhead before she can yak all over the woman of the hour and tug her away just in time to launch her lunch onto the floor.

A wail splits the air.

A shrill, piercing, blood-curdling cry from the bride.

"I can't believe you did this! I told you not to drink so much."

Tania clutches her stomach. "I didn't know the cosmos were so strong," she cries before she christens the tile with more of her stomach contents.

My nose crinkles. Yes, those cosmos were indeed bodybuilder strength.

Sasha stomps her foot. "I knew you were going to ruin my wedding. You're a total bridesmaid-zilla. And you can't walk down the aisle now, barfing all the way up to the front of the cathedral."

Yeah, that'd be bad.

Sasha whips her head to me as I aim Tania as far away from the bride as possible. "What are we going to do, Piper?"

It's the most desperate question I've ever heard from a bride.

Tension flares through every nerve in my body. Worry threatens to strangle me. I need this wedding to go off well. I need it to be talked about. I need to become part of the whisper network in New York's bridal circles.

This is one of those do-or-die moments. This is when I rise to the occasion or fail.

With my arms circled around a heaving bridesmaid, I weigh the options, limited as they are.

Send hungover Tania down the aisle to potentially hurl on the minister, the bride, the mother of the bride, and/or any and all assorted guests.

Let one groomsman make the walk solo, which will

rattle Sasha's OCD need for an even number of men and women.

Enlist someone from the wedding attendee list who's the same size as Tania to stand in.

Run away from the problem.

Or something else entirely.

I rub Tania's back and raise two fingers of my free hand, smile apologetically, and offer myself as tribute. "I'm about the same size."

Dawn's lips part. Praveen emits an impressed "Whoa." Madison claps. Jessica shrieks. And Sasha beams, like I've delivered Ryan Gosling on a platter to her. "Oh my God, you *are* the same size. That's amazing. And I know you'll look incredible in lavender."

Yep. That's part of that blend factor. That's what everyone always says about me. I'm always about the size of the dress that somebody else can no longer wear. I always look good in every hideous color because, again, my face is merely pleasant.

Sasha's big blue eyes plead with me. "Please, Piper. Can you please be my final bridesmaid? I have to have the same number of bridesmaids as groomsmen."

I cast my gaze downward at abject Tania, her lovely updo already undone as Adrien's assistant tuts and flutters, attempting to clean up a mess no one wants on the tiled floor of a Parisian-styled Upper East Side salon.

Tania moans, dry heaving. Maybe there was moonshine in her cosmo.

Adrien's gray eyes make a quick appraisal of my brunette shoulder-length do. "Piper, I can have your hair done in a flash. Give me five minutes and I will make you a bridesmaid."

By 4:15, my hair is swept up on the sides.

"It's like it was meant to be," Sasha says.

That's because I'm the everything fruit.

I slip Adrien an extra Franklin as we go, and I slide into my new role as the replacement bridesmaid.

Evidently it's now one of the many à la carte services offered by this up-and-coming wedding planner.

Later that evening, my heart rate has slowed to normal, I've ticked most of the items off the wedding checklist, and I've nearly reached the end of a successful socialite event.

Like a good understudy, I slipped into the role unnoticed by the audience, following the choreography to a T as I walked down the aisle, elbow linked with the fourth groomsman.

All that's left is the toast, the dance, and the cake.

And the dance is going to be perfect here on this rooftop garden in Gramercy Park with twinkling lights flickering along the wrought-iron fence as a swing band plays love songs.

Jessica pops over, squeezes my shoulder, and whispers, "You're going to be a rock star wedding planner, girl."

"You're going to be a rock star lit agent," I tell her, and she already is, inking deals left and right for her clients, just as she'd told our friends she would when we plotted our futures over fro-yo and beer in the campus snack shop. "Also, thank you so much for the referral. This is golden."

She shakes her head, flicking some strands of silky black hair from her face. "No, *thank you* for being my wedding planner too."

I shoot her a curious look. I didn't even think Jessica was dating anyone. "Are you holding out on me? Who's Mr. Chen?"

She laughs. "Who knows? I haven't met him yet. I'm just planning ahead. Someday I'm going to hire you. Also, you're a witch for looking so good in lavender. I look like a curtain, and you look like a Febreze commercial."

I arch a brow. "I'm not so sure Febreze is an improvement over window coverings."

"Febreze is fabulous." She laughs, shakes her hips, then points to a groomsman, adding in a wink.

"Go get him, witch," I say.

"I plan to get him and bed him."

"Yeah, I figured as much."

True to form, Jessica has the groomsman wrapped around her finger in minutes, chatting him up on the other side of the garden.

A little later, a fork clinks against a glass, and the best man rises. Sasha gazes at him intently during the speech, watching as he toasts to the happy couple.

I breathe deeply. I did this. Wedding number ten, and a bona fide success. As a Sam Cooke tune floats through the night air and the dancing begins, I head to the bar in the corner and ask for an iced tea.

"Coming right up," the bartender says.

"And I'll take a scotch, Ted." I know that voice, and I angle toward the deep, raspy rumble. It belongs to one of those *too good-looking* men.

You know the kind.

Cheekbones carved by the gods.

Eyes an unfair shade of blue.

A jawline that could cut granite. Name? What's his name? It's been a few years since I saw him at the campus snack shop with the crew.

He raps his knuckles on the bar. "Ted, what's the over/under on this one working out?" Mr. Too Good-Looking asks the bartender.

Shock snaps my gaze fully to him, wide-eyed then narrowing in disbelief. "Excuse me? Are you placing bets on my wedding?"

He turns to me. Oh, God. I remember him now. Zach Nolan, the superhero look-alike from our group of friends, and the first to marry. He was the cockiest bastard in college, and based on his opening line to the bartender, it looks like he's still operating at the same level of dickhead. I don't know how he ever snagged a kind, smart woman like Anna to marry him. I swear, if I'd been the keeper of our circle in college, I would not have let him in. But alas, I was on the caboose end, and he was a few years older than Jessica and I were, so I had no say.

Zach looks at me with suspicion. "Your wedding? You're not in white, Miss Lavender."

I groan inside. Men who call women nicknames have another think coming. "Oh my God. You mean this

you see how she gazed at him during the speech? Like he was the one she wanted. As for the groom, I see a guy who doesn't respect his bride. And I see a couple who wants everything but each other. I see a perfect wedding . . ." He cuts his gaze to me knowingly, and fine, pride does suffuse me because, hello, this is a glorious event and I created this moment. "And this seamless, flawless, gorgeous wedding," he goes on, "is simply to cover up a perfect lie of a marriage. Who the hell kicks a friend out of the wedding party because she was hungover?"

"How do you know that?" I ask, indignant.

"Heard the groom talking. Seems he thought it was a crap move."

"And what should she have done with a barfing bridesmaid, since you know so much about doomed weddings?"

"Give her some ginger ale and crackers and have her do her job."

"That's all anyone is trying to do, his or her job. So what the hell is yours? Irritate the wedding planner?"

Dipping his hand into the inside pocket of his tailored suit jacket, he hands me a card.

I take it, annoyed, but I don't look at it. "Business cards? Do we still do those?"

He chuckles. "You never liked me, did you?"

"You're just now figuring this out?"

"No. I'm just confirming it."

"Why do you care? You're married."

"Happily," he adds.

"So yours is the one marriage no one gets to judge or place bets on?"

He squares his shoulders. "Mine will last. I'm not worried."

A shocked laugh bursts from deep within me. "You better mark your words."

A shrug is his only answer. "I'm just saying, Mrs. Nolan didn't long for the best man. I didn't ignore her at our wedding. And she didn't give a rat's ass if the bridesmaid was upchucking."

"If you're so happy, why are you standing here and judging everyone else?"

"It's what I do."

Intrigued, I flip over his card. "You're a divorce attorney. Why am I not surprised?" Everything about Zach Nolan makes perfect sense. "That's why you're here. You're like an ambulance chaser."

He gestures to the setting, as if to say I called it right. "And you put the bodies on the stretcher."

Red billows from the corner of my eyes. Fumes roll off me.

Must disengage.

I pretend I'm on a miniature golf course, focusing on nailing the par. I'm cool, calm, and dead-focused. No time for distractions. I tap the purple ball and watch it go.

I draw a deep breath, plaster on my best society smile, and extend a hand. "Good to see you again, Zach. I hope you never need the services of someone like yourself."

"I won't," he says, cocky through and through. He checks his watch. "And on that note, I need to go. The wife's due any day."

"Wish Anna luck from me," I say, because his wife is a sweetheart.

"Will do."

He leaves, and I couldn't be happier a year later that Sasha and her hubby are still together.

Even if they're hanging on by a thread.

1

ZACH

Present day

A gruff voice right outside the door shouts, "Delivery!"

I glance around the front room of the office. Where the hell is Edward?

The bearded guy in the brown uniform steps into the doorway, hauling a big box.

"Thanks. You can just leave it here," I say, gesturing to Edward's empty desk. Where the hell is he? Would it kill him to actually work, say, at his damn desk?

Evidently.

He prefers working anyplace else, as far as I can tell. I only popped out of my office hoping it was the Thai food delivery man.

But there's no spicy beef salad in this gigantic box. The guy thrusts a tablet at me, asking for a signature. I sign, thank him, and say goodbye.

I survey the box. I've no clue what this is or who sent

it. Our deliveries are of the paper variety, not the boxed kind, and not from . . .

Wait. The side of the box says it's from Lucky Rice? What the hell? I peer at the sticker from the manufacturer. Twenty containers of . . .

Are you kidding me?

I check the delivery address and groan. "Edward? Are you hiding under your desk again?"

The office is empty.

"I'll do it myself. Don't worry. That's why I hired you. So I could do everything myself while you get your hipster drinks. Also, no one needs that much tea."

Talking to an empty desk is unsatisfying. It's just me talking into the void.

I grab the box, carry it over to the door at the end of the second-floor hallway of the brownstone in Gramercy Park that's the nine-to-five home of several small businesses. The sign on the ajar door reads "Wedding Designs by Piper" in calligraphy font, and I rap on it.

"I have one of your boxes again."

A voice calls out from a back office. "Ooh! I hope it's a sample from Vera's new spring line."

Piper pops out of her office wearing—what the hell is that?

I arch a brow. "Is it Halloween?"

She shoots me a withering glare. She's most excellent at withering glares. "No. It's May. There's this thing called a calendar. You look at it and it tells you the dates. I know it's hard to figure out sometimes, but there are people who can help you, Zach."

I roll my eyes. "Why are you wearing that thing? You look like a Peep."

"Many people enjoy Peeps, so thank you very much." She curtsies in her cloud of yellow.

I wave at her with my free hand. "I can't stand Peeps."

"Shocking. Utterly shocking."

"Seriously, is someone actually going to wear that to a wedding? It's like it's made of baby chick fluff."

She sighs, picking at the cloud of skirt material. "One of my brides is considering it for the bridal party. She sent it to me and asked for my opinion. I tried it on to get the full effect."

"And you're going to tell her the effect is that of a life-size Easter bonnet walking down the aisle?"

"No. I'm going to tell her it's lovely, but not quite right. Because there's this thing called tact. I like to use it when I have conversations with, for instance, *people*. Now what can I help you with?"

"Your rice cakes are here." I set the box on the coffee table in her reception area, next to a set of mini-golf clubs and a container of purple golf balls. More weird wedding favors probably. I scratch my head. "I have to say, I've fielded a lot of deliveries for you since Steven gave us a deal on this office space. You've had shipments of purple, orange, and polka-dot dresses; of Jordan almonds, which, incidentally, no one on the entire planet likes; of pickles, which are the oddest wedding favor I've ever heard of. Oh, and the *Lord of the Rings* ears for that bride who wanted everyone to dress as if they were from Middle Earth.

But rice cakes? Are these decorations? Appetizers? Favors? Variations on a wedding cake? If so, then this is clearly the end times for the entire institution of marriage."

Piper sighs as she grabs her keys to slice open the box. "Weddings aren't doomed. Marriage isn't doomed. I just have a bride who's requiring her wedding party to go on a diet. They can only drink water and eat rice cakes. Those who aren't successful need to wear pashmina shawls to cover up their fat arms."

I blink in surprise. I'm speechless.

Piper holds up her keys as if in surrender. "Those were the bride's words, not mine. I don't care about fat arms. Or chubby bridesmaids. Or porky best men."

I rein in a sliver of a grin. "Good to know you're not a sizeist."

"Unfortunately, this bride is."

I rub my palms together. "All right, I can't resist. This is too easy. I have to go all in on this one not lasting longer than—"

She cuts me off. "Don't. Don't go there. I'm doing everything I can to stop her."

I park my hands on my hips. "C'mon. Even you have to admit this has zero—"

She shakes her head. "Nope. Do not spew your negative energy on my bride."

"She started it. That's like one of those bridal requests that goes viral. Like that one where the bride wanted everyone to wear orange suede pants and green turtlenecks or something."

Piper scoffs, but there's a laugh tucked into it. "'She

started it'? Seriously? Go back to your lair, Grim Reaper."

"Enjoy the rice cakes." I make a gagging sound.

"I'd say enjoy the spicy beef salad, only it was delivered here an hour ago when I was out, and when I returned at the same time your assistant popped by—in a fit of mortification that he might have to serve up bad news to his ogre of a boss—he was so devastated to learn that it was cold that he put on his running shoes and took off to the Thai place to get you another one."

I snap my fingers. "That's where he is."

"Oh wait. You thought he was off ignoring you and getting his Earl Grey latte?"

"No," I say, denying, denying, denying. Of course I thought he was getting an Earl Grey latte. He inhales that wretched beverage.

"And he was actually serving his master."

"Hey, he wanted the job."

"And you've successfully terrorized him."

"That's what lawyers do."

"Good luck with your spicy beef salad. I hope it's burn-your-tongue-off hot."

I turn around. "Good luck with the rice cake–zilla. I give it a month."

* * *

Later that evening, after I finish the spicy beef salad, tell Edward to get an Earl Grey latte on me as a thanks for his problem-solving, and finish reviewing some documents, the sitter brings my daughter by the office.

The first thing Lucy asks is if she can see Piper.

"Really? You don't want to read here in my office while I finish these papers?"

Lucy laughs, shaking her head. "Her office is filled with pretty things. Yours is so blah it's like a double serving of blah."

"Well, just take me down a few notches, why don't you?"

She waves happily and trots down the hall.

I stand, reach into my wallet, and grab several bills to pay Miranda, a clever, fifty-something woman who's been taking care of kids in Manhattan for ages. She's one of those people who knows every activity, every class, and every workshop for kids at every museum. She also knows my sister and worked for her when her kids were younger.

"Thank you so much, Mr. Nolan. I'll pick her up tomorrow too? I can take her and Henry to the open studio hour at the Whitney Museum."

"That would be great."

She turns to go then spins back around, a little twinkle in her brown eyes. "Also, one of the ladies at school was asking about you. Hannah's mother . . ." Her voice trails off, like she's just going to leave that little chocolate chip right here on the table to see if I'll pick it up.

I don't. Nothing against chocolate chips—or a pretty single mom I've run into once or twice at school events —I'm just not interested. "How good of her to inquire."

"You know, it might be fun to take the kids to the pottery class together this—"

"I have plans this weekend. Thank you. See you tomorrow. Same time."

Miranda leaves, and a few minutes later, I hear my daughter announce that she now looks like a baby chick and she's swimming in this dress, then she giggles, and Piper laughs too.

I smile, liking the sound of Lucy's laughter.

2

ZACH

On Wednesday evening later that week, I'm multitasking, dashing some pepper onto the chicken as I sauté the meat while cradling the phone. "I promise you, Taylor, I'm going to protect your assets like a shark. A tiger shark. The most feared tiger shark in the seas." I toss in some rosemary, and the pan sizzles. "You started your bistro before the marriage. I know he thinks he's entitled, but now you have someone tougher on your side, and he won't want to deal with me." I add a pinch of salt. "Because he's going to be an overcooked chicken when I'm done with him."

Taylor chuckles lightly on the other end of the line, and it's the first time I've heard my client emit any sort of laugh since she came to me with her case after the "soft touch" attorney she first hired suggested she discuss asset distribution with her soon-to-be ex over a nice Chianti, since Chianti makes everything better. His words, evidently.

"With a balsamic glaze and skewered with a sprig of rosemary through the heart," Taylor, who's a chef, adds.

"Exactly," I say as I flip the chicken breast with a spatula. This chicken is a perfect shade of golden because I don't see the point of cooking unless you can cook well. "New York might be an equitable distribution state, but your restaurant is separate property."

My son, Henry, appears in the kitchen and tugs at the hem of my shirt. "Daddy, can you please check my math homework?"

I turn to the little towhead who's thrusting a sheet of . . . basic addition? Oh, hell yeah. I can definitely do that.

"Just a sec, buddy. Let Daddy finish his call," I tell Henry, and he flashes a gap-toothed grin then runs to the living room. Because why walk when you can run?

"You really think we can protect the restaurant and still get the apartment?" Taylor asks.

I add some artichoke hearts and green beans to the dish, stirring as I reassure her. "You started it with your own money, prior to the marriage." I take a beat before launching into the next topic. "As for the apartment, do you truly want that, given what went down in it?"

What went down was Taylor's husband banging his assistant every night while Taylor was making butternut squash soup at the Tribeca restaurant down the street.

She sighs. "I'll ask my shrink. My shrink thinks we should try to have a collaborative divorce."

I grit my teeth. Of course the shrink thinks that, and in many cases, I recommend it too. But not in this one. "If you give him an inch, he'll take a mile. Do you want that? You came to me because you didn't want to settle this over Chianti and candles and affirmations."

Her voice is stretched thin when she answers with a shaky "No."

"I didn't think so. But look, if you decide you want to be able to hold hands with him when this is done, I'll send you down *that* path. If you want to make sure he stares down at the carcass of his dead marriage with regret and pain—as much pain as you felt when you first found those filthy, disgusting text messages he sent to his assistant—I can march down *this* path."

A small laugh is her answer. "The dead carcass path." She takes a deep breath. "Does that mean you'll rip him to shreds?"

Well, that isn't entirely what a good divorce attorney does, but the perception sometimes is what matters. "If you want him torn to shreds, I'll do my damnedest. Now listen, I need to finish up this chicken and veggie masterpiece before the residents grow too restless. We'll meet on Friday, review everything, and finalize whether you want the kumbaya path or the carcass-torn-to-tatters route."

I say goodbye as my daughter yanks open the utensil drawer, reaches for forks, and sets the counter without even being asked.

I put the phone down and gesture to Lucy, amazed. "Fine. I'll admit it. You're a perfect child."

As she slides a butter knife neatly to the right of a plate, she stares at me, her blue eyes inquisitive. "Daddy, why do you want to rip everyone to shreds?"

Ah, I long for the days when I didn't have to have

after-hours conversations with clients in front of my kids. But then again, I long for a lot of things I can't have anymore.

I turn off the burner, kneel, and dot a kiss to Lucy's forehead. "Because it's how I pay for your school, and for your brother's school. Because it's how I pay for our life. Because it's how I afford everything."

"By being mean?"

I bare my teeth. "Daddy's a shark." I pretend to nibble her arm.

She squeals. "Ouch, ouch. Don't eat my whole arm."

I take another bite of her elbow. "I only want half of it, I swear."

She narrows her eyes at me. "Now, Daddy, is half my arm equitable distribution?"

My jaw drops. Holy shit. My ten-year-old is starting to understand the finer details of New York divorce law.

"Daddy, can you check my math now?" Henry shouts from the living room. "Lucy wouldn't do it."

Lucy heaves the indignant sigh of an almost tween. "I told you I would do it as soon as I set the table. You're such a dweebmeister."

Dweeb is a popular insult now? Or rather, dweebmeister? I've barely mastered Instagram lingo, and now I have to learn trash talk. "Henry, my man, bring it on." I smack my palm against the island counter, and he motors on over, shoving the paper at me as I serve the chicken and veggies.

"But what if Taylor's husband doesn't deserve being ripped to shreds?"

I look up from the paper, meeting Lucy's curious gaze as I keep pace with our ping-pong conversation. "But what if he does?" I toss back. "He was a bad husband. That's not cool, is it?"

She shakes her head, her brunette ponytail swishing back and forth. "No. That's totally not cool. You should be a good husband. *You* were a good husband, right?"

"Of course he was," Henry answers, picking up his fork. "He was the best, right, Daddy?"

"Obviously." I set down the math paper, focusing on *that*, on questions with clear-cut answers. "What's fifty-two plus eighteen?"

"Seventy, obviously," Lucy answers.

"Luce, let Henry answer."

"It's seventy, obviously," he says, mimicking her.

I stab my finger against the page. "Just fix that one problem and everything is perfect."

I sit down to join them, and we eat, catching up on the details about life in second and fourth grades, respectively.

After Lucy finishes her chicken and puts down her fork, she furrows her brow. "Hannah's older sister told us at recess that we need to get tampons soon. Do I need to get tampons?"

I freeze, fork midair, jaw hanging open. Where in the single parent handbook does it say your prepubescent daughter is going to ask about period supplies *well before she's supposed to*?

"You just turned ten, sweetie pie," I say, dodging the question, because holy fuck. Is ten when girls get their periods?

I grab my phone and google it.

Average onset of menses—okay, seriously, who names this shit? That is the worst medical term ever—is twelve and a half. I have time.

I put the phone down. "First of all, not yet. But when you do, we'll deal with it, okay?"

That seems sufficient for her. "Sounds good."

And it'll have to be good enough for me since it buys me enough time to research the hell out of how to handle *that*.

"Daddy, are you still a shark?" Henry asks.

Lucy sighs as if she just can't take him asking that again. "Of course he's still a shark, Henry. He's the sharkiest shark in Manhattan."

"Can't you be a lion instead?" Henry bares his teeth, tosses his head back, and emits a roar. A very high-pitched Tiny Tim one.

I ruffle his hair as I swing behind him to pick up plates. "When it comes to you, I'll be your lion, your shark, and your king cobra. You've always got me on your side. Now, help clean."

Henry wiggles back and forth, sticking out his tongue like a snake and hissing.

"Henry, don't do that," Lucy chides as she slides a plate into the dishwasher.

"Do what?"

"Pretend to be a snake."

"Why?"

"Because I don't care for snakes," Lucy says primly.

"But I'm not really a snake." Henry points out with the cool and unassailable logic of a seven-year-old.

"True, he's not a snake, Luce," I add.

"But we have an understanding, gentlemen." Since she declared herself "woman of the house," it's become important to her to put us men in our place.

"And what is that? I don't recall a memo of understanding about snakes." I scratch my head. "Can you show it to me?"

"We had a verbal agreement. We don't play with real snakes or pretend snakes. We don't pretend to be snakes in any way, shape, or form. Don't you boys know that?"

Henry rinses his plate. "Fine, then Daddy can be a bear."

"Mama bears are fierce," Lucy points out.

I offer a smile, one that's filled with far too many memories. "They are. They're the fiercest thing I've ever known."

3

PIPER

My heels click against the sidewalk as I press my cell phone harder to my ear, as if that will emphasize my point to the person on the other end. "No. The artichokes need to have just the right amount of purple to their leaves. They need to be the center of the centerpiece, surrounded by the dahlias and the daisies. But none of those filler leaves or twigs. Bud, you know that."

Bud sighs from the other end of Manhattan. "I just wish you didn't hate twigs so much."

"I have nothing against twigs. I love twigs. Twigs come from trees, and trees are awesome." I scan the concrete jungle around me as I march up treeless Park Avenue on Thursday afternoon. "What I wouldn't give to hug a tree right now. Yet, I don't want tree branches in my farm-to-table centerpieces."

"Farm to table," he groans. "The worst combination of three words ever created. It's made my job as a florist a living Hades."

I laugh. "Remember the good old days when couples just wanted mums or stargazer lilies?"

He shudders over the phone line. "No one ever wanted stargazer lilies."

"Fine, peonies," I concede.

He sighs wistfully. "What I wouldn't give for peonies to make a comeback. Just this morning I had to try to make an attractive arrangement out of kumquat, cabbage, and brussels sprouts for a wedding this weekend in Prospect Park."

I scrunch my brow, trying to picture that unusual assemblage. "I'm getting stuck on the brussels sprouts. I think I'm going to require a photo."

"Never. It's like a photo of all my pain. I've had to become a fruit and vegetable broker these last few years. I became a florist because I like to arrange flowers. You know, lilies, mums, roses. Not cabbage patches."

"Are you sure you weren't tempted to eat the brussels sprouts? Just steal a few from the arrangement?"

"Raw brussels sprouts? No, thank you. They're only in the arrangement because they're in season. It's like the bride is showing off that she knows what veggies are growing this time of year. I might have to retire soon."

I cringe at the thought. He's my best florist. "Look on the bright side. All I'm asking you for are purple-leafed artichokes. And you know I'll Instagram the hell out of them," I say, dangling my Insta-following at him, since it's not too shabby for a wedding planner.

My other line beeps, and the screen flashes that it's

Jonathan from the Luxe Hotel, who's next on my call list. "Bud, give me one minute. I'll be right back. And we'll plot the future of artichokes." I switch to the other line as the May sun beats down on me.

"Jonathan, I bet you're calling to tell me you'll have the Raphael Room for a ten percent discount, since I'm your best client?" I flutter my lashes, even though he can't see me.

"You're killing me." He heaves a sigh. A most dramatic sigh. "And you say you want it in September?"

"Naturally. I know that's tight, but I'm sure you'll find it's free, say, the second weekend?"

"Why do I bend over backward for you?" I can hear him flipping through the pages on his register. He's one of those old-school guys who prefers a datebook rather than a computer calendar.

"Because you're flexible. And because you love me."

"No. Because you bring me the best brides."

"Whose photos you use to advertise your hotel as one of the city's premier wedding sites," I add, reminding him of why I deserve the date of choice, plus a discount.

"Then it's yours."

I pump a fist. "I love you madly, Jonathan. More than any other hotel event manager in the city."

"I bet that's what you say to all the boys when they give you their best rooms."

"Keep giving me good rates, and you'll be at the top of my list."

"That's the only place any event manager wants to be."

And that's how I like it. I want the hotel managers, restaurateurs, and wedding venue coordinators wanting to partner with me. Most do, and I've worked my ass off to reach this point.

I say goodbye and return to Bud Rose, diving right back into the thick of it. "Bud, I feel for you. But the world is changing, and you either change with it or get left behind, sweetie. You don't want to be left behind, do you?" I ask, since he seems to need a pep talk, and that's the least I can do for my main flower wizard.

"I don't. You're right," he admits.

"Good. Then the way I see it is this: there's no one on the eastern seaboard who can arrange pomegranates, artichokes, figs, and mums like you, with your floral artistry. So embrace the farm-to-table change."

He chuckles. "Flattery will get you everywhere."

"Wonderful. Right now, I need to get a decent price on the artichoke arrangement."

He huffs. "I can give you a ten percent discount if you let me add twigs."

I huff right back. "You can add twigs for fifteen percent."

After a few minutes of Manhattan-style negotiation, wheeling and dealing as I weave my way through crowds of New Yorkers barking on cell phones, we agree on twigs and terms.

"Long live artichokes," I say.

"And figs and brussels sprouts."

"That's the spirit."

I hang up, and a few minutes later, I reach my destination, pushing open the door and sweeping in to see my favorite man. I give Adrien a kiss on each cheek. "I missed you."

He pats my hair. "Your hair missed me. It's been four weeks. That's far too long." He flicks the ends of my locks. "When are you going to let me give you red highlights? I swear your hair is calling out for it." He leans in close, pretending to whisper to my brown hair. "Give me red color. Please make me more beautiful."

I clutch my hair, keeping it out of his grasp. "Never."

He sighs heavily. "Darling, some wine-red highlights will only make you more beautiful."

I scoff. "I don't aspire to beauty."

"What do you aspire to, then? Greatness? Dominance? Becoming an all-powerful force of nature? Oh wait, you already are."

I smile. He knows me so well. "The last one, of course. At least, I try to achieve it."

He squeezes my shoulder affectionately as he guides me to the chair by the basin. "Speaking of, how are my brides doing?"

I love that he feels the same ownership of them as I do. That he refers to them as his, just as I refer to them as mine. We've worked on countless weddings together over the years, and he is my comrade in arms.

"Fabulous," I say, and I rattle off the names of some of the brides he's styled. "Marie just found out she's pregnant."

He coos in delight. "And you had to be a last-minute bridesmaid for her too."

I stepped in at that wedding when her best friend

from China wasn't going to make it in time. "Connecting flights are the worst."

"And how is Brenna? She looked so lovely in that A-line dress."

"She just had twins, and she could probably fit in that dress again soon if she wanted."

He gives a delighted "Ooh."

"And Gigi and her husband just took off on another trip to Italy."

"Can I stow away in their bags, please?"

"You and me both," I say as I close my eyes and relax into the sensation of strong fingers lathering shampoo in my hair. "I want to go to Tuscany."

"Then you should go, love. What's stopping you?"

A laugh bursts from my chest. "Oh, you know, responsibilities and all that."

"Someday you'll go to Tuscany."

"Someday," I say wistfully.

"And what about Jessica?" His voice rises with hopefulness as we resume our catch-up. "Will she be needing my services?"

I cross my fingers, hopeful that one of my closest friends has finally found the one. Opening my eyes, I answer, "She's been in London the last year for work. I hope she's met some fabulous Englishman, and he'll whisk her away to his estate or castle." When we've had the chance to catch up, being an ocean apart, Jessica's hinted that there might be someone special, but she hasn't spilled the details yet.

"Jessica would look amazing as a lady of the manor.

Maybe her man will be a castle-owning earl or a baron or a Windsor."

"Pretty sure if he were a Windsor, we could arrest her for robbing the cradle. But yes, it would be just like her to score a prince and a fabulous palace."

"Isn't that what we all want?"

"Or just to look as good at our weddings as Kate and Meghan did."

He hums his approval. "I still can't decide who was prettier."

"Don't try to pick. Both were beautiful in their own unique way." I sigh happily, picturing my happy place: a royal wedding. I've only rewatched Meghan and Harry's five times. "In any case, Jessica texted me the other night that she's coming back to New York soon, but she won't give me a date."

I grab my phone from my pocket and show him her texts.

Jessica: Witch! I'm going to be back in NYC soon, soon, soon.

Piper: When, when, when?

Jessica: I'll tell you the second I know! But I promise you'll be seeing my smiling face before too long.

Piper: You're so cruel to leave me so long without you.

Jessica: I am, but life is good, and I can't wait to catch up with you on everything. I miss you terribly.

Piper: I miss you madly, awfully, and also desperately.

Jessica: But if you had to pick one adverb to define your missing, which would it be?

Piper: Abjectly.

Jessica: Good one!

"See what I have to deal with?"

"She's a double witch."

"Try triple. But I love her, even when she's stirring her cauldron and not sharing her newts."

"And I love her hair. I want to do her hair for her wedding."

I shoot him a smile. "I want to braid her hair at, like, every sleepover from now till the end of time. So, I feel you."

He chuckles. "Please tell me you don't have sleep-overs anymore."

"Not with girlfriends."

"Does that mean there's a boyfriend sharing a pillow? And you haven't told me?" He bats my shoulder with an admonishing elbow before he returns to washing.

I scoff. "Please. Obviously, there's no one."

He arches a brow as he rinses the shampoo. "Are you sure? You've tried to keep secrets from me in the past. Are you keeping them again?"

I swallow roughly, trying to avoid thoughts of

secrets—the ones I keep and the ones I've shared. "Never from you."

"You better not."

"I swear there's no one. Besides, I'm focused on my sister and my brides and everything I need to get done."

He hums as he works in the conditioner. "You say that, but someday you'll walk down the aisle and let me do your hair."

I flash him the biggest grin. "Please. You'll do more than my hair. You'll be my man of honor."

"Ah, you always know the way to my heart." He plants a kiss on my cheek. "And what's the latest with Pukezilla?" He nearly always asks me about her, since there's nearly always something to say.

"She's getting married again. Third in ten years." Tania didn't hire me for any of her weddings. No surprise there. But Jessica kept me updated, since Jessica knows everything.

"Seems like it was only yesterday when she was begging me to do her hair for her first."

"And you wisely refused."

"A stylist must have standards. Yak once in my salon, shame on you. Yak twice, shame on me."

"Rules to live by."

"And how is Sasha doing on number two?"

"Good. Let's hope it sticks this time."

In the end, Sasha's marriage self-destructed, just like Zach predicted. The wedding fortune-teller was off by a full month, though, so I took some solace in the fact that Sasha and Robert hung on for all of 396 days.

But Zach was right about everything else. Sasha had

a hankering for the best man, and now she's married to him. She loved my work and hired me for that wedding too. Second time's a charm, I hope.

Zach's been accurate about a few other weddings too, as he plays his swami of doom game. I still hate him for it, even though lately it's become harder to do.

I've tried, trust me. Especially since I now share office space with him on the same floor of the most adorable brownstone in Gramercy Park. That came about thanks to a fabulous deal our mutual friend Steven offered us on real estate a few years ago. Charlie, Zach, and I jumped all over that opportunity, and we have the same business address, though Charlie's rarely around.

As Adrien rinses conditioner from my hair, I do my best to shove thoughts of Zach and his frustratingly spot-on wedding predictions from my head.

But it's tough. I do wish more unions lasted. I wish that half of my work didn't flame out, or worse, go up in a five-alarm fire a few years after the *I do's*. Or in my mom's case, a few months after each one.

"It's an occupational hazard," I muse, thinking out loud.

Adrien moves me to the chair and begins snipping my hair. "What is, love?"

"That so many marriages fail."

He sighs knowingly. "So many do, like, oh, say, my first. But so many don't too."

I shoot him a sympathetic look. "Your first husband didn't deserve you."

"That is definitely true."

"But even so, I just wish that *most* lasted."

"Of course, but what can you do? Don't let it get you down. I try not to let the end of mine ruin my outlook. Look at it as a good thing at the end of the day. A marriage might fail, but then the bride and groom often try again with someone new. It is a universal condition that we humans keep reaching for the brass ring of love."

"Yes, I suppose that's true. Most do want to take another ride on the merry-go-round of love."

"Love and beauty. They make the world go around."

But there's something else, too, that makes us keep moving forward.

Family. That tie can make us go, go, go.

When I'm finished with my cut, looking suitably pleasant as always, I say goodbye and head to my next appointment, a meeting with a stationery shop, the final item on today's nearly finished to-do list.

As I walk down the block, my phone brays.

My sister's ringtone.

My pulse quickens.

Please let it be good news.

I answer. "Hey, Paige."

She greets me with tears.

4

ZACH

While Lucy brushes her teeth at bedtime, I find an unread text from my buddy Charlie.

Charlie: Basketball tomorrow? The courts near you?

I glance at the date. Shoot. He sent this two days ago. On Tuesday.

Zach: Sorry, man. Missed the message. Hope you found someone else who abused you thoroughly on the court, beat your ego into a bloody pulp.

Charlie responds immediately. He's good at that, unlike me evidently. But in my defense, Lucy downloaded some game to my phone, and I can't find anything on it anymore. Between all the filters and trivia games and list keepers, it's a miracle I can locate my email most days.

Charlie: No. I found some ten-year-olds. Schooled them.

Zach: You lie. Even grade-schoolers kick your ass on the court.

Charlie: Why do I bother inviting you to do anything anymore? I swear, I see your kids more than I see you. But I don't squander my time with them. When I took Henry to the bookstore the other day, I showed him all the money and investing guides that could open up worlds to him. Never too early to start indoctrination. But where were you as I taught my godson the finer points of becoming a tech genius?

Zach: I believe I was taking my daughter to her gymnastics class. Thanks again for training him on how to be the Zuck at age seven. You're a world-class godparent.

Charlie: Please. Call me Godfather.

Zach: I will only call you Godfather in person so I can say it with an accent. In any case, I'll check my calendar and find time for basketball soon.

Charlie: Gee, thanks. Appreciate you checking the calendar. Maybe in November you can fit your old friend Charlie in.

Zach: Fine. We'll go tomorrow at lunch. But I will destroy you.

Charlie: Excellent.

Zach: It's amazing how you can be so damn good at so many things and suck at basketball. And yet you always want to keep playing. You're a glutton for punishment.

Charlie: That I am. Also, my sister said to tell you she has a friend she wants to set you up with.

Zach: And in other news, how's work?

Charlie: Message received. The hunt is on for the next great start-up. And I'm working on a group dinner soon. Would be great if you could come.

Zach: Let me know the date and I'll see about a sitter. But if the dinner is just a ruse for meeting your sister's friend, I will know.

Charlie: And would that be so bad?

Zach: Yes. I don't want to be set up.

Charlie: Got it, but you should know ALL OUR FEMALE FRIENDS are salivating for the chance to set you up.

Zach: Then they should get drool bibs.

I set down the phone as Lucy finishes, then I check on Henry. He's curled up with his dinosaur blanket, so Lucy and I settle in to read a book in her room. When I finish the *Goosebumps* story—a brilliant performance by me, costarring all my character voices—I tap the cover. "Do you think it's ironic that you hate snakes, but love being scared by ventriloquist dolls coming to life? Those are super creepy. Way worse than snakes, in my opinion."

She snuggles deeper into her pillow. "But see, that's your opinion. I have a different one."

"And you contend ventriloquist dolls aren't creepy?"

She wiggles her eyebrows. "They're creepy awesome."

"And the creatures who shall not be named are not creepy awesome?"

She shakes her head. "Nope. They're creepy gross. Creepy gross is unacceptable."

I set the book on her shelf. "It's confirmed. You're definitely my child. There's nothing you won't argue about."

"It's not an argument. It's a discussion."

I kiss her forehead. "And you keep making my point."

"Fine. But it's your fault," she says, laughing.

I laugh too. "I accept the blame. Now go to sleep."

"I will." She stretches across her bed, reaching for a notebook. The front cover says "Dream a Big Dream" in a curly silver font. Lucy loves notebooks and has written more letters to herself than she can count. "But first, I want to show you something," she says with a mixture of worry and excitement.

"A new letter?"

She shakes her head and bounces a little nervously on her mattress. "It's a list."

That makes sense. She doesn't show me her letters. Lists? Yes. Letters? No. She doesn't offer, and I don't ask. They're personal.

I rub my palms together. "All right, little list-maker. What have we got on this one?" I place the back of my hand against my forehead like I can read her fortune. "Wait. Don't tell me. It's a list of favorite cupcake bakeries that you want me to take you to."

Laughing, she shakes her head. "I did that last week. I showed you that one!"

"And I took you to Sunshine Bakery."

"And the strawberry shortcake cupcake was *so* good."

"It was delish." I furrow my brow. "So then, is this a list of names for the dog you want to adopt someday?"

"You saw that too. And you agreed that Pedro was a good name."

"Pedro is an awesome name for a someday dog."

She takes a deep breath. "This is a new list."

I hold up a hand to stave her off one more time. "I've got it. It's a list of everything that's as creepy awesome as a ventriloquist doll?"

She shakes her head once more, giggling, then pats the notebook proudly. "This list is all the things Mom wanted me to do this summer."

It's a punch in the gut, the mention of Anna. It's been a few years, but now and then Lucy says something about her mom that knocks me to my knees. "This summer specifically?" I ask, swallowing roughly, trying to figure out how to tackle whatever this is. Have I missed some preteen milestone?

"No." She shakes her head as if I'm the child. "Any summer. When I was ready. And, well, now I'm ready."

"Okay. And how did you come up with the list?"

Lucy smiles brightly. Too brightly. "I worked on it with her."

My heart squeezes. "When did you work on it?" Lists are Lucy's thing, and a recent one. Lists weren't Anna's thing at all.

Lucy looks at the stars on her ceiling, swallowing. "A while ago."

I take a beat. Take a breath too. "Before? You worked on it with her before?"

"Yes." Her voice wobbles a bit. "Well, we talked about it. I only wrote it down just now. I was finally ready to."

My throat tightens. Not for Anna, but for this girl, who's had to make sense of the insensible. "Do you want to show it to me?"

She nods, her pitch rising with excitement. "I do. Do you want to see it?"

"Heck yeah," I say, with more gusto than I feel. Besides, I *do* want to know what's on her list. Because I want to know what's on my daughter's mind.

Slowly, she flips through the pages, and as she does, I brace myself, hoping this list will be of the cupcake shop variety, rather than the latest bullet I don't know how to deflect. Too many surprise barrages I don't have the armor to withstand: periods and mama bears and memories that sneak up on me.

Lucy finds the page and shows me. I read her pristine handwriting.

Things I Want to Do This Summer:

Swim with turtles

Go to London

Eat a sundae with all the flavors and extra toppings

Share something that's hard to share

Snorkel

Stay up past midnight

Turns out, I've braced myself for something that didn't hurt at all. It's not the first time. Not only is it painless, it makes me smile. I can see Lucy doing all these things, having a blast, moving on, letting go.

I hand it back to her. "That sounds like an excellent summer."

A smile spreads across her face. "You like my list?"

"Love it."

"Can we do it?"

I read the list again then look at the clock. "It's nearly ten, and it's a school night. But I promise some night this summer you can stay up past midnight."

"What about everything else?"

I point to her list. "Is there something you've been wanting to share?"

She shrugs, a shy look in her eyes. "Maybe. Someday."

I arch a brow. "Is this something I need to know?"

"No. It's just a letter. I'll show you soon. When it's right."

"A letter, huh?" I keep my voice neutral, even though part of me wants to see the letter *this second*. But I want her to do this on her terms. "There's no rush on my part. You can share when you're ready."

"I will. I promise. I've had one for a while that I want to show you." She takes a beat. "But we can do the rest of my list?"

I stare at her quizzically, making sure this list comes from her heart. That these are things that truly matter to her and not simply a whim. "You really want to do all this?"

She nods vigorously. "I do."

"Let me think about it."

Lucy smacks her forehead. "Oh, wait. There's one more thing."

She grabs the notebook and adds an item, then shows me her addition.

Master mini golf

"That's something you think your mom wanted you to do?"

She smiles impishly. "No. That's just something I want to do."

Kids. They zig, then they zag. "What's with the sudden interest in mini golf?"

She rolls her eyes. "Piper, silly."

"Piper?" I ask, incredulously.

"Yes. When I saw her in the office the other day, she said she would teach me. Did you know she used to play competitively?"

"I did not. I didn't even know that was a thing."

"It's definitely a thing. Also, she's pretty cool. I like

her. Plus, her office is filled with pretty things. And she keeps lots of lists too."

Freaking Piper. The woman from college, the woman from the weddings, the woman down the hall in the same office building who despises me. The woman who weirdly looked hot wearing an Easter bonnet for a dress. How the hell is that possible?

"And does she have a list about mini golf?"

"She has a list of all the best places to play in the city."

It figures. Piper probably wants to teach anyone how to whack a ball hard enough to smack me in the head with it.

And she'd probably look good doing it too.

5

PIPER

Deep in the heart of Queens is a musty old school that gives away every secret in its walls.

Everything in here echoes.

Voices carry from room to room.

Shoes sound on the next floor.

You have to whisper at ten decibels below the ambient noise level unless you want the gym class in the basement to hear.

Paige slumps on the green vinyl couch in her office, where she serves as the vice principal of this private high school.

I double-check to make sure the door is locked. We're alone since it's evening. But you never know. That might be even more reason to close up tight.

She heaves a sigh, grabs a tissue, and dabs at her eyes. "I don't know how long I can do this," she whispers.

I sit next to her and squeeze her shoulder. "For two and a half more months. That's how long."

She lowers her head, her shoulders sagging. "Every day, it's something."

"Well, it's not really every day." I flash a cheery grin. "It's been more like every month. So look on the bright side: you only have ten more weeks of the biological mom trying to extract every single penny from you that she can."

Paige groans. Another tear falls. "Ten more long weeks."

I pat her thigh. "Have you told Lisa about this new request?"

Paige shakes her head. "No. She's so stressed. She's been wanting this for so long, and I don't want to worry her. That's why I called you."

I wrap my arm around her shoulder. "It's good that you called me. I'm like one of those fix-it chicks. Jodie Foster would play me in a movie—all badass and tough, taking no prisoners."

"You're totally the fixer. But Jodie Foster would wear a suit. Don't wear a suit."

I flub my lips and make the sign of the cross like I'm warding off vampires. "As if I'd ever wear a suit. Fixers like me? We wear trendy tops and cute skirts and sexy heels."

Paige looks me over and smiles. "That's definitely you." She sighs again. "I'm sorry, Piper. I hate that I have to keep asking for your help."

"Hey. I want to help. That's what I do. That's our deal." I take a beat. "How much does she want this time?"

"She says she needs another three thousand dollars

for maternity clothes," Paige says, tugging on her blonde ponytail.

I whistle in shock. "Damn, maternity clothes aren't cheap. Is she shopping for them in the Hamptons with the Kennedys?"

Paige laughs lightly. "And it's for living expenses too."

I shake my head, frustrated for her, but what can you do?

Paige and her wife, Lisa, are adopting a baby, and the biological mom has been draining them dry with her requests that border on emotional extortion. It stresses Lisa out, and it worries Paige.

Understandably.

It's not their first time on the baby rodeo, but they're hoping this time sticks.

They tried to have a baby through in vitro first, but it didn't work, so they chose to go down the adoption path. The trouble is, they're out of money after the in vitro attempts.

That's where I've come in.

I've been paying for everything.

I offered. I'm glad to do it. I want my sister to have her heart's desire, and she and Lisa want to be parents so badly that their want has its own weight.

But they're stretched thin in their jobs, and adoption is insanely expensive. I dip my hand into my cavernous bag, grab my phone, and PayPal the money to her.

She sighs, clasps her hand to her chest, then yanks me in for a hug.

A wet hug.

Since she's crying again.

On my shirt.

It's silk, and one of my favorites.

Gently, I try to move her face away from the fabric as I stroke her hair.

"Thank you. I feel terrible asking." She takes a deep breath and collects herself.

I shake a finger at her. "Don't feel one bit bad. I offered to pay for it. That was the deal. Don't you remember?"

"I do," she whispers.

We sat down one afternoon more than a year ago, after their last failed attempt at in vitro, and I made the offer.

"We can take out a loan. Or put it on a credit card somehow," Paige had said.

"Stop. Credit cards don't work like that, and you know it. Plus, I'm doing fine. I've tucked plenty away. I'm like a squirrel with her nuts, only I remember where I left them. I have it, and I'm going to cover the costs. Every single penny."

"Are you sure?" Paige had asked.

"Positive."

It was the least I could do for the person I love most.

I smooth her hair. "I knew it was going to be like this. And you have enough to worry about. Don't fret about me. But you do need to tell Lisa, okay?"

She nods, squares her shoulders, and nods again as if telling herself she'll find the strength. "I know."

"Now is not the time for secrets. Got it?"

She arches a brow, nudging me knowingly. "But some secrets are okay to keep?"

"Hey! I keep secrets about myself. Secrets no one needs to know. This is different. This is something you need to share with your wife."

She nods. "You're right. I just don't want to stress her out more. And she gets stressed when she knows what you're paying for."

I brandish my claws. "Tell her never to stress. She'll just owe me a life debt in her child. But hey, no big deal."

"I'll let her know you're claiming your stake in the baby."

"Hell yeah. I'm going to shower her in everything. Incidentally, your little girl is going to have the best wardrobe ever. I'm already buying her everything. It satisfies every desire I have to be an aunt."

"You might want to be more than an aunt someday," she says, her voice rising like she's leading the witness.

I stare at her. "First, no partner. Second, have you seen my daily to-do list? It's stuffed. Third, let me just focus on aunting for now. And getting you your baby. That's my number one goal."

"Thanks again, Piper. If I could ask anyone else, I would."

I arch a brow. "Like Mom?"

She laughs heartily. "That's a good one."

"Why, thank you very much. I've been working on my comedy routine."

"You know she'd want to though."

I roll my eyes. "She'd want to. She'd dip her hand

into the ceramic pig cookie jar, grab some rolls of quarters, and say, *Here's what I saved for you.*"

"Mom and her cookie jars. She means well at least."

"She does mean well. But she doesn't always do good. She doesn't always, how can I put this delicately, make the best choices."

A laugh bursts from Paige at the callback to what one of our teachers said about our mom when she took us out of school for a week for her fourth wedding. We've since adopted it as our slogan. "So we make better ones."

I knock fists with her. "Radcliffe sisters. Making better choices," I say.

Paige and I made a vow to each other in high school: do better than Mom. And we don't mean financially.

On that note, I say goodbye and grab a Lyft back to Manhattan. Along the way, I catch up on emails, hoping to reschedule the stationery shop appointment for tomorrow since it's far too late now.

Tomorrow morning works, the owner replies quickly.

I sigh in relief, grateful for the easy switch. I need events to run smoothly and business to keep coming in. I have to be able to pay both my bills and any more unexpected costs for my sister.

That's a promise I made her and it's one I intend to keep. Fortunately, business is good, but I can't rest on my laurels.

That means I must get back to work.

I settle into the back seat, check my phone, and find

a text from someone who seems to have adopted me lately.

Lucy: I totally want to take you up on your offer!

She's not a prospective bride, obviously. Spending time with her won't net me more business.

But that's not why I reply with a time and a date.

I don't even do it because I knew her mom.

I do it because Lucy's a cool kid.

Then I zoom in on work, work, work. I touch base with my brides and prospective brides, set appointments, schedule meetings, and see if I can help them with anything at all.

I need to be the best.

No.

I need to be even better.

6

PIPER

The couch in my office is pink and plush. The space is half Martha Stewart, half Barbie Dream Home, and that makes it 100 percent delight. Brides love meeting me here, and I love meeting them here. It's a win-win.

From my spot on the pink couch a few days later, I listen intently as Katya details her grand plans. I nod at the right moments, take notes at other times, and continue to work on my list of all the ways to make her wedding the most fabulous activity-strewn event in all the land.

Because that's what she wants.

"So . . . what do you think?" Katya practically bounces on the cushion. With wide green eyes, she waits for my response.

I tap my purple pen against my chin, forming my answer. "There are some really terrific ways that we can weave in games," I tell her, then detail some of the more successful strategies I've used. "Wedding Mad Libs are a blast. You leave them at each table and the guests give you marital advice. Often hilarious."

Katya squeals. "I love Mad Libs."

"Who doesn't? Just expect a lot of advice about birthing monkeys and guidance about where to put a candlestick, as well as wisdom about all things slippery."

Katya gives a confused blink. "Advice about slippery candlesticks? Is that supposed to mean . . ." She trails off, blushing as pink as the sofa cushions.

"I think that's the idea. According to research, *monkeys*, *candlestick*, and *slippery* are some of the most popular words people use in Mad Libs." I tap my list and continue. "You can also have board game centerpieces, bride and groom trivia, and a couple of crosswords for guests to play."

Her magnetic smile returns, and she clearly loves those ideas. "And what about games at the rehearsal dinner and bachelorette party? Galen and I want to do that too." She tucks her feet under her on the couch.

"If you'd like to initiate your guests into the games theme early, then go for it," I say.

"You're so good at this. How are you not married?"

I cringe internally. How does being skilled at planning a wedding equate to *being* wedded? But alas, this is an assumption I get regularly—if I'm helping a woman plan a wedding, I *should* be happily married.

I flash her a practiced smile. "Because I'm busy planning fabulous weddings. Don't you spend a second worrying about my dating life. Someday it'll be me walking down the aisle."

She grins too—that was what she wanted to hear.

That reaction wasn't new to me either. People in love want everyone to be in love.

"Now, tell me more about the games you want to play," I say, steering her back to why we're here.

She nibbles on her lip, glances around as if she's about to reveal a secret, then stage-whispers, "I thought we could also play Never Have I Ever."

I die a little bit inside. Because I'm going to have to squash her dreams.

"You know," she says, mistaking my expression for unfamiliarity with the game. "It's that drinking game where one person says 'Never have I ever . . .,' then says something embarrassing. And everyone who's done the embarrassing thing has to drink."

"I know the game," I say stone-faced, raising a stop-right-there palm.

There are certain hard limits in my business. That game is one of them. Every now and then, a bride wants to play that bad idea disguised as a pastime, and I must find a way to stop her. Katya is no different.

Fortunately, I've developed a preventative with a 100 percent success rate.

Here goes.

I look Katya straight in the eye. "I'm going to level with you, practice some tough love. That was what I told you the first time we met, right?"

She nods like a good girl. "You said you might have to give me tough love at some point, but it would be in my best interest if you did."

"I meant it, and the time has come. Are you ready?"

"I'm ready." She perches on the edge of her seat and reaches for my hands.

Oh, okay, this is how we're doing it. We're holding hands.

So be it.

I squeeze hers. "Katya, repeat after me."

She nods. "I will repeat after you."

"You will not . . ."

"I will not . . ."

"Ever play . . ."

"Ever play . . ."

"That game at your rehearsal dinner, your wedding, your bachelorette party, or at any time within a one-week window around your nuptials."

She sighs morosely. "Really?"

"It's the Never Have I Ever wedding pledge. You can play it on a girls' night out one-month post-wedding. You can play a kid's version with nieces and nephews. But you can't play it with friends or your spouse or the wedding party. I need you to finish. You have to take the pledge."

She repeats my final lines, and when she's through, her shoulders sag and she fiddles with the cuffs of her white blouse. "But why? It's such a fun game. Don't you love that game?"

I choose a diplomatic answer. "It's a fun game at times, especially with kids. But games have a time and a place. *Halo*, for instance, is great in a man cave. Trivial Pursuit belongs with your brainiac nerd friends who love to show off." (Full disclosure: I do like Trivial Pursuit, and my friend Kristen in Florida kills at it.) "Monopoly is the granddaddy of family night bonding games. Even Would You Rather can be a fun game. But Never Have I Ever is what we in the trade call 'a recipe for disaster.'"

"But we played it all the time in my sorority. We had the best time."

I can only imagine that sort of "best time" resulted in one hell of a hangover the next day. "I'm sure it was fun, and I'm sure it's tempting to play. But it's not a wedding game."

Katya keeps pressing. "Why would it be so bad at a wedding? It's all my friends. I know all their business."

And I'm going to have to set the table for her, soup by salad spoon. "Here's why. Picture this: you're at a lovely rehearsal dinner. Maybe it's an after-party with just your friends so you let loose, you have a few tequila shots, and you decide to play Never Have I Ever with the guys and the girls in the wedding party. It starts to go like this." I draw a deep breath and imitate a participant in the game. "'Never have I ever blown the best man.'"

Katya's eyes widen and she shakes her head. "I've never blown Benji."

"Trust me. Someone in the wedding party will have blown Benji, and you'll all find out who has had his dick in her mouth."

"Oh my."

I adopt a manly voice. "'Never have I ever sent a dick pic to the maid of honor.'"

She clasps her hand over her mouth and giggles. "Oh my God. I bet Tristan did send one to Haley. Galen told me Tristan loves to send dick pics."

"My point exactly. And the last one." I pause dramatically to clear my throat, adopt my most intensely serious expression, and bring it home with my never-fail Never Have I Ever killer. "'Never have I ever had sex up the butt.'"

She cringes, and perhaps that's her hard limit. "But Galen and I have talked about all this. We're not interested in butt stuff."

I point at her. "Exactly. And if you play that game, do you want to know that maybe he has done butt stuff? Or Tristan has? Or Haley?"

She covers her ears. *Monkey hears no evil.* Then she uncovers them. "Haley says it's a no-fly zone."

"But what if it's not for Tristan? Or Benji? Or your bridesmaids? Do you really want to know that about all of your friends? Do you want to know who likes butt stuff and who doesn't? Do you really want to have the image in your head of who likes butt stuff when everyone's walking down the aisle?"

She sighs. "Maybe I don't."

I lean forward and pat her knee. "Personally, there are just some things that belong between God, me, and the lamppost."

She laughs and agrees, then checks her watch and gathers her purse. "You're right. I've never done butt stuff, and I never want anyone to know. Butt stuff is between God, me, and the lamppost."

I rise and walk her to the door. "Butt stuff is definitely in that, and only that, three-way."

Laughing, she tells me she'll see me in a few days at her fitting and heads down the hall. I return to my favorite place on the pink couch, sending off some emails about Katya's wedding to-do list. A few minutes later, there's a knock at my door.

"Yes?" I say without looking up.

"So your butt stuff is between you, the lamppost, and your Maker?"

I grab a bridal magazine from my coffee table and do my best to fling it straight at Zach's head.

He dodges my effort easily, and the magazine wings its way to the hall. He turns around and grabs it, then sets it on my glass coffee table. "I mean, I'm just curious. I didn't realize this room operated as a confessional."

I arch a brow. "I didn't realize you saw fit to eavesdrop on all my conversations."

"I was walking down the hall. She was leaving. The door was open. Ergo . . ."

I nod. "Ergo, the next time you're consulting with a client about how you're going to rip his or her spouse to shreds, I'll remind you that the door was open."

"I don't have those conversations with the door open."

"Or do you?" I fire back. "Maybe I've overheard some."

He stands in the doorway, leaning against it, looking too good-looking once again. That's his true special talent, besides being completely odious. He's odious as he looks too cool for school. Today it's courtesy of tailored slacks, a crisp blue shirt, and his tie, slightly undone. What is it about slightly undone ties that are too sexy to be fair?

His tie sports a design of penguins, and that doesn't help matters. Cartoonish, adorable penguins.

Not fair indeed.

Especially when he smooths a hand over said tie, drawing my attention to his flat stomach. Is there a rule somewhere that says men this handsome must also be dreadful? "Well, you've clearly overheard some of my finest work. I'll assume you were impressed. Negotiation is my strong suit. Wait, everything is my strong suit."

I roll my eyes. "One, I was not impressed. Two, I can negotiate my ass off too, thank you very much. Three, humility is certainly not your strong suit."

"And may I remind you, *never have I ever* said it was." A teasing glint flashes in his eyes.

"Hey! You were eavesdropping."

He shrugs, but he's grinning. "I only eavesdrop on good things, like butt stuff."

I glare at him, narrowing my eyes. "Did you come here for a reason?"

He sighs then drops his lawyer demeanor and turns on some sort of sweet voice I rarely hear him use. "I stopped by because Lucy's on her way. You sure you're cool with this? With the mini golf stuff?"

I smile. "Of course!" I adopt a nefarious tone. "I've been looking for a mini golf acolyte."

"You've definitely got one. She's set on this." He's quiet for a moment as he jams his hands in his pants pockets, looks away, then back at me. "Listen, thanks. I appreciate this."

And I soften. It's hard to hate a widower who's good

with his kids. It's hard to hate a widower who's walked through hell and back. Even though I contend he's still odious, I suppose he's a little less than he could be. "Lucy is always welcome."

He grins crookedly. "Unlike me, right?"

I smile. "Exactly. Exactly unlike you." I wave him off. "Move along, shark. Move along."

But he doesn't leave right away. He stares at me as if he's studying me. Raising one eyebrow, he peers more intently, like something is out of place.

"What?" I swipe a hand over my cheek, my mouth. "Do I have something on my face? Is there a sesame seed stuck in my teeth?"

I didn't eat anything recently, so I've no clue what's off.

He points at my face, then makes a rolling motion with his index finger. "Your hair."

Raising a hand, I pat my strands. "Is there a bug? A piece of lint?"

He shakes his head. "You cut it."

"Yes. The other day. But it was . . ." *Wait. What the hell just happened? He noticed my hair?*

"Just a trim?" he asks, finishing for me.

A flush sweeps over my cheeks, heating me up with the strange realization that he pays enough attention to notice.

But then, just as quickly, I tell my cheeks to chill out. He didn't even compliment my hair. He simply observed that it's one centimeter shorter. That's part of his job. To pay attention to details. It means nothing more.

"Just a trim," I repeat, returning to my crisp, you-drive-me-crazy tone as I gesture to the door. "The door is that way."

He makes a show of checking out the doorway. "Yes, this is indeed the door. Thanks for the tip."

A few seconds later, as his footsteps sound on the hallway, he calls out, "The haircut looks nice."

That flush? That heat?

It comes back for an encore.

Even though I want to punch him for saying something not horrid.

Not horrid at all.

* * *

Lucy hops up onto the pink couch, sitting cross-legged. She glances around, like she does every time she's here. "Your office is so pretty. You have so many pretty things. I'm going to make a list of all the pretty things from your office that I want to have in my office someday."

"Why limit it to your office? Why not just make a list of all the pretty things you want to have in your room right now?" I say as I grab my favorite purple golf balls and drop them in my purse.

Her eyes brighten. "You're right. I'll tell my dad."

"He'll be delighted, I'm sure."

She whips out a notebook from her backpack and begins writing. She shows me the list: pink couch, white curtains, a whiteboard.

"Whiteboards," I say, sighing happily as I snag my

golf clubs. "They're the best. Make sure to get many colors of dry-erase markers."

"Ooh, I will," she says, then writes that down. "Also, I'm super excited, because I've never had a pink couch."

"Never have I ever had a pink couch," I offer.

"You need candy now!"

"I do?"

"I play that game with my friends, and we eat candy when we've done it."

I shake a finger at her. "You'd better be playing a kid-friendly version."

She rolls her eyes. "Obviously. Also, I have gummy bears. We can use them." She dips her hand into her backpack and grabs a plastic bag of gummy bears as I usher her toward the door. "Don't tell my dad, because he doesn't like it when I eat candy. But I picked some up after school today."

"Why doesn't he like you having candy?"

"Because he says it's going to send me to the dentist, but I brush my teeth all the time, so I'm fine."

"I have to tell you something," I whisper as I lock my office door. "I love candy."

"Me too. Okay, let's play. You go first."

As we walk to the waiting Lyft, I try to think of something to stump her. "Never have I ever licked a frozen pole."

Lucy laughs. "Why would anybody lick a frozen pole?"

"To see if your tongue sticks to it."

"I think your tongue would stick to it. I'm definitely not licking a frozen pole."

I grab a piece of candy and pop it in my mouth.

She points at me. "That's not fair. You knew you licked a frozen pole, and you just wanted a piece of candy."

I wiggle my eyebrows as the car arrives. "Exactly."

We hop into the car and Lucy goes next. "Never have I ever retaken a selfie ten times to make sure I look better in it."

"Please, girl. One hundred retakes is more like it."

We both reach for gummies and pop them in our mouths.

I hold up a finger, taking my turn as the driver heads toward the closest mini golf course. "Never have I ever had dessert for dinner."

Again we both reach into the bag.

Lucy clears her throat, and a twinkle gleams in her blue eyes. They're an ice blue, like her father's, and they're quite stunning. I mean, on her. Her eyes are stunning on her.

"I've never tried to convince my brother that he was born on the moon."

I huff. "That's so not fair. I don't have a brother."

She shimmies her shoulders, reaches for a gummy, and chews it proudly.

"Fine. I have an excellent one." I go for the pièce de résistance. "Never have I ever pretended I won an Oscar."

We both reach for the candy bag at the same time. I laugh and then say, "What's your Oscar speech? Do it right now."

She straightens, clasps her hands to her chest, and

begins. "Oh my God, I'm totally shocked, I didn't expect this at all, and I didn't even prepare a speech because I was so sure I was not going to win. This is such a surprise. But I'd like to thank the Academy. I'd like to thank my agent and my manager and the producers, and I want to thank Marvel for casting me as the most awesome superhero of all time, and I want to thank the producers of *Girl Power* for making such a great movie about how awesome girls are. I'd like to thank all of my best friends. I'd like to thank my daddy. And most of all, I'd like to thank my mommy." She stops, and her voice catches, then turns somber. "She's my inspiration."

And on that wobbly note, my heart hammers and a wave of sadness crashes over me. "You still miss her a lot." It's not a question. It's an acknowledgment of the truth.

"I do. Will I always?"

I squeeze her arm as the car slows at our destination. "She was one badass lady. And you will probably always miss her in some way."

"I think so too," she says, and we head to the course.

While there, I turn my focus solely to the sport, telling her how I played for fun with my friend Kristen when we were growing up in Florida, then I turned more serious in high school. I show her the tricks of the trade, how to plant her feet, how to hold the club, and the most important tip of all: how to hit rather than whack the ball to the next county. Admittedly, smacking the hell out of a ball can be a blast and a great way to blow off steam, *but* it doesn't help your game.

And on a mini-golf course, whacking usually translates into striking something you shouldn't be striking. The next obstacle or, say, a person.

Lucy's no prodigy, but she's a quick study, and she improves as we move through the course. I'd like to think her mom would be proud, and I tell her as much.

"Thanks, Piper. Also, will you keep it a secret from my dad that I ate so many gummies?"

I hold up a hand to high-five. "Obviously, that's vault."

When we return, my phone buzzes as we head up the steps to the brownstone. It's Charlie.

I pick up and say hello. "What's cooking, good-looking?"

"Group dinner tomorrow night. Are you in? I have some big news to share."

"Better not be that you're entering the wedding planning business, because you're the last person I'd want to compete with," I say, unlocking the front door.

"You think I'd make a good wedding planner? I'm not sure if I should be honored or offended."

"Silly man, it's a compliment. Obviously. I don't want to go head-to-head with you in the battle for business. You have the Midas touch. You'd somehow find a way to be the best in two days."

"That's kind of you. But it would take three days."

I laugh. "What's the news?"

"I'll unveil all my wedding business plans tomorrow night." He gives me the time and location.

"I'll be there."

I walk with Lucy down the hall to her dad's office, and when we go inside, he's on the phone, Henry in his lap, coloring on his desk. "You're sure it's just a group dinner?"

Zach waits.

"I know, but I have to ask."

He pauses.

"All right. No drool bibs. I'll see you tomorrow night."

He looks up at me and our eyes meet. I raise a hand like I'm going to ask a question in class. "Why would there even be drool bibs?"

A lopsided grin is his answer. A grin that's far too crookedly sexy for my good. "Long story."

Parking my hands on my hips, I stare, letting him know *I'm waiting.*

"You don't need a bib anymore, Daddy. I don't need one. Bibs are for babies," Henry says, without even looking up from his drawing.

Zach shrugs amiably. "And that's the long and short of it."

I'm getting nowhere on the drool bibs, so I return to the matter at hand. "I take it you're going to Charlie's group dinner?" I wouldn't be surprised—we run in the same circles. But I want to make sure.

Zach nods. "Charlie said he has news to share."

"I have an idea. You guys should go together," Lucy suggests, pointing from her dad to me and back, in case there is any confusion who she means.

"You definitely should," Henry seconds.

A cough bursts from my throat. "I have an appointment beforehand."

Even though I don't.

But I don't want Zach to be the one to say how ridiculous Lucy's idea is.

I don't want to hear him reject me when I haven't even asked him out.

Not that I would.

But I especially don't want to be laughed off while he's sitting there being all effortlessly handsome as his son draws on his desk.

I swivel around. "See you there."

Zach nods. "See you there." Then he calls out, "And thank you."

"Thank you, Piper," Lucy adds.

I leave, wondering what to wear.

7

ZACH

My mother gasps. "You. Look. So. Handsome."

My sister nods so vigorously she's making nodding a sport. "Sharp. You're totally sharp."

Lucy bounces on her toes. "You're adorable."

Seriously, why is everyone here in the kitchen? Are they gathering a coven of Nolan ladies?

I only asked my mom to come over to watch the kids tonight. And naturally she dragged my big sister, Emmy, along. My daughter *was* two floors down at her friend Melanie's house, but she mysteriously popped back up a few minutes ago after I finished getting dressed for Charlie's big dinner.

And now Lucy stares at me with wide eyes as she perches on the edge of a kitchen stool alongside the two other women.

Who all gawk at me.

Like I'm a zoo animal.

Watch Zach getting ready for dinner!

Be amazed at how he can dress himself!

Prepare to be dazzled at the way he hails a cab!

Why, yes, the modern male can indeed accomplish basic tasks on his own.

Only Henry is uninterested in my attire: dark jeans, blue-and-white-striped button-down, and wingtips. My son plucks blueberries from a bowl, arranges them in a circle, then pops them in his mouth as he flips through pages in an early reader book on baseball. Like father, like son—he knows our nation's pastime is the best sport ever. Full stop.

"Thanks," I say to the ladies as I head to the cupboard, grab a glass, and pour some water from the tap. I turn around, take a drink, and am greeted by three still-smiling faces.

Yup. Coven.

I down the water, set the glass on the counter, and cross my arms. I can go toe to toe in any staring contest. Like a cat. So I do. They stare back at me, wide grins still intact.

Satisfied grins.

What the hell?

Fine. I crack. "Okay, what's with the giggly faces?"

"I'm just excited that you're going out," my sister declares, yanking her brown hair from its hair tie, then refastening it in a bun on top of her head.

"You do know I've gone out before," I point out.

"I know. But it's still exciting," my mother chimes in as she pushes the coffee pot against the counter back-splash, then adjusts the toaster's position just so. My mother can't resist straightening things. *Any* thing. *Every* thing.

I arch a brow. "Really? Why is it exciting?"

"Because you're doing stuff with your group of friends again," Emmy adds.

"I've done stuff with them before." Haven't I?

I scratch my jaw, trying to remember. Admittedly, I haven't been the most social cat in the last couple of years, but who can blame me? Still, I must have gone to a bowling night or a beer-tasting event or a brunch?

Wait. I hate Sunday brunch. Who has time to wait for a table in Manhattan or Brooklyn just to order avocado toast and poached eggs to take pictures for Instagram?

Emmy shakes her head. "I don't think you have though."

"Do you track my social life?"

"Well, seeing as you usually ask Mom, Miranda, or me to take care of the kids if you have plans, and you've only asked us to watch them when you have work, it's not that hard to track," Emmy says, like it's normal to remember these details rather than, say, incredibly nosy and overly interested.

"She's right, dear. You haven't done much besides work and take care of the kids," my mother says.

"That's sort of how it goes when you're a single parent," I deadpan.

"It's just nice to see you socializing," Emmy says.

Wait! I've got it. I did do something. "I went to David's fundraiser last year. I donated one thousand dollars too. There. I have socialized."

My sister scoffs. "You lasted all of forty-five minutes.

You came home early, when we'd just started watching *Mythbusters.*"

Henry's gaze snaps up. "You can lift a car with duct tape, but you can't stop it with duct tape."

I hold up a hand to high-five. "You know it."

Then I gesture to my sister. "See? We finished the episode and learned something valuable. Plus, those forty-five minutes felt like hours."

My mother shoots me a motherly look. "Dear."

That's all. Just "dear." It says so many things, mostly that she vastly disagrees with everything I'm doing in my life.

Emmy shoots me a look. The *I'm older and know better* one. "You're proving our point. You don't socialize much. And when you do, you only do stuff with the guys. Basketball and that sort of thing."

"You really only have playdates with Charlie and David," Lucy adds. The little rat. "But not girls."

I hold up a hand, jumping in immediately to make the most vital correction. "One, they are definitely not playdates. Two, so what? Charlie and David are cool."

"Yes, they're lovely gentlemen. We're simply happy you're going out with boys *and* girls tonight," my mother adds.

I grin, fully onto them. All of them. Maybe especially my daughter. But I can't toy with her. "Lucy, sweetie pie, can you and Henry find a tie for me? You're so good at picking out ties."

I'm not planning on wearing a tie tonight, but it'll keep them busy for a few. She hops off the stool, grabs Henry's hand, and hustles him to my room.

When she's out of earshot, I decide to have fun with my mom and sister. "You're so right. And you know what? I'm so glad you're both here." I clasp a hand to my chest and affect a little squeal. "Because I wanted to let you know I'm finally ready to date again." I flash the biggest smile. "So I thought, what better place to start than with the big group of people I've been connected to since college?"

My sister's breath catches. "Yay!"

My mom beams. "Oh, sweetie, we've been hoping you'd be ready to get back out there." She throws her arms around me. "I'm so happy for you, honey."

Wait. They believed that load of crap?

My mom's embrace tightens, ratcheting to full vise-grip level. Yup, the rumors are true. I am an asshole. Also, clearly I have no heart. But I do have a brain, and it's yelling loudly at me to fix this mess I've made.

I disentangle from her. "Mom, I was joking. I'm sorry."

She tilts her head like the dog at the Victrola. "You're joking?" Her tone is the definition of despondent.

"I'm just not interested in dating."

"But it's been two years," she says gently, running a hand down my arm like I need comfort.

But I'm not. I'm fine. "I'm well aware of the time frame."

"Are you still . . .?" She lets her voice trail off as she pats her cheeks.

I blink. "Am I what? Crying myself to sleep at night?"

My sister whimpers. "Ohhh. Were you crying yourself to sleep?"

I heave a sigh. "Emmy. Mom. I love you both. But I'm not crying myself to sleep. I'm not crying in the shower. I'm fine. When you check in with your grief books, feel free to take some solace in the fact that I'm in the acceptance stage. But that doesn't mean I'm going to dinner with friends to scam on women."

My mother furrows her brow in a question. "Is that what they call it these days? *Scamming?*"

"I think they just call it *pick up* women," my sister says helpfully. Then she lowers her voice to a whisper. "Also, people mostly just swipe right and left. Do you want me to help you get on Tinder?"

"You could try a matchmaker too. I've heard of a very successful one who helps men in your situation," my mom puts in.

My sister thrusts her phone at me, showing me Tinder. "I downloaded it just for you. Let me help."

Groaning, I shove my hands roughly through my hair. "I don't want your help with Tinder. Or PlentyOf-Fish. Or a matchmaker. Especially one who helps '*men in my situation.*'" I stop to sketch air quotes. "Nor do I want to go out with Charlie's sister's friend, or Hannah's mom. I'm not interested in any of those because I have my hands full with the law practice and the kids. Dating is the last thing on my mind, and if it were higher up, I assure you, I would *not* be *scamming* or *picking up* or *swiping left, right, up, or down* on someone in my group of friends from college, especially since tonight is about Charlie."

"But are you sure? So many singles are having loads of success." My sister's voice rises with the last vestiges of hope. She's relentless. But that's the highest compliment from one attorney to another.

Exasperated, I slump against the counter. "Seriously, what is it about being a widower that makes everyone—literally everyone—want to set me up?"

Emmy's lips twitch in a grin. "Well, that's exactly what makes everyone want to set you up. Being a widower."

I shake my head in disbelief. "Let me get this straight. That's why I'm the hot commodity in the meat market? Because I have a dead wife?"

Emmy takes a step back. My mom grabs the edge of the counter. Was my bluntness too much? But what's the point in tiptoeing around the obvious? "Let's just call a spade a spade. You want to set me up because my wife is underground? Does that make any sense?"

"Zach," my mother chides. "Don't talk that way."

"Why?"

The answer comes in Henry's low sniffle.

He's back, a purple tie in one hand.

His whimper turns into a louder one, then it's muffled as Lucy tugs him in for a hug. "It's okay, little bub."

"I don't want Mommy to be underground," Henry says between tears.

My heart slams to the floor. I squeeze my eyes shut for a second, as if I can will this away. I've made my son cry. I'm a terrible shark. I'm a snake.

I cut across the kitchen, kneel, and wrap my arms around both of them. "Guys, I'm sorry. I'm so sorry."

Henry sniffles more, louder, and wetter.

"Forgive me," I whisper, my throat tightening. "Please, forgive me."

"It's okay, Daddy," he says, swallowing his sadness, it seems.

But soon, my shirt is covered in tears.

And I don't have to worry if I have a black heart. I know I do.

* * *

The great thing about being seven is you're like a rubber band. Henry bounces back a few minutes later. He wipes away his tears, helps me pick out a new shirt, and insists on me going even when I tell him I can skip the dinner and watch that *Mythbusters* episode on how to make an airplane from duct tape.

"It's okay. I'm all better. Aunt Emmy and Grammy said they're taking Lucy and me out for ice cream."

Ah, ice cream. God bless. It's the universal salve. It makes nearly everything better.

Before I know it, the four of them are pushing me out the door and telling me to have fun, even though fun is the last thing on my mind.

Emmy follows me down the hall to the elevator, setting her hand over the panel. "Listen, don't think twice about it," she says, exonerating me before I even have to ask for absolution.

I scrub a hand over my jaw. "Sorry."

She clasps a hand to her chest. "No, I'm sorry. I pushed you. We piled on you, Mom and me. You need to take things at your own pace. I was honestly just so stupidly excited that you were going out. I let it get the better of my judgment, and then I pushed you, and I'm not surprised it upset you."

I try to wave it away. "It's fine. I get it. I mean, let's be honest—I was a total catch before Anna. I'm still a total catch. It's not a surprise that men, women, and matchmakers of all ages want to try to snag a piece of me." I smack my ass for effect.

She gags. "I think my lunch just came up. Wait. No. That's breakfast. I'm so grossed out my oatmeal is threatening to make a return visit."

I laugh, and she laughs harder, and all is forgiven. She tugs me in for a quick hug, then straightens my purple tie. Henry wanted me to wear it. Given that I made him cry, it's the least I could do.

"Anyway, it just makes me happy that you're doing better. And that means going out, whether you're going out romantically or with friends."

I smile. "I'm definitely better. And tonight, I'm definitely going out with friends."

After I head downstairs and hail a cab, it hits me that I'm going to be thirty minutes early for dinner.

I guess that gives me time to *scam* at the bar.

Right. As if I want to do that. I'll just grab a drink and catch up on work on my phone. I'll answer emails, read files, and check in on cases.

When I arrive at the restaurant, I tell the hostess I'm here for Charlie McGrath's dinner. She flashes a red-glossed smile and tells me there are others from the party waiting at the bar.

When I turn my gaze, I catch a glimpse of wavy

brown hair and legs that go on for days. I catalog the rest: a leather skirt that hits mid-thigh, dark-gray suede heels, and toned arms on display in a short-sleeve black blouse.

The brunette is chatting with a blonde.

When Piper laughs, her lips curve up and her eyes twinkle. She hasn't even noticed me.

I stand and stare as a realization lights up for me like a neon billboard flashing above a bar on a dark country road. You drive for miles and miles on winding, hairpin turns till you see it, and when you do, it's bright and beckoning.

Piper Radcliffe is the first woman I've been attracted to since Anna.

And I'm pretty sure the attraction didn't begin tonight.

I've been noticing her for days.

For weeks.

For months.

8

ZACH

Charlie has chosen a bistro off Park Avenue, in the East Sixties. It looks like a farmhouse in the French countryside with long wooden tables, white linens, and wine, everywhere, wine. The bar is lit in the kind of light that suggests gas lamps are flickering, casting the space in a twilight glow. The kind that shows no imperfections. That makes everything look soft, inviting.

Hell, maybe that's why my world just went ass up.

Perhaps the light is tricking me into thinking something, feeling something, when I've felt so little for so long.

That's what I tell myself—that this sensation in my chest is temporary insanity—but when Piper turns around, catches my gaze, and shoots me a curious look, I know it's not the light.

Something else entirely is taking shape. Something that feels foreign. Because it's been ages since I felt a spark.

I feel a ton of them right now. That's exactly what

this is. Exactly what's been brewing for the last several weeks.

And precisely why it'd be a mistake to do a damn thing about it.

Especially since she clearly still hates me, judging from her *if you have to, you can join me* wave.

I head straight for her, doing my best to shove this bizarre attraction to the far corner of my head. Wait. Make that farther. Make that all the way out of my mind.

Yes, it's gone.

"You're early," she remarks with a deliberate huff. "I guess you can hang out with us for a minute."

"Thanks. I appreciate the heartfelt invite." I turn to her friend and extend a hand. "Zach Nolan."

The blonde shakes my hand. "Sloane Eliza—" She stops herself, laughing. "Sloane Goodman."

I arch a brow. "Recently married and adjusting to the new last name?"

"Exactly. And it's been three months, so you'd think I'd be accustomed to it now."

"Three months. That's great. Congratulations."

Piper holds up a hand and slams it to my shoulder. That's unexpected too. The contact. Has she touched me before? I don't think she has, at least not like this, and not for longer than a second.

She's already passed the five-second mark and she's still touching me. She's not letting go. She curls her hand over my shoulder and squeezes. "Do not do it."

Her warning is stern, and her brown eyes are full of fire—the hellfire she'll rain down on me if I *do it*.

Sloane chuckles, casting a curious glance at her friend. "Do what?"

Piper tips her forehead in my direction, still clasping my shoulder. "Zach, who, incidentally, is Zach Nolan, *Esquire*"—she drags out "Esquire" so it drips with the mockery that it deserves—"doubles as an oracle of doom when it comes to marriages."

Sloane's smile turns upside down. "Keep your predictions far away from me."

I raise my hands in surrender. But not so high that Piper takes her hand off me. Nope, her hand is definitely still on my deltoid. "I promise I reserve this party trick to amuse Piper, since, well, it drives her crazy."

Sloane chuckles then lifts a brow in a knowing kind of way. "And do you pull her pigtails too, and dip them in ink?"

"Of course," I answer.

Sloane turns to Piper. "And do you leave frogs in his lunch box?"

Piper shoots her friend an *are you crazy* look. "What does that mean?"

Sloane stares right back. "Figure it out."

"Fine. I will." Piper crosses her arms, taking her hand off my shoulder.

Well, that's sad. My shoulder enjoyed that moment a hell of a lot.

The women are silent, studying each other's faces. I watch them intently as they seem to communicate a million things in one long stare. It's impressive, really. The way their eyes lock, their brows rise and fall, their lips quirk. They're having an entire conversation in facial expressions and laser eye holds. Women truly are more highly evolved.

Piper holds up a finger. "Got it. But I disagree."

What does she disagree with?

Sloane shrugs happily. "Disagree all you want, but I know the truth."

Tell me. I want to know.

"There's nothing to know," Piper adds.

Holy shit. I'm witnessing a mind-meld, a conversation conducted half out loud and half via brain waves.

I jump in. "What did you guys just say?"

"Girl talk," Piper mutters.

Sloane checks the time on her phone. "I should head out of here. Malone is performing in thirty. That's Mr. Goodman to you," she says to me.

"Malone? You and your husband have rhyming names?"

She lifts her chin. "We do. And I love him madly. Wildly, incandescently, insanely, intensely, immensely."

"So there," Piper chimes in, then sticks her tongue out at me.

Sloane laughs, shaking a finger at Piper. "Like I said, I know the truth."

Piper waves her off. "You may leave now."

"Wait." I point my thumb at Sloane then meet Piper's gaze. "Did I ever tell you that rhyming names trumps everything? Any couple with rhyming names definitely will love each other forever and ever."

Sloane clasps a hand to her heart. "Aww. See? He's not as bad as you say, Piper."

I chuckle. "My reputation precedes me."

Piper waves a hand dismissively in my direction. "Your reputation wafts off you."

I pretend to sniff my shoulder. "It's a most excellent cologne."

Sloane laughs then leans in to give Piper a kiss on the cheek. "Have fun tonight, and don't be such a good girl."

That piques my interest. Is Piper a good girl? In bed? I'll just stuff that thought under the rug in my brain too.

Piper shoos away Sloane. "Say hi to that handsome man. Tell him to sing, well, anything, since everything he sings makes you swoon."

"That is true."

Once she leaves, Piper gestures to her friend. "Her husband is a vet who moonlights as a lounge singer. Like she stood a chance. Plus, she runs an animal rescue, so it's pretty much fate that brought them together."

I give her a steely stare. "Wait. Don't tell me you believe in fate."

She raises a palm and slams it to my chest. *Hello, hand. Nice to see you again.*

"Do not," she warns.

"Do not what?"

"Do not ruin my buzz."

Ah, that explains her touchy side tonight. Just to be sure, though, I ask, "Are you drunk?"

She scoffs, gesturing to her half-filled champagne glass and letting go of my chest. Damn. Maybe I can get her to the third-time's-a-charm stage. "Please," she says. "I've had half a drink. I'm buzzed on life, happiness, and the possibility of tonight. After all, it's the *big news* night, and big news is usually good news. Also, why are you here early?"

I toss the question back as I take the stool next to her. "Why are you here early?"

She arches a brow. "Did I invite you to sit down?"

I lean a little closer. "No. But I did it anyway."

She keeps her eyes locked to mine. "I'll try again. Why are you here twenty minutes early?"

I decide to cut through the bullshit. "I'm here early because all the women in my family kicked me out of my house."

"Why did they kick you out? Were you mean to them? Did you insult your sister's hair, dress, clothes, or lifestyle choices? Did you tell your mom her new recipe for lasagna tastes like sand? Did you inform Lucy there's no such thing as Santa?"

"Whoa. You do think I'm terrible. But I'll have you know, Lucy is well aware of the lie of old St. Nick and has been for two years."

"And the other possibilities?"

I scratch my chin. "Hmm. Why do I get the feeling you're trying to tell me I have nothing nice to say, ever? And yet I seem to recall recently telling you your haircut looked nice." And since she's been on a touching spree, I decide it's my turn. I lift a hand and touch the ends of her hair.

She freezes then swallows, glancing down at her heels.

"Soft too," I add.

Her breath seems to catch.

I let go.

Because I don't know where this moment goes next, or where I want it to go. Or even what the hell I'm doing. Am I flirting with her? Should I be doing that? And do I even know how to anymore?

Piper gazes at the shelf of wine bottles behind the bar, like she's orienting herself, then turns her attention back to me. "I kept meaning to ask if the pod people had taken you over that day when you complimented me. Had they?"

Here goes nothing. "It's possible. Or maybe I actually thought your hair looked pretty," I say, upgrading from nice as I kick my doubt temporarily to the curb. I'll see what happens with these strange new feelings.

"I find that hard to believe." But before I can ask why, she zooms back to the issue. "Why did they kick you out?"

The bartender swings by and asks if I want beer or wine. I opt for a beer, and then answer Piper's question. "They seem to think I need to do more than work and parent."

Piper's brow knits, and her expression shifts from playful to serious. "Is that the case? Is that all you do?"

I shrug. "Maybe. I read a lot though, and I also work out."

"Working out is important. You have to make sure you look good in a tie."

I narrow my eyes in confusion. "How does regular exercise make me look good in a tie? You're going to need to spell that out."

She lifts her glass and tips back some champagne. "Working out helps when you do that"—she drops her voice to a masculine tone—"*I'm gonna smooth my hand over my tie* move." She demonstrates, running a hand over her imaginary neckwear.

"Ah, like this?" I imitate her, running my hand down the purple silk, slow and seductive and totally over the top.

She cracks up. I do too. And it feels good. Really fucking good to laugh with a woman. It reminds me of good times. It reminds me that times can be good again.

I lift a brow. "Did it work?"

She pouts sexily and fans her face. "Oh, yes. I'm so turned on now."

Now that's an interesting thought. What face does she make when she's turned on? I probably should sweep that thought under the carpet, along with wondering what Piper is like in bed. Should, but don't want to. I like it too much.

I meet her brown-eyed gaze straight on. "Level with me, Piper. You noticed the tie move. Clearly you've been checking me out."

She nearly chokes on her drink. "Yes. You caught me. I've been observing you for the study I'm doing on the mating habits of the cocky male."

"Tell me more. I'd like to know about my mating habits."

She shoots me a stare. "They're . . . habitual."

I reach for my beer and take a long drink. "I wish."

She tilts her head. "Really?" Her voice is stripped free of teasing.

I decide to cut the bullshit. "Take this for what it is.

A number of people have tried to set me up in the last few months, and I've said no every time."

She screws up the corner of her lips, as if she's noodling on what I just said. "Makes sense. You're not ready."

I shake my head. I don't want her to think I'm damaged goods. "It's not that exactly."

"It's not?"

"I've said no because I haven't been interested. But my mom and sister kept pushing, and they were pushing tonight, and it got to be too much. I wound up saying something kind of shitty." I bite off each word, shoving a hand through my hair, frustrated with myself once more. But telling Piper is freeing too. Sharing the fact that I acted like a dick feels weirdly good. I can breathe again, like I'm not coiled tight. "I'm pretty sure they all wanted me gone. That's why I'm here early. I guess they needed space from me."

She smiles sympathetically, running her finger along the bar. "It can't be easy to keep it together all the time."

"Yeah. But I should do better," I admit, my shoulders relaxing. I don't even think I was aware that I was tense. But maybe I'm usually on high alert with Piper because of the sharp words we sling at each other. Right now though? We've both dialed down the digs a notch or two. And that's a relief, just to talk.

"That's not what I mean." Her voice is firm. "What I mean is, don't be that hard on yourself. You're juggling a lot. Kids, a business, loss."

She's right, but she's also not right. And I want her to

know that. "But at some point, you're no longer juggling the loss."

She arches a brow. "Yeah? You feel like you're doing okay?"

I nod, managing a smile. "What else can you do? You move on, you keep going."

"That sounds healthy. And I have to imagine at some point, that's what you want most: to feel normal again."

I take a drink. "Exactly. That's what you aim for. I suppose that's moving on. Feeling normal rather than numb."

"Was that how you felt for a while?"

I nod, thinking about that first year—the fresh, raw pain, like my insides were being excavated. After that, the cold numbness set in. And somehow, that numbness became the first step in finally coping, and I thawed.

Now, I'm on the other side. Not the same as before. Never the same. But a new normal.

"Definitely," I say. It's a one-word answer that conveys the whole truth.

Piper purses her lips, then blurts out, "My father died when I was five. I don't remember him. I don't think my mom ever truly moved on."

Wow. I didn't expect Piper to share that. We've never really talked like this before, without our armor or our weapons. I've laid my guns down tonight, emptied the chambers, and it seems she's done the same. "Why do you think she hasn't moved on?"

"She's been married six times since then."

I scrub a hand over the back of my neck, absorbing this new data. This explains so much about her. Only,

I'm not sure now is the time to psychoanalyze her, so I keep my response simple. "Holy half dozen weddings."

She laughs, then grabs my arm, squeezing. "If you ever repeat what I just told you, I will deny, deny, deny."

I look down at her hand on my forearm. I'm three for three tonight. "Sharing secrets? Are you trusting me now? That would be scandalous."

"Never. Please. You and me, we're mortal enemies. Lex Luthor and Superman."

"I wonder which one I am."

She wiggles her eyebrows. "Maybe we take turns."

"I'll drink to that." I raise my beer and take another drink while she finishes her champagne.

She sets down her glass and sighs. "By the way, that sucks that everyone is pushing you to date again. Only do it when you're ready."

"Hey. Don't feel sorry for me."

"Did I say I felt sorry for you? Never."

I flash her a grin. "That's the Piper I know."

"You'll get no sympathy from me." Ah, now we're back on familiar ground, and I don't mind this territory either. I know the terrain, can navigate it without a map.

"Good. And don't you play the Pity the Widower game."

"As if I'd ever do that."

"You better not. I want full license to be the asshole you think I am. No pity. Never."

"You get zero from me. I assure you."

"Excellent." I take a beat then lift an eyebrow. "By the way, how long have you had it bad for me?"

An eye roll is her response. "By the way, how long has it been since you lost your mind?"

"You have a huge, insane crush on me. Just admit it."

She shoots me a concerned look. "Was it rough? When you hit your head earlier today? Clearly you're a little disoriented."

"Absolutely. It was like my world was knocked sideways." I circle my hand around her arm, taking my shot in the handsy game. "Because that's the only reason I'd say this." I look her up and down, my eyes lingering on her short leather skirt. "You wear leather ridiculously well."

Her brown eyes widen in surprise. I'm a little surprised I said it too, but evidently leather on her body makes me quite bold.

"I do?" Her voice is feathery.

I take my time before answering, enjoying the way she parts her lips and seems to be poised on the edge of this moment, of my words.

"You absolutely do. It suits you."

She breathes out a quiet "Thank you."

And she knows. Knows that I meant that last bit. That it's real.

Which makes absolutely no sense to me since I can't stand her.

At least, that's how it's been. That's how it's supposed to be.

I shouldn't be able to tolerate this much time with her at all.

But evidently I can.

9

PIPER

I try.

But it's hard.

Still, I've done hard stuff before—I climbed the Empire State Building in the annual race up its steps. I took a graduate seminar in English while only a junior in college and nailed it, and oh yeah, I built a kick-ass business in Manhattan, supporting myself and helping my sister finance an adoption, all while moving on from the heartbreak of my twenties, and the string of failed relationships left in its wake.

Yup. My past is littered with the shards of my own broken heart.

But those accomplishments pale in comparison to tonight's feat of strength.

This evening, I'm Hercules. No, make that Athena, because I'm channeling all that badass lady-goddess's strength as I do my damnedest not to look at Zach during dinner.

This should not be difficult.

This ought to be a tra-la-la-skip-through-the-spring-woods kind of thing. Hell, I've been navigating my way through those woods for years, even in the dark, blindfolded, hopping on one freaking high-heeled foot.

But tonight, I can't find my way on the path.

When did the Zach-shaped roots spring from the forest floor to trip me up?

Is it the wine? I lift my glass. It's only my second drink, and I'm less than halfway through it, so I can't blame the vino for this war between my brain and my body.

As I chat with the always peppy Dina Hopkins, I'm fighting—dare I say, grappling and wrestling with myself—not to look at Zach at the other end of the table.

What would I see anyway? Just a man in a crisp button-down that hugs his frame, with sandpaper five-o'clock-shadow stubble, and dark, lush hair that swoops over his forehead.

Grrr.

This is the problem.

He's too handsome.

Clearly his looks are like those weather vortexes you hear about. He's that location on the map where low pressure collides with hot air, and women experience an atypical rise in temperature when they're near him.

It's a secret weapon. His looks are a stealth bomber. A fancy spy gadget.

Like the kind a movie villain would possess.

How does opposing counsel—man or woman—

manage with him across the table? That must be how he's so successful. His looks disarm any opponent. Because no one can be that good-looking, so you spend the whole time wondering how it's possible.

"And that's when he said, 'Mommy, you're my favorite.'"

Dina.

Right.

Dina is speaking.

I paste on a huge smile that says, oh sure, I've absolutely been paying attention the entire time.

I clasp my hands to my chest. "So sweet."

"What about you?" Dina asks.

Uh oh.

I've been working so damn hard not to check out Zach that my brain cramped. I have no idea what Dina and I were discussing.

Or really, what Dina was discussing.

"What about me?"

"Do you want to have kids?"

Oh. *That* question. That million-dollar question. For someone who has kids—like Dina—there is only one acceptable answer, and that's *of course, oh my God, please tell me what parenting secrets you've gleaned, since you're obviously amazing at it.*

But my answer? It's a little more muddled.

I like kids, but I don't know if I want to have them.

Maybe because of how I was raised. My mother molded me into her personal flower girl, her most dependable maid of honor and *her closest friend.*

She treated me like her bestie and her accessory all

rolled into one bridesmaid-dress-wearing doll—pink at age five, lavender at eight, pale yellow at ten, periwinkle at thirteen, black at seventeen, and aqua at nineteen.

She came to me when her heart was broken, she cried on my shoulder, and she even offered me a second spoon and asked if I wanted to join her in drowning her man sorrows in a pint of Ben & Jerry's when I was only a sophomore and hadn't had the chance to get jaded on love in my own time.

She meant well, I suppose.

She's a hopeless romantic, always searching for the love she'd had with my father again.

But even though I *understand* her choices, that doesn't mean I want to make them.

What if I have kids and learn I'm lacking the skills? What if I bring a child into the world, and it turns out—oops—I'm just like my clingy, have-some-Cherry-Garcia-with-me-since-Rafe-didn't-turn-out-to-be-the-one mom?

The fear is real because I'm already like her in some ways. She's a social butterfly and counts a big group of friends in her circle. She loves pretty things, the smell of old books, the scent of lilacs, and the lure of Europe, even though, like me, she's never been.

I'm the same in bigger ways too. We've both been involved in countless weddings. Fine, she was usually the bride, I was usually behind the scenes. But still, I've been drawn to marriage ceremonies since Mom, Paige, and I watched Princess Diana's wedding in reruns after her tragic death. We have this bond, and it's an odd one —one I don't care to psychoanalyze.

What if I'm the same as my mother in other ways?

The prospect terrifies me.

But there are other reasons that parenting scares me too. I've made my own mistakes, and I've made choices that, in retrospect, were the wrong ones at the wrong time for the wrong reason. Am I better off alone?

It's possible.

I simply don't know, so here I am, marinating on Dina's question: do I want to have kids? Dina, who knew when she was a sophomore in college she wanted to balance a corporate job in project management and be a mom. Dina, who seems to have succeeded.

"Someday," I tell her, and it feels like a half-truth, half cover-up.

We make small talk about work, and as we do, I'm remembering Jensen, the man I was madly in love with in my twenties, the man I thought I'd be with forever and ever.

I was stupid.

I was foolish.

I was in love.

Surely Zach would have predicted the failure rate of that relationship at 100 percent.

He'd have been right. Jensen and I never stood a chance.

"What do you think Charlie's news is?" Dina whispers as the waiter brings another round of small plates. Charlie's holding court at the head of the table, but he's yet to reveal his big news. Maybe he cashed out of yet another venture. The man sold his last company for a mint. He's been living the good life since then, traveling to Europe often, surfing in Costa Rica, and enjoying the best of Manhattan as he searches for the next company he wants to start.

"Something good, that's for sure," I say.

Dina bats her blue eyes. "You must have an idea."

I have several, but I don't want to jinx the ones I'm hoping for, so I toss out the most obvious possibility for the Midas man.

"I bet he started a new business."

"Maybe he's becoming a monk."

And here is Zach with his opinions.

My natural instinct is to roll my eyes when I hear him. But my body doesn't listen. It has instincts of its own. A shiver has the audacity to roll down my spine.

God help me.

This is unfair. It is cruel and unusual punishment to make me suddenly responsive to this man.

I turn my head. He's standing next to me. Leaning near me. I catch a faint hint of his scent, and it's not cologne. It's aftershave, I think. Something woodsy and clean that reminds me of snow and cedar.

The smell is intoxicating.

Great. I'll never be able to go for a walk in the woods again.

I gird myself, arming myself with a comeback. Barbs —that's what we do. "Charlie is more likely to give up all his creature comforts and move to Ecuador to build homes for the poor than to become a monk."

"True. He does love the ladies more than his material goods. Does that make him an *immaterial guy*?" he asks, riffing on the Madonna tune.

I chuckle, despite my best intentions to remain unamused by Zach. "He's a material guy. But he's a good guy."

Zach nods. "True that. Still, I say he's either going full monk, becoming an ultra-marathoner, moving to the South Pole to research the effects of global warming —also, how the hell do you *not* fall off Earth when you're on the South Pole?—starting a new venture he wants us to crowdfund, or . . ." His eyes darken, and he trails off.

"Or what?"

Zach drags a hand through his hair. "It better not be cancer. He fucking better not be announcing it to all of us tonight, telling us he's dying but embracing it, so he's celebrating."

My heart lurches toward him. I reach for his arm, gripping him tightly, like I can send my certainty into him. "That's not it. There's no way. He's not doing that. Tonight is for good news."

He bends lower, so we're at eye level. "Better be," he mutters.

I squeeze again. "He would never do that—gather us all to tell us that. He wouldn't set us up to think everything was fine."

Dina chimes in, her voice soft. "It's going to be okay, Zach. It's going to be fantastic news. I bet he started a charity or something. Wouldn't that be great?"

"Yeah, it would." He heaves a sigh, then shakes his head like a dog. "I'm good. It's all good." He flashes a grin, and it feels forced. "I'm voting for monk though. That's my prediction, and I'm sticking to it."

I laugh because it's necessary. "I'm casting mine for Ecuador."

He extends his hand. "Bet on it."

I shake. "A gentlewoman's bet."

"Yoo-hoo! I want in on it," Dina says, lifting her chin. "I vote for he just bought this restaurant and we can eat here for free anytime."

Dina and Zach shake on it. "I'm all for that. Free food rules," Zach says.

"I want to bet on Dina's idea. Please, please, please let it be free food for all of us. Also, gravity is why you don't fall off the South Pole."

Zach snaps his finger. "Gravity. I knew it had to be something."

The three of us smile, and this time when I scan Zach's face, his grin feels real. And I'm glad.

When Dina lets go of his hand, she hums. "Hey, you know, seeing you reminds me of something."

"Yeah?" His tone is noncommittal.

Dina taps his hand with hers. "Are you on the dating circuit again?"

I glance at him. He smiles at me with his eyes, lifting a brow as if to say, *See what I mean?*

He meets Dina's gaze. His answer brooks no argument. "No."

His gaze swings back to mine. His blue eyes twinkle, and my stomach flips.

Okay, that's it. I'm arresting myself for mutiny. I've had enough of my traitorous body for one evening. This kind of treachery is unacceptable. I believe my brain gave my libido the memo not to lust after Zach.

And yet . . .

"Dina! I want to take a picture." Heather waves from the other side, and Dina pops up, joining Heather and her husband, Freddie, as our real estate friend, Steven, takes a seat next to them.

In a heartbeat, Zach grabs Dina's vacated chair. "Hey. Did you notice that?"

"The way Dina went after you for the dating mill?"

He shakes his head. "Nah. Who cares about that?"

"I thought you did. Isn't that why you just asked me?"

He shakes his head. "When I said, 'Did you notice that?' I was referring to the way you and I had a mind-meld."

"We did?" I laugh lightly.

"Hell yeah. Like you and Sloane talking through your crazy-powerful female minds." He grips his skull dramatically, like a telepathic superhero. Or super villain for that matter.

I laugh. "I guess we did."

"See? We did too."

"We communicated with our female brains? Zach, is there something you want to tell me? Are you transitioning?"

"Yes, from jaguar to cheetah." He holds up two fingers, pointing from my eyes to his. "We spoke with our eyes, Piper. We spoke with our goddamn eyes. That was brilliant."

"Well, don't start getting any ideas that we're suddenly going to have a secret language."

He snaps his fingers aw-shucks-style, then lowers his voice to a deep and smoky rasp. "A man can dream."

His voice sends tingles along my arms. Reflexively, I tug at my sleeves like I can hide the effect, the goose bumps. I hope he doesn't notice the flush traveling along my skin either. But mostly I hope I can figure out what to do about this strange attraction to the enemy, because it's incredibly inconvenient.

Fortunately, Charlie rises, clears his throat, and shoves his wire-rimmed glasses higher up his nose, providing the perfect distraction. He's a handsome man, a Michael Fassbender once removed, with his ginger hair and chiseled face.

His smile is stitched with secret glee. "You're probably all wondering why I asked you here tonight."

"Ya think?" Zach calls out.

Charlie smiles devilishly. He's good at smiling that way.

He holds his arms out wide. "I won't keep you waiting much longer. But I wanted all my closest friends gathered round to hear my news at the same time. I've been friends with you turkeys for several years."

"Try a decade and a half, math genius," Freddie calls out.

"Yeah, have you forgotten we're all pushing thirty-five?" Zach barks.

"Speak for yourself," I say. "I was acquired by your crew when I was two years younger than most of you." I point a thumb at myself. "Pushing *only* thirty-three."

"Thirty-three, and even hotter than when you were twenty," Steven adds with a salacious grin.

I laugh, adopting a husky tone. "And so are you."

Zach shoots me a steely look.

"What?" I whisper.

"You think Stevie's a babe?"

"What if I did?" I ask, challenging him.

"But you don't."

"How do you know?"

He shakes his head. "You just don't."

Charlie resumes his speech. "In any case, I suppose the only thing that would make tonight a more fitting one to share my big news would be if Jessica were here. But our good friend has taken to life across the pond, which makes it harder to convince her to join group activities."

I miss that witch. I wish she were here.

Heels click across the floor. Loud and purposeful.

My eyes bulge.

Am I seeing things?

10

PIPER

If this is a mirage, my new hallucination is fabulous, and it's delivering one of my good friends.

That witch is marching toward the table like Lucy Liu striding onto a movie set, silky black hair flying like a flag, a determined stride in her step, a glint in her big brown eyes.

"You're here," I shout, a smile sweeping across my face.

"I'm here," she declares.

I bet she just stepped off a plane. I bet she always planned to crash Charlie's party and surprise the hell out of him. Charlie does love surprises.

He jerks back, then nearly stumbles against the table. Yup. He's shocked, and this is the pièce de résistance of tonight: Jessica catching wind of the dinner and showing up unannounced.

"Holy shit. You're here," he utters in disbelief, and my grin grows the size of a continent.

Jessica smiles at him, then grabs his hand. "Oh, stop. You're not surprised."

Charlie laughs wickedly, then yanks her close for a . .

.

My jaw drops. My breath ceases.

Is this happening?

Charlie brings Jessica in for a kiss.

And there's nothing friendly about it.

He's giving her the full Charlie McGrath tongue-treatment, and she's giving him the Jessica Chen arms-wrapped-around-his-neck medicine.

My eyes drift to her left hand, and I gasp.

I'm nearly blinded. The diamond on her ring finger is the size of a dinosaur egg.

They're engaged. Holy smokes. Charlie and Jessica pulled off a surprise engagement.

"Whoa," Zach utters. "Someone's going to be Mrs. Charlie McGrath."

I snap my gaze to him. "You didn't predict this."

He smiles, shaking his head, holding up a hand. "I definitely did not predict this."

I smile back, enjoying that Zach Nolan wasn't two steps ahead of this couple. Yes, he can still make predictions on their marriage, but right now, he's not.

Right now, he's responding like the rest of us.

As they kiss, we cheer and hoot. Zach whistles, and his mood is ebullient and genuine. It's everything Zach's reaction to Sasha's wedding wasn't, and the change delights me.

When the couple separates, the man of the hour shrugs and smiles. "I guess things are better already,"

Charlie says. "Because I convinced Jessica to be my wife. We're getting married, and you're all invited."

The table erupts into more cheers, more toasts, and more happiness. Because this is the good stuff. These are the joy-filled moments. The times when we aren't thinking of who we've lost, who's not here, and who didn't make it through their unions.

All I'm thinking is my good friend looks incandescently happy, and that's precisely how you should feel when you're promising to love someone for the rest of your life.

Charlie cups Jessica's cheeks, plants one more kiss to her lips, then turns to the table. He holds out his hand toward Zach. "Nolan, my man. You asked me to be the godparent for your children, and that was one of the most important moments of my life. Would you do me the honor of being my best man?"

Zach blinks, straightening, like he wasn't expecting that.

"Absolutely." His answer is swift, covering up any surprise. "Thank you for asking."

Jessica turns to me, and my heart speeds, my pulse spikes. No lie—I've been dying to do her wedding for years. The twinkle in her eyes tells me she's about to ask me. I cross my fingers, wishing on a star. "And I would be so honored, Piper, if you'd be our wedding planner." She pauses and takes a beat, even though I'm shouting *yes* internally. "And also my maid of honor."

I thrust my arms in the air. Double duty. "I've been waiting a decade for this. Yes. I'd love to. It'll be my gift to you two."

Jessica kisses Charlie's cheek, her smile reaching to the end of Manhattan and back.

When they separate, she clasps her hands together. "And what we really want is to celebrate with our friends. We want you guys"—she gestures to the table—"to be a part of our new love, our happiness. And that's why we want to have some pre-wedding parties at our favorite places, and all you have to do is come along for the ride. It's all on us. Or Charlie Warbucks," Jessica says, pointing a thumb at her fiancé.

The table erupts into a wild rumpus of toasts and yeses.

Charlie and Jessica grab seats across from Zach and me. "And you guys will help us with all the events? As best man and maid of honor?"

"Of course," I say, delighted as a friend and tickled pink as a professional that Jessica wants to have this kind of wedding fiesta.

When Charlie and Jessica kiss again then head down the table to hug our other friends, I sneak a peek at Zach, and he flashes me that *what can you do* grin.

I tilt my head to the side. "What was that for?"

"What was what for?"

"That little grin?"

"Oh. You know. Just the realization that we're going to be spending a whole lot of time together."

"I'm sure we can handle our best-man and maid-of-honor roles via text message," I say coolly, returning to the familiar ice and fire that is us.

"Because it'll be easier that way?"

I give him a curious look. "What'll be easier?"

"For you to resist me. What with your insane crush and all."

"Let me put it this way," I fire back. His eyes dance with mischief, like he can't wait to hear what I'm about to unleash. "It'll be as hard for me to resist you"—I tap his chest—"as it is for you to resist me."

"Ah," he says, nodding sagely, as if he's taking in my comment and weighing it.

He leans near, brushing my hair away from my shoulder, clearing his throat. I tense, because this has to be when he hits below the belt.

Instead, his voice is low and dirty. "I guess we'll have to place a bet, then, on whether it'll be hard or easy."

I stare right back at him, refusing to give an inch. We might have had a moment earlier—fine, a few moments, a few wonderfully touching moments—but we're back on familiar territory now. And here on this terrain, my job is to hold the hell out of my ground, heels dug in and unbudgeable. "You picked monk. I picked Ecuador. Seems our last bet was a draw."

"Indeed it was."

I cross my arms. "Maybe this will be too."

"Maybe it will be." He lifts his chin, his gaze studying mine, like he's looking for answers in my eyes. "So what's your bet, Piper? Hard or easy?"

I'm not sure if he's asking if I think it's hard for him to resist me, or for me to resist him. But now isn't the time to parse out the language of this absurd bet. I choose the well-trodden path.

"Resistance? It'll be a piece of cake," I add in a satisfied grin. "And you?"

He twists the corner of his lips, like he's considering the answer, then he nods crisply. "I'm going all in on my bet."

"And?"

"I'm betting the answer will surprise both of us." He inches closer once more, his tone disarmingly vulnerable. "Thanks again for earlier. For all of it. The things you said."

"Of course," I say, as his whispered words spread warmth over my skin.

He rises and walks around the table, clapping Charlie on the back, then embracing his good friend in a man hug.

As for me?

Like an archaeologist hunting for clues, I'm studying the last minute of our conversation, digging into my satchel for the right tools to excavate its meaning.

Did he mean anything by it at all? Is he saying it's hard to resist me? Or easy? Or that he wants to find out? That he wants to be surprised?

Gah. Men. Why can't they communicate through mind-melds that make sense?

There's no time to linger, though, because Jessica rushes over to me and flops down in Zach's spot. "Musical chairs!"

"It's what we've always played," I add, sliding right back into our routine. Whenever our group of friends gets together, it always goes like this—moving around the table, catching up with whoever we need to catch up with, snagging chairs and stealing moments.

She throws her arms around me and sighs happily.

"I'm a bad friend. Do you forgive me for not telling you in advance?"

I laugh and pet her hair. "Hmm. Good question. Depends on when he proposed to you."

She pulls back and flashes me her monster-size ring. "Last night. At the Cloisters, since he knows it's my favorite museum. But we had talked about it, so I sort of knew he was going to, and he really wanted this whole night with everyone to be a surprise. Charlie loves surprises, and parties and celebrations."

"He sure does," I say, recalling both the impromptu fetes he threw in the dorms as well as the unplanned dinners and birthdays he spearheaded for friends. "But hello! How long have you been seeing him, and why did you keep it from me?" I give an exaggerated pout, all in fun, but honestly, there's a part of me that wishes she'd told me.

"It happened so quickly." A touch of guilt curls through her tone.

I blink. "It did?"

"He came to London a few months ago. We had dinner, and before we knew it . . ."

My jaw drops. "Dirty girl."

She bats her lashes. "It was one of those things. Everything sort of collided, and then we had this very whirlwind romance, and . . ."

I raise my brow, staring at her belly, then meeting her eyes. "And does that mean you'll have a whirlwind birth in nine months?"

She swats my thigh. "Hey! I know how to use protection."

"Just making sure."

"Anyway, it's been a magical sort of courtship in London. He took me to all my favorite museums. You know how I love museums."

"I do. You dragged me to all the local museums in college."

"And you loved them as much as I did. And Charlie and I toured little bookshops, and smelled yummy old books, and then had afternoon tea."

"And did you eat fish and chips and roast beef in little pubs?" I ask in my best grand-old-dame English accent.

"Please. I'm all about the curry. Love me some spice."

I laugh. "It sounds very *you*. And very *you* in London."

"And we loved every second of it. We wanted to tell everyone together. Like this."

"I couldn't be happier, although I'm going to require more details on the little bookshops. How did they smell? Wait. Don't tell me yet. I might swoon, and I don't want to do that at your party. And don't you dare say a word about palaces or jewels, or I might faint from second-hand happiness. For now, tell me, how is being engaged?"

"It's a dream. And listen, in case it wasn't clear, I'm paying you to plan the wedding. I know you said it was a gift, but I'll have none of that."

"Don't be silly. Your money is no good here."

"I insist."

"You don't have to insist, and you don't have to pay me."

She sighs and squeezes my arm. "Hey. I want to. Let me. Also . . ." She drops her voice to a whisper. "Have I mentioned my fiancé is rich? We are paying you, and that's that."

Who am I to argue? I'm not hurting, but I do like the way money is useful—to pay bills, for instance, especially the unexpected ones that have been coming my sister's way lately. "Thank you, Jessica."

She tucks a strand of jet-black hair behind her ear. "Do you think you can tolerate Zach though? I know you never liked him."

I bristle at the question, oddly protective for some reason. But why would I feel protective of Zach?

"I can handle him. He's still the same old Zach," I say with a shrug.

And that's true.

Mostly he is the same.

But it's also untrue.

Because lately, he's a different Zach.

A Zach who has a softer side, a kinder side, a thoughtful side. And a flirty side too, apparently. A Zach who shows those sides every now and then.

A Zach I'm wildly attracted to.

That's the problem.

I've managed working down the hall from him, no problem. Heck, I've hung out with his kid, and that's been fine. But now that I'm suddenly strangely drawn to him, how the hell am I going to handle being maid of honor to his best man in this let's-make-it-an-ongoing-party type of wedding?

My traitorous body is going to love this, but my too-smart heart is going to have to install a barbed wire fence.

Oh wait. I have one. I only hope it holds.

11

ZACH

The next morning, I demolish Charlie in basketball at the local community center, while Lucy and Henry take an intro to tae kwon do class in the gymnasium.

"It's not even fair for me to play with you," I say as I land another jump shot.

He grabs the ball on the rebound and dribbles, then misses a dribble.

I stare at him. "Just take a mulligan. I can't keep destroying you this harshly."

He shoots me a steely stare as he stalks to the edge of the outdoor court. "I'm off my game, that's all. Late night with the woman."

I roll my eyes as he retrieves the ball. "Please. I crush you often and easily, regardless of your late-night escapades."

He dribbles again and shoots. The ball flies through the net. "Oh yeah. Who's the man?" Charlie gloats. "He shoots. He scores. Just like last night."

I snag the ball, stopping to scratch my jaw. "Please. I don't need to hear about you getting lucky last night."

Charlie chuckles. "What can I say? I'm a happy bastard."

I clap him on the back. "Glad to hear it."

"And listen, thanks again for being my best man."

I arch a brow. "As if you were going to ask anyone else."

"Never. But I do appreciate it. And thanks for helping out with the pre-wedding activities. We want to make it fun."

I shoot, the ball whooshing effortlessly through the net. "It's amazing I'm not in the NBA." I turn to my buddy as he grabs the rebound. "And it'll be fun. It'll definitely be fun."

A ridge forms in his brow. "You sure you're cool with all this?"

"With you getting hitched? Yeah, I'm one hundred percent down with it." I laugh. "What on earth would I have against it?"

"No, I just mean—well, I know you and Piper have never really gotten along well, and now you have to do all this social stuff together."

"I'm an adult. I can handle doing things with her."

"You sure?"

I steal the ball from his hands. "Positive," I tell him, but the dirty little secret I keep to myself is that I'm looking forward to spending more time with Piper.

Because the other dirty little secret?

I had fun last night.

I haven't had fun in ages. The flirting kind. That's

exactly what it was. The touches, the moments, the sexy little comments. I regret nothing. Not a word. In fact, when I returned home and it was just me and Netflix in my quiet home, since the kids were sound asleep, I replayed my favorite scenes.

Her hand on my shoulder at the bar.

The conversation when we let down our guard.

The bet.

And that moment at the end, when we tangoed around resistance. Is resisting me easy, like she said? Or is it getting tougher for her to wrangle the lust, the desire, the burgeoning—

What the hell?

There's no debate over resistance. There isn't a need for it. Piper and I aren't one of those hate-to-love-you bickering sitcom couples who don't realize they really dig each other.

Piper and I know the score.

There isn't even a scoreboard for us.

We aren't a thing. We aren't going to be any kind of thing whatsoever.

My newfound lust for her is just getting ahead of itself.

That's all last night was—a surprise bout of lust that's over. Done. Finished.

With a determined laser focus, I take the ball down the court and deliver it through the net.

When I turn around, Charlie's holding out his hands. "You won. And you showed me up. Man, that's what I love about you, Zach. I can always count on you to be a cold, determined bastard on the court." He strides over and claps my back.

"Happy to school you every time."

"You're reliable as fuck. With that, and with everything."

Reliable.

That's what I need to be as his best man. Reliable, dependable, and a good friend.

Charlie is my closest buddy. He's been here for me through the darkest times. He's helped with my kids. He's helped with my sanity.

The last thing I want is to cause a problem while he's heading into the most important moment of his life: marrying Jessica.

Pushing forward on something with Piper—a night, a flirtation, *anything* at all—would be stupidly risky.

My best man role is all about Charlie. And, Lord knows, if I give in to anything with Piper, we'll be warring again the next day, but ten times worse.

It's for the best that resistance is easy for her, because that'll make it easier for me to stuff these feelings in a storage unit and throw away the key.

As we head off the court, Charlie says, "So, the first thing we want to do is throw an engagement party in London."

I flash back to my daughter's list for the summer. London was at the top of it. That's what I need to focus on—my friends and my family. Making things happen for the people who are still here.

"I'll be there with the monsters."

And in the back of my mind, a little voice reminds me that Piper will be there too.

No shit, little voice.

Like I don't fucking know.

That's why when Piper messages me about another time for her and Lucy to play mini golf, I reply curtly, letting her know to go ahead and set it up with Lucy.

Her response is equally short: *Okay.*

As if last night didn't happen.

That's how it needs to be.

Whatever last night was—flirting, touching, teasing . . . just fucking *feeling* something for the first time in years—it can't happen again.

There is too much at stake.

I need to turn around and retreat. To hoof it far away, like my feet are on fire.

Piper and I are better off as enemies.

Or, really, as frenemies.

When Lucy arranges a time with her, I do what I need to do. I call Miranda and make sure she handles the drop-off and the pickup.

I have to be a shark.

Because Taylor's husband is the worst. He's hitting below the belt, playing underhanded games, trying to mindfuck her. Which means I'll have to take the gloves all the way off.

I put my head down and focus on work, rather than on this stupid sensation I get in my chest when I see Piper.

So I do my damnedest not to see Piper.

Confession: I've never been to London.

Well, okay, fine. I've been to London in my mind. In my fantasies. In my freaking dreams. And it's not even because of the whole sucker-for-a-British-accent thing. That's not my thing.

It's because of Harry and William. Meghan and Kate. And Diana.

And because of jewels—glorious, gorgeous, bright, shiny jewels. After my mother introduced me to the pomp and tiara of a royal wedding, I was sold.

Sign me up.

Send me there.

I didn't want to be a princess, though I wouldn't have kicked Harry out of bed for eating raw onions and liverwurst, I assure you.

My dreams were simpler: to gawk at the ceremony; gaze upon the crown jewels; see the castles, the moats; and imagine what it would have been like to live amid all of that.

When I meet Jessica for tea at her favorite shop on the Upper East Side the day after the dinner, she tells me she wants me to help her plan a little engagement celebration across the pond. I'm cool and calm, and I don't let on it's a dream come true.

After all, she's a friend, but now she's a client, and I don't want her to think I can't handle the sheer and absolute awesomeness of what she's offering me.

I flash a professional smile. "I have plenty of contacts in London. Some of my best colleagues here have counterparts in England, and in the luxury hotels and hip restaurants there, so this will be a piece of cake. Or should I say, a piece of scone."

"You should definitely say 'a piece of scone.'" She winks, then holds up her Earl Grey for a clink.

"I'm already getting in the spirit. Drinking my English breakfast," I say, holding my tea ever so properly.

"Do you think we should do an afternoon tea, maybe the day after the engagement party?"

I nearly squeal. But somehow I manage to keep my giddiness inside. I tap my chin thoughtfully. "Tea and cakes and petit fours. Gee, I wonder."

She laughs. "I guess that's a yes."

"It's a yes, but only if we can get one of those three-tiered cake stands that holds all the little cakes and biscuits and treats."

Her eyes seem to sparkle. "I knew you'd be perfect for this, my Anglophile friend. And Zach is already helping Charlie plan manly stuff."

Zach. The name makes me bristle. I've barely seen

him since the dinner, though I've spent time with his daughter. Admittedly, I was a little disappointed that he didn't sweep into my office a week ago, tell me that resisting me was damn near impossible, and then sweep out.

Just because, well, who doesn't want to be irresistible?

But he didn't, and that's for the best.

Because he's completely resistible, and I'm wholly focused on my friend and my business.

It's that simple. I have zero brain space to allocate to Zach Nolan's whiplash flirt/no flirt behavior.

Jessica and I chat more about her vision: an engagement party in London, a celebratory fete here in New York, then perhaps a destination wedding somewhere exotic.

When we're done, I tend to work then meet up with my sister in Central Park, since she's in Manhattan for a meeting. We stroll through the Conservatory Garden, a spot teeming with flowers, as I update Paige on Jessica's plans.

My sister squeals, maybe even double squeals, and the sound delights me. It's so much better than the tears that rained down her face the last time I saw her. "Are you going to see the crown jewels and go to Buckingham Palace and see Windsor Castle, where my bestie Meghan was married?"

"But of course, love," I say in my best British accent.

"I'd say you're a lucky bitch, but I know luck doesn't have a thing to do with it. It's all hard work. *Your* hard work. Can I also just say, this is so much better than Sea World?"

I crack up as we wander past dazzling orange daylilies and rich purple irises. "Hey, that's not fair to Flipper and friends. Dolphins are cool too."

"I know, but London? Wedding stuff in London? C'mon. That's what we dreamed of as kids."

For two girls growing up in Florida, London was like another planet. We didn't cross the Atlantic or the Pacific. We went to Busch Gardens and Sea World on vacations.

"We did drink a lot of royal Kool-Aid," I say.

"But never princess Kool-Aid." She offers a fist for knocking, and I knock back.

"Hell no. I'm still annoyed that Ariel didn't just write Eric a note. That mermaid made poor choices."

Paige nods, her blonde ponytail bobbing. "I know, right? Instead of just batting her eyelashes, she could have used a thingamabob or a dinglehopper or whatever to write him a letter or draw him a picture. Also, he sucks for falling for Ursula just because she had a pretty singing voice."

"Eric sucks the most of all the princes," I agree. My sister and I picked apart every fairy tale when we were kids. We dreamed of castles because we wanted to be princesses. We just didn't want to live in a tiny two-bedroom apartment in Homestead, Florida.

But hello! We absolutely would have thought of writing a letter to Eric if our voices were banished.

"Also," Paige says, "while we're on the subject, why

on earth didn't Snow White stay with the seven dwarves?"

I shrug. "I always thought she'd have been better off in a reverse harem situation with the men who loved her and who she truly loved."

"A different man for each mood," Paige adds.

"And each day of the week."

"Of course, who's to say the princess shouldn't marry another princess?" She nudges me.

"As long as true love conquers all." I add an eye roll since I know my sister and Lisa are still ridiculously in love.

"What can I say? I found my princess and kept her."

"Ugh. You're such a show-off with your perfect marriage to a perfect woman. Also, did you have to snag the hottest babe ever?" I ask, since Lisa is a knockout.

"She is pretty awesome." Paige pauses and adjusts her ponytail, her expression turning more serious. "And I followed your advice. I've been more open."

"Good. Always follow my advice. I know best on literally everything."

Paige squeezes my arm. "Want to see something amazing?"

"Is it a two-headed man? Because the answer is no."

Laughing, she grabs her phone, swipes her finger across the screen, and shows me an alien. I mean, a baby. A beautiful baby in a 4D ultrasound. "Stacy had to get an ultrasound. Doesn't the baby look great?"

"Why did she need an ultrasound?" My alarm starts ticking, tensing my shoulders. Is Stacy jerking them around again? I've read up on pregnancy, and ultrasounds aren't common at this stage. "That's not typical in the third trimester."

"She thought she was having contractions. But it turned out to be heartburn."

"God bless heartburn."

"Exactly. They did one just to be sure, and the good news is there's nothing to worry about. Plus, I got another baby pic, which I can't complain about. The doctor said everything is on track and looking good."

"That's terrific."

Then Paige's smile fades. "Sorry though."

"For what?"

"For the ultrasound. I was hoping to ask you . . ."

I drape my arm around her. "I told you, it's fine. I've got it handled." The birth mom doesn't have anything beyond basic insurance, so Paige—ergo, *moi*—is covering the above-and-beyond costs.

And it's all for the best.

"How did Lisa react when you told her about the last request?" I ask.

"She threw her arms around me and said I had the best sister ever."

I shimmy my shoulders. "You really do."

She bats her eyes. "Great. So you'll bring me back one of Kate's hats?"

"You want me to go to England and pilfer one of Kate's hats?"

She raises her chin, going full Brit. "No, I want you to *nick* it."

As we walk around the fountain, debating baby names, I tell myself it's a damn good thing I didn't let

Jessica talk me out of accepting money for her wedding. These ultrasounds aren't paying for themselves.

It's an even better thing that I intend to deliver an absolutely awesome engagement party for my friend.

That's why on my to-do list, I have a note to deploy one of my secret weapons.

* * *

My friend Jason moonlights in the wedding business, and he hails from Old Blighty, so I meet him at his favorite pub later that week.

We help each whenever we're able, since we're not competitors. As an "undercover groomsman," he serves an entirely different niche than I do. A narrower one, but it works for him as his side gig. And he's excellent at it, organizing stag parties like a pro and standing next to the groom when the occasion calls for it. For those weddings, his job is simple and incredibly hard: be 100 percent believable as a friend of the groom, even though he's not.

After we order two pints, I swivel around on my stool, facing his hazel-eyed gaze. "Debrief time," I tell him.

He rubs his hands together. "Excellent. Shall I give you all the clandestine details on my last gig? Like when the bride nixed the original best man because of a row he'd had with the maid of honor over whether either of them wanted to see the other naked again?"

My interest is thoroughly piqued. "I must know everything."

He shares all the scandalous details, and I ooh, ahh, and recoil at the appropriate times.

"Bless you for sharing a juicy story," I tell him, bowing my head.

"Always happy to oblige in that regard. But enough about randy best men. What can I do for you?"

I take a deep breath and dive into the heart of why I wanted to meet with him. "I've been talking to my contacts in London, checking on any new hotels or eateries that have popped up recently. But I wanted to know if you heard any buzz the last time you were back home, or from your friends there." He's lived in Manhattan for a while, but he makes his way back to London every now and then. "And, of course, let me know if there are any spots to blackball."

"You want the blackball list? That's a mile long."

"One mile? Are you going soft? I'd have thought twenty miles."

"Soft? Me? Never. I'm always hard. Always ready."

I hold up my palm. "I don't want to hear about your tensile strength. We've already established you're not allowed to hit on me."

It's our running joke, since the two of us have never been attracted to each other, even though Jason, with his dark hair and amber eyes, is a looker. We've only ever been colleagues, so it's easy to rib each other.

"But it's so hard to resist you." He's teasing, but I feel a wistful pang. Because there is someone I wish were truly having a hard time resisting me.

But that's foolish. I don't have time to be a fool. "I know, I know. But didn't you say you had your sights set on someone? Your best friend's sister or something? Has she succumbed to your charms?"

"Not yet. And he would likely kill me. But I'm not opposed to a challenge."

"Or being murdered, it seems."

"I'm willing to die trying for this one."

"She must be special."

"She drives me insane."

"Sometimes those are the ones we want most," I say.

The bartender brings us our drinks, and we set to work catching up on the savviest concierges in Kensington and the best eateries. I make list after fabulous list.

"This is amazing. Where did you amass all this fresh intel?" I ask.

"From my master spy network. Or possibly because I did a virtual consult with a groom in the homeland recently. Wrote him a best man speech, and he shared details on all these new places. Now what about you? Have you had any more bridemergencies?"

I smile. "Every now and then, a maid of honor goes rogue or a bridesmaid goes full Godzilla. I'd say once or twice a year, I step in, in one capacity or another. I've played nearly every part in a wedding. Thanks to the internet, I'm an ordained minister, so I've done everything now except play the bride or the groom."

He shudders. "That last one's a role I'll never play either."

"But I thought you were smitten with your best friend's sister?"

"Sure, smitten works. But that doesn't mean you'll ever see me walking down the aisle."

"Don't worry. I'm sure you'll be happy being single for the rest of your life."

"And you too, pot to kettle."

I shrug. "I'm not opposed to marriage. I just haven't met that someone."

He hums then takes a drink, staring off in the distance. "But I bet everyone still assumes you ought to be successfully betrothed, right?"

"Yes. Yes. Yes," I groan. "Everyone expects wedding planners to be happily married, or thinks we've never suffered a single unsuccessful relationship."

He takes a drink. "But isn't that true of you, Piper? Your love life is a fairy tale."

I nearly spit out my drink. "It's the furthest thing."

He arches a brow. "And is there anyone on the horizon who could make it a nearer thing?"

An image of Zach flashes before my eyes.

I send it away. "There's no one."

* * *

That's what I tell myself when Zach pops into my office a few days later.

He's *no one* to me.

His voice rumbles. "Hey."

I glance up from my pink couch. He's doing his standard Zach pose. Leaning against the doorframe, looking business-sexy.

I grit my teeth. *Must resist.*

"Hello." My voice is ice.

"So . . ." He cracks his knuckles, all casual and laid-back. "Are we supposed to do planning stuff?"

I scoff at his description of my job. "I can handle it all." As if I need *his* help. "The *planning stuff*."

He arches a brow. "Including the stag party?"

I shoot him a glare. "First, we both know there's no stag party during the engagement party weekend. Second, even if there were a stag party, I could handle that too."

He lifts a brow. "That so? Have you planned stag parties?"

"I have. Sometimes my friend Jason helps me."

"Who's Jason?" He straightens, the accordion of his body stretched out as if he's trying to occupy more space. No more Leaning Tower of Zach. He's over six feet, so he fills out the doorway quite nicely.

Wait. I'm not noticing his peacock moves. I'm definitely not paying attention to the *mmm, just right* fit of his charcoal shirt and tailored slacks, and the tuga-bility of his cranberry tie with the—I squint—what are those creatures? "Do you have hedgehogs on your tie?"

He glances down, running his fingers along the silky material, then smiling like he just remembered. "Hey, look at that. I do."

"What's with the cartoon-animal theme for most of your ties?"

"You noticed?"

I sigh heavily. "I'm not inventorying your ties. I don't have a database of your neckwear and whether you have duckies or piglets or porcupines on them. But I did notice you had penguins the other week."

"Lucy picks out my ties. She likes to go tie shopping. She always has. She actually chooses most of my neckwear."

An image skips through my head, a picture of his clever little daughter scanning the displays at Bloomingdale's or Barneys, determination in her blue eyes, Daddy's little helper. My heart thumps from the cuteness overload. That is the sweetest thing I've ever heard.

But I can't tell him that.

"That's adorable," I say, choosing a simpler compliment.

But he doesn't seem interested in my remark. "Who's Jason?" he asks again.

Oh, right. I didn't answer. "A friend of mine. He does some work in the business."

"A wedding planner?"

I shake my head. "No. Why do you want to know?"

"Is he gay?"

I laugh. "Why are you asking? He's not gay. He's super straight."

He draws air quotes. "And what is 'super straight'?"

"A ladies' man. A player. You know the type."

"So he's interested in you?"

I stare at him, slack-jawed. "That's your conclusion from me saying he's a player?"

"I assumed that was what you meant. Players make plays, ergo . . . I'm only being logical."

"You're being illogical. He's not interested in me, and I'm not interested in him, and men and women can be just friends. He's a work colleague. He's British, and he's helping me scout out some venues in London so I can put together a lovely party."

Zach's shoulders seem to relax. "Do you need me to do anything? You're so great at the planning. I mean, of course you are," he says, and I forgive him a little for the "planning stuff" remark. "I organized a golf outing with the guys. And I looked up a few pubs. But I've been crazy busy with this case. The defendant is threatening to take it to trial . . ."

"A golf outing sounds great, and so do pubs. I've got the rest. Don't worry."

"Are you sure?"

"I'm positive." I study his face for a minute. Worry lines crease his forehead. "Is the case weighing on you?"

He scratches his jaw. "Nah."

He's lying. It bothers him. But he doesn't seem to want to say why.

He takes a deep breath and turns to the door, rapping on it as if he's stalling. "So, we're leaving in a few days."

"Yes. I'm going a day early."

"Same here. It's easier for the kids. We're on the six-thirty flight."

A grin attempts to take over my face. I fight it off. Valiantly. So damn valiantly. "Me too."

"Yeah? Same flight?"

"Same flight. I'll probably sleep the whole time."

"Lucy and Henry love red-eyes."

"They do?"

He shrugs almost apologetically. "I take them on a lot of trips. They sleep like criminals on planes."

"The old adage about how a guilty man gets a full night's rest?"

He flashes his crooked grin. "They're outlaws."

I return his smile, wishing briefly that we were sitting together on the plane.

13

ZACH

Lucy squeezes my hand. "Can I get a sundae with all the toppings? Do they have those on this flight?"

"We sure do." The flight attendant greets Lucy with a polished smile. "Especially for the best-behaved passengers."

Henry's eyes light up, and the little ice cream lover jumps in. "I'm excellent on planes. What flavors do you have?"

The flight attendant peers at the ceiling of the galley as if she's only now learning of these flavors. "Let's see. For the seasoned traveler, we have chocolate, vanilla, and guess what? We also have coconut."

Henry bounces on his toes. "I love coconut. Can I please get coconut with chocolate and caramel and nuts and whipped cream?"

The woman laughs.

I pat my son's shoulder. "They probably don't have all those toppings."

The flight attendant gestures to her setup in the galley. "Actually, we do. I would be more than happy to make sure you have a sundae with all your toppings, once you've had your dinner. If it's okay with your father?"

"I want two, pretty please," Henry says.

Lucy tugs on my hand. "A sundae with all the toppings is on my special summer list. But you're already doing so many things on my list by taking me to London. If you want to give my sundae to Henry so he can have two, I'm okay with that, because you're the most awesome dad."

I ruffle her hair. "Aren't you magnanimous today?"

"What's 'magnanimous'?" Henry asks.

"Generous. It means generous. And we'll figure out the sundae distribution later. Thanks so much," I tell the attendant, as we settle into our seats. We're in 3A, 3B, and 4A, so I point ahead to the fourth row. "Lucy, why don't you take 4A so you can sit by yourself, and I'll sit next to Henry."

"Oh my God," Lucy shouts, "I don't have to sit by myself. Piper's here."

My heart jumps at the same time that the universe smirks and says, *Good luck, sucker. Resist that.*

When Lucy reaches the fourth row, Piper raises her face from her book. She's looking casual and fresh-faced in jeans and a white V-neck T-shirt.

Is there anything better on a woman than a white V-neck T-shirt? Maybe a gray one, or pink, or black. Honestly, the color doesn't matter. All V-neck T-shirts look fantastic on beautiful women. And with that, I realize I'm not just attracted to Piper. I think she's stunning, and that is scary as hell.

I focus on the shirt rather than my terrifying thoughts.

"Fancy meeting you here," I deadpan.

She smiles brightly. "I was supposed to be in economy premium. But Charlie Warbucks bumped me up." She pats the seat next to her. "And I have been saving this seat for either one super cool seven-year-old or one super cool ten-year-old."

Lucy doesn't give Henry a fighting chance. She plunks herself down next to Piper, and the two of them quickly fall into a round of Never Have I Ever about plane food. A smile tugs at my lips the whole time as they talk about different plane foods they've supposedly never had.

As I settle Henry in next to me, I listen to their game.

I've never eaten a five-layer cake on a plane.

I've never drunk a chocolate milkshake on a plane.

I've never consumed three dozen Cokes on a plane.

For a moment, this whole scenario feels like it *should* remind me of Anna and Lucy, as if Piper could be some sort of replacement. But I'm not looking for a replacement, and there could never be one. More than that, Piper and Anna aren't the least bit interchangeable. Anna was a great mom and loved reading to the kids and having long talks with them. But when Anna flew, she liked to listen to music or books rather than chat.

Piper seems to like to just . . . talk.

And I like the way that Piper and Lucy have a

rhythm that is uniquely theirs, one that they've figured out on their own.

I sneak another glance at them.

But if I keep looking, I'm going to keep thinking too much about Piper, and I'm trying to get her out of my brain, even though she's in my physical space.

Good luck with that.

I settle in with Henry, and we quickly get lost in a round of *Minecraft* on his phone. Perfect. All I have to do is build walls till we land.

But one hour, a chicken risotto, and a sundae with the works later, my kid is zonking out hard. The sundae with all the fixings seems to have had the opposite effect —the sugar high crashed into a sugar low—and his eyelids flutter closed. Half-heartedly, Henry pushes the button to turn out the light and slumps against the armrest, stretching out his little legs in the capsule-like seat.

With a yawn, Lucy taps my shoulder. "Can I switch seats with you? I'm tired too, and I don't like the light on."

"I can turn it off," Piper offers.

But I don't want her beholden to my kids' rhythms. "I'll switch."

Lucy and I change seats, and my little girl blows me a kiss then whispers, "Good night."

"Like criminals," Piper whispers, nodding at the two monsters who are sliding into snooze land.

"Guilty little scofflaws," I say. She sets down her book on the armrest, and my eyes drift to the cover. "You like J.D. Robb?"

"I like badass lady cops."

I laugh. "Of course you do."

"And why do you say that?"

"I could see you as a badass cop."

Her brown eyes narrow, and her lips imitate a ruler. Her voice goes gruff, no-nonsense. "You're under arrest for disturbing my peace."

I laugh at her police officer impression. "Are you going to lock me up?"

She lifts her chin, keeping the tough demeanor. "You have the right to tell me why the hell you think I'd make a good cop."

I point at her. "For that right there. For your tough-as-nails approach."

She shoots me a doubtful glance. "I'm a softie."

I scowl. "You are not a softie."

"You're not a softie either," she counters.

"Never claimed to be. So what's the opposite of a softie?" I answer my own question. "A hard-ass, obviously."

Her eyes stray over her shoulder, as if she's checking out her own rear. "That's me. Spin class three times a week."

"Do you really go that often?" I ask, liking the image of her riding her butt off on a bike.

"I do. I really do."

"You are definitely a hard-ass, tough-as-nails, badass cop."

She taps the cover of the book. "I am."

Is she giving me a hint?

"If you want to go back to reading, I won't be

offended," I say, since I did just horn in on her reading time. I glance around the first-class cabin. Nearly everyone is dozing off. The lights are low, and only a few reading lamps are still lit. "We don't have to talk."

She tugs her blanket higher on her waist. "You really know how to make a girl feel welcome."

"I just didn't want you to feel obligated."

"I don't." She cocks her head, peering at me. "But also, is obligation such a bad thing?"

I shove a hand through my hair, unsure of what she's getting at. "No, obligation is not a bad thing. I just . . ."

The airplane hums in the silence I can't think how to fill. We soar across the night sky, the ambient noise from the engines a low-key soundtrack.

"Zach, did you feel obligated after the dinner? Because we talked so much that night? Is that why you kind of stopped talking to me?" she asks.

Whoa. Way to hit the nail on the head, but not exactly.

I meet her gaze head-on. "I didn't feel obligated. Everything turned crazy busy. I'm sorry." It's not the whole truth—because I'm not dumb enough to admit I need space to resist my desire for her—but it's true.

"The trial? The case you mentioned?"

"It's not going to trial yet, but it turned messy. The soon-to-be ex keeps calling my client and trying to get her to back down with threats. I don't want him talking to her at all. I want it to be just his attorney and me, but the ex is the ex for a reason, and the whole situation is way more shitty than I expected," I say, thinking of the way Taylor's husband decided to start playing hardball, and the way it reminds me of someone in my family.

"That sucks," she says sympathetically. "Do you think you can, I don't know, tear him a new one?"

I laugh at her crudeness. "I would really like to, Piper. I would absolutely love to."

Her eyes turn curious, as if she's searching my face. "What drives you?"

"To be a lawyer?"

"Yes. I assume you have a pugilistic side. But what specifically drove you to be a divorce lawyer? You must have known what you wanted to do as soon as you finished law school because you were practicing right away. But it's not as if you hate marriage, since you got married pretty young too, right?"

There's something refreshing about her frankness, her willingness to dive into life's meatier topics. "I finished law school at twenty-four, married Anna a few months later."

"And you guys were happily married."

I nod. "We were."

"What's the story, then, counselor? Why do you enjoy your job so much?"

I exhale, looking away from Piper. The flight attendant checks on the passengers in the first row, then returns to the galley. Otherwise, the cabin is awash in the quiet of an overnight flight. I focus my attention back on my seatmate. No need to dance around the answer. When you're suspended in the sky, moments like this are for honesty. "My parents divorced when I was ten. My father was a complete and absolute asshole to my mother during it."

She gasps quietly. "Oh God, really?"

"He was a relentless son of a bitch. For no reason. There was no cheating on her part, nor his. She was simply unhappy because he worked all the time and was never involved in our lives. And when she left him, he let her have it. He punished her financially, taking a lien out against the house they owned, claiming his parents had given him the money for the down payment, then going after her income, claiming she earned more."

"Did she?"

"She owned a boutique, and he worked for a bank as a manager. He said she had higher earning potential."

"Did you overhear all this when you were only a kid?"

My jaw clenches. "Like I said, he was an asshole. He didn't hide it from us. He just lit into her. He wanted her to pay for leaving him, and she did."

"How did she manage it all?"

"She's a tough woman. She rode it out. She knew she needed to leave the marriage—she wasn't happy with him the last few years they were together, and who could blame her? He wasn't there for her then. He wasn't there for us then either."

"And was that it? Was that what it took for you to know what you wanted to do?"

I lean back in the seat, stretching out my legs, recalling my younger years. "I don't think it was a light bulb moment, but over time, the roots grew deeper within me. And when I was in high school and started on the debate team, that's when I knew. I had the power to stop that. I had the ability to fight with words and knowledge and my brain. I could use logic to prevent assholes from ganging up on someone. I wasn't going to let that shit happen. Not if I could stop it. I didn't want women like my mom to be without options."

"Do you only represent women?"

I shake my head. "I have some male clients. But my business is word of mouth. Women tell their friends about me when their friends need a killer divorce attorney, so I represent a lot of women, because a lot of guys are assholes. They want to make their wives suffer. They want to punish them in a divorce. You might think I'm a shark, and the truth is, I am. But I'm a shark because I can't stand people who take advantage of someone else who's simply trying to have a better life, make a better choice."

She swallows and takes a deep breath. "Wow."

"Wow, what?"

She shakes her head, a small smile forming on her lips. "I had no idea anyone could make being a divorce attorney seem noble."

I wave a hand, dismissing the idea. "Please. I'm not noble. I like the money the job brings."

"You can't say that. You can't say this thoughtful, wise, considerate thing, and then go back to being a dick." She lifts a hand, pinches her thumb and forefinger together, moves them an inch from my lips, and then pretends to zip them closed.

I laugh. "Fine. I have a tiny bit of nobility in me. Not much. But I meant everything I said. I'll go to the mat for my clients because I don't want to see them being punished for simply wanting to move on. If I can prevent it, if I can fight for them, I goddamn fucking will."

She shudders.

"Did I scare you?"

She leans closer and drops her voice. "No. It was kind of hot, truth be told. Your whole *defender of those who need me* speech."

That sends a dart of lust down my spine. That warms me up on this cold plane—the idea that she likes the fighter in me. My lips quirk up. "Is that so? You think it's hot?"

She smiles, a little shyly. "It kind of is."

I want to push in this direction. I want to explore what she thinks is hot. I want to tell her I think she's on fire. But this is a time to focus on my friends and on my family. Not to risk ruining a wedding with an awkward situation.

So I don't let myself get caught up. I lean forward, checking on my kids in the row ahead. Snoring.

"Outlaws," I whisper.

"Bandits," she seconds.

"Lawbreakers."

"Perps."

But I also don't want to just toss words back and forth. Because that conversation with her felt good. It felt as good as flirting with her at the dinner did. I want to keep digging deeper. "Your turn," I say. "Why do you like weddings so much?"

She fidgets with her blanket, then meets my gaze. "I told you my mom was married six times."

"You did say that."

"I've always been drawn to weddings. Royal weddings. Soap weddings. Real weddings. I used to walk past a church in my neighborhood in Florida on Saturday afternoons and try to catch glimpses of brides and grooms."

An image of a young Piper, spying in the pews, flashes before me. "I can see that."

"It just seemed like the perfect job for me, and I felt like a bit of an expert given I was in so many weddings because of my mom."

"Has she found love again?"

A sad look pierces her eyes. "I don't think so. I don't think she's ever found anyone she's loved like my dad. She keeps trying, but she comes up short."

"And with your mom getting married so many times, that didn't turn you off to the institution?"

"No. I'm sure Freud would say I'm trying to get it right."

"Do you think you'll ever get married?"

She licks her lips, takes a breath, then speaks softly. "Do I think I'll ever get married again, you mean?"

I blink. *Married again?*

14

PIPER

Maybe it's the night. Maybe it's the way the airplane operates like a cocoon. This sleek metal tube is a secret chamber, shooting us across the starry sky where secrets are safe.

Or perhaps it's that he shared something with me.

Something big.

Something important.

In moments like this, when Zach lets down his guard and lets me in, it seems like we're no longer the barbed wire Zach and Piper that we usually are. We're these softer, friendlier versions of ourselves.

Sometimes I like these versions better.

He stares at me, mouth agape, shock etched across his face. Quickly he recovers, and I suspect it's the lawyer in him, the training that tells him never let them know you're surprised.

"Can you say that again?" he asks, his voice a little scratchy.

"You heard me right."

He scrubs a hand across the back of his neck. "You were married? As in, husband and wife? Bride and groom?"

"It surprises you that someone would marry me?"

He narrows his eyes, shooting me a *c'mon* look. "No. Not in the least." He wiggles his fingers, motioning me to serve it up. "But you've got my complete attention, and I'm going to need the full details of how it happened."

I take a deep breath and confess. "My dirty little secret is that I was married for six months."

"And it's a *secret* secret?"

Laughing, I ask, "What's a *secret* secret?"

"When it's vault level. Lucy says it's for the deepest of secrets."

I nod crisply. "Then this would be five-stories-underground, undetectable-by-radar, zombies-can't-find-you, bunker-level secret."

"Got it. Why? Who? When? Where? What?"

I lean back against the cushy leather seat and prepare to share my albatross as a wedding planner: not only am I *not* happily married, I'm also divorced. "His name is Jensen. I met him when I was twenty-six. I was crazy about him, wildly in love," I say, imagining Jensen's shoulder-length hair, his raspy voice, his man-against-the-world mentality. "He was a violinist."

Zach rolls his eyes. "Musicians."

"Yes, they're attractive."

"Go on."

"We met. We fell hard and fast. We were tangled up in each other."

He makes a *speed it up* gesture. "Feel free to skip the whole *we had sex every second and I loved him like crazy* bit."

"Ooh, jealous much of my sexcapades from seven years ago?" I tease.

"Moving on."

"Anyway, I thought he was the one. I thought it shortly after I met him."

"How did you meet?" His voice is a tightrope.

I trip back in time, remembering Jensen's intensity, the way he drowned himself in music, how his brown hair fell over his eyes when he massaged the bow across the strings like he was making love to the instrument. The way he poured his entire body into Brahms, Bach, Beethoven. "He played for the New York Philharmonic. We met at a bookstore. I was thumbing through a book of sonnets—a gift for my sister. He was reading poetry."

One look at Zach tells me he is working hard to rein in an eye roll. I pat his arm. "It's okay. You can mock me. I'm well aware that it's like saying our eyes locked across a crowded room and the world melted away."

"Or that you were both reaching for the last slice of cake at the same time."

"Hey! I never let anyone else get the last slice of cake. My cake-snagging skills are top-notch."

"Mine are even better. But back to the story. Keep going. I want to hear it." The urgency in his tone tells me that for some reason he *must* know this.

I give him the full truth. Nothing held back. "It was very . . . *passionate*. Very romantic. Like something out of a book or a movie. I fell for him because it was everything I thought love was supposed to be."

"You mean, it was what you saw your mom do?"

"Yes. It seemed like the hopeless romantic was getting her happy ending. We went for walks together in the park, and I had my hand in his back pocket and he had his hand in mine. We were laughably in love. I'd watch him perform, and I'd wait for him backstage, meet him when he was riding that performer's high. We'd go out to bars or speakeasies, to lounges, and we'd soak in the romance of the city. I was so wrapped up in it, and so was he."

"So he proposed?" It sounds like he's chewing on gravel.

I sigh, clucking my tongue. "Sort of?"

"Ah, the plot thickens."

"We went to Vegas."

A *ha* bursts from his lips. "What happens in Vegas . . ."

"We went there for the weekend, and we'd been together maybe four months. He wandered past the chapel in the Bellagio, and he said, 'Let's do it. Let's get married.'"

"And that was all it took?"

Honestly, that was all it took. I was caught up. I was swept up. I was in love. I nod, answering Zach. "I thought he was my forever. I thought he was my happily ever after, my prince, my fairy tale."

"What changed? What was the twist in the story?"

I smile faintly, liking that he puts a spin on the fairy tale gone awry. "We returned to New York, rings on our fingers, lives supposedly entwined, but every day it became more obvious that we weren't a good fit."

"What made it obvious?" He's relentless, like he's parched and I can quench his thirst with my answers.

"Little things. Big things. We'd go out to dinner and have nothing to say after appetizers. He'd come home after a performance, and all he wanted was to talk about the music. But when I tried to talk about my day, he had little interest. He was lost in his world, and truth be told, I was lost in mine."

"Your marriage had intensity, but no depth."

I tap my nose. "Exactly."

"How did it end? Was there a fight?"

"No." A stitch of sadness marks the word, a vestigial emotion from a time when I ached, knowing we weren't going to last. My marriage fizzling out was an open wound, and it didn't heal for a long time. "There was no epic fight, no burning of his clothes, no tossing my things out the window. Just this realization that we weren't meant to be, that we'd jumped the gun. We were fools in love who fell out of love." I adjust my seat, letting it back an inch or two, then return to the story. "We divorced amicably, went our separate ways. He's performing in Russia now and is married with two children."

Zach hums, staring off into the dark of the tiny oval window. "So you keep your marriage a secret?"

"I do," I whisper, that old shame surfacing. "I mean, 'Quickest Marriage Flameout since Kim Kardashian's First Wedding' doesn't look great on a business card. Only a handful of people know. No fanfare, since we married in Vegas. My sister knows, of course, and my friend Sloane. And Jess too, but she's been sworn to secrecy." I bring my finger to my lips. "She's a good secret keeper, unlike Charlie."

Zach nods, understanding exactly how our friend is.

"And honestly, by the time it started to unravel, I was embarrassed. Of all people, I should have been able to make a marriage work. Or at least have avoided making my mom's mistakes. I didn't want to tell anyone I hadn't managed it. Certainly not clients. Brides want to believe in the fairy tale. Heck, I believe in the fairy tale. But my clients want me to fit into it. They don't want a fairy godmother who makes stupid mistakes. And they definitely don't want any reminders that marriage can die."

He shifts a little closer, his expression thoughtful. "It's not stupid. It's not shameful. You loved him once upon a time."

"But not like you and Anna. I remember seeing you guys at parties in college. That was real love."

His eyes meet mine. "It was."

Two words. *It was.* No doubt, no question.

"Do you still love her?" I ask softly.

He sighs. He holds up his hands, like he's surrendering. "I don't know how to answer that without sounding like an asshole."

I reach for his arm, pressing my hand to it gently. "Try."

His eyes latch onto mine, darkness shrouding his irises. "This is life. You can only play the hand you're dealt. This is mine. I played the cards. I had a great hand for a short time. I have no regrets. But here I am, maybe with a new deck."

He lifts a hand. Is he—is he going to sweep my hair back?

He is.

His fingers brush against the ends of my hair, moving the strands behind my shoulder. My skin sizzles. Maybe it even glows beneath his touch.

I bite the corner of my lip and hope he can't hear the hitch in my breath. I'm not supposed to respond to him like this. I don't want to be attracted to him at this molten level.

"Your hair was about to be stuck in the seat," he says, but it sounds like an excuse, and a part of me loves that he's making one.

"Thanks," I say, wobbly, as butterflies whoosh through my insides. Damn butterflies.

"Now you're safe."

"Thanks for saving my hair."

"That's what I'm here for."

"You're a prince," I say, going full playful, as if that will stop the onslaught of feelings slamming into me.

He lets his hand drop, resting it in his lap. "Hey, Piper?"

I swallow thickly. "Yes?"

"You know love isn't a fairy tale, right?"

I sigh. "I do know that. And I know it doesn't have to be a fairy tale to work."

He nudges my arm, winking. "Thanks for sharing your dirty little secret."

"Don't tell a soul," I say, miming zipping my lips.

"I'm a vault."

I poke his chest, stabbing his sternum. "You better be."

In an instant, he circles his fingers around my wrist. My heart stops; my breath catches. His eyes lock with mine.

Is the entire plane asleep? We're the only ones awake in this cabin. Perhaps the only ones who want to be. And I *want* right now. I want so much. I am a woman comprised solely of *desire.*

My gaze swings down to our hands.

He slides his thumb along my wrist, stroking me. Tingles rush across my body, lighting me up, sparking every nerve ending, unraveling me.

He moves in slow motion, the pad of his thumb tracing a line up and down my skin. He's mesmerizing me with his touch. I swallow, wondering, waiting.

Is he going to kiss me on the plane? With his kids a row ahead of us? Instinctively, I check to see if they're awake.

I've broken the spell.

Even though they're sound asleep.

He drops my hand. "Never have I ever fallen asleep on your lap on a plane."

I smile. "Is this your way of telling me to sleep on you?"

His grin is magnetic as he answers me. "Yes."

Perhaps I'm more tired than I thought, because the

next thing I know, I'm dozing off on his leg, and I swear, I can feel his fingertips gently stroking my hair.

I tell myself it's nothing, he's no one, because once we land, we have to don our armor again.

But we don't.

15

PIPER

The line at the Tower of London stretches for miles behind us. Miles in front of us.

"This is going to take forever." I shift from one foot to the other, bemoaning our state of affairs.

"I promise I'll get you an ice cream cone when we're done." Zach pats my head as if I'm a child.

I stomp my foot, acting like one. I can't wait much longer. Waiting and I are not friends.

Lucy peers around at the crowd. "We're almost there, Piper."

Literally every tourist in London has decided to flock here today. Didn't they get the memo that I was coming and will require a moment alone with the tiaras? A personal audience with the crowns?

Evidently not.

"You really don't do lines well, do you?" Zach observes.

I moan like a balloon letting out air. "I'm terrible at lines. I hate them. They're the worst."

"We've only been waiting thirty minutes."

"Feels like an eternity."

Zach arches a brow, a grin dancing on his face. "I bet you're one of those people who makes plans to go to brunch at some thoroughly hip place named something super trendy, like Fox and Fig or Oak and Orange, then if you arrive and there's a line of guys in skinny jeans next to Instagramming girls, you bail?"

"No, I wouldn't bail, because I wouldn't even go."

Soon enough, we make it through the queue and inside to the stones and precious metals, and when at last I gaze upon a gold crown inlaid with rubies and diamonds and sapphires, I float. I fly. I beam. The riches are as stunning as I wanted them to be.

Glittering and glorious, the crown jewels speak of another time, another era, when gold and silver were currency, when they paved the way for truces and treaties.

Reverently, I explore the gems, Lucy by my side. We stop at a purple velvet crown set with topazes, rubies, sapphires, and more. "That's St. Edward's crown. It's used at the actual moment of crowning itself," I tell Lucy, gazing upon the stunning head-topper for the monarch. "It's the most important of all the crowns."

"I bet it's super heavy." Henry rubs his head like he's experiencing associative pain. "I think it would give me a headache."

"I've no doubt it would," Zach says, squeezing his son's shoulder. "But how about that scepter? I could see you wielding that at the office, Piper."

"Yes! Me too." I move closer to peer at a dazzling

gold scepter with a diamond the size of my fist on top. I pretend I'm brandishing it, issuing orders, declaring edicts. Lucy laughs delightedly, and Henry squirms away in a fit of giggles. He bumps into a squat English woman, who shoots him a wrinkled smile.

He makes a little bow of apology. "Sorry, ma'am."

"Quite all right, young man. I see your mum has a lovely make-believe scepter."

Henry shakes his head. "She's not my mom. She's just my daddy's friend."

The woman blushes, quick and red, from cheek to jowly cheek. I laugh and wave. "Daddy's friend. That's me. And I have a scepter."

I pretend to bonk Zach with my imaginary gold baton.

"Ouch." He doubles over in mock pain.

The woman clasps her hand to her chest. "I'm so sorry. My apologies."

"It's all good," Zach says.

"You're American?"

"We are."

She pats his arm. "You have a lovely accent, lovely children, and a lovely lady friend."

Then she ambles the hell out of dodge.

Daddy's friend, I mouth, and Zach simply shakes his head.

I spin around, turn my focus to the real scepter, and read the placard. "That diamond weighs five hundred thirty and two-tenths carats."

"And it's said to be the largest cut white diamond in the world," Lucy says, reading along.

I turn to her. "What's so amazing is these jewels have been around for ages, for centuries. The monarchs in the sixteen-hundreds wore them, used them, touched them. The world was so vastly different, but these jewels were here."

"It's weird to think about the sixteen-hundreds. They probably didn't have phones or cake."

"Oh, they definitely had cake."

"But no phones. Or sneakers. Or exercise pants." She looks down at her leggings, standard girl attire.

"They definitely didn't have yoga pants. The only leggings they had were an uncomfortable and weird sort of pantyhose. Nor did they have equal rights for women, so given all that, I like this generation."

"Me too," Lucy says.

"Nowadays, we can like pretty things and admire jewels and still be awesome at school, our jobs, and at taking life on our own terms."

Lucy flashes a big grin and raises her fist. "Girl power."

I knock back.

After we finish giving the sparkly stones a thorough gawking, we leave and grab a black cab and head over to Kensington Palace, where we tour the state rooms. Lucy and I pretend we are in charge of everything.

Literally everything.

We decide how we want to rearrange the palace and which heads of state we'll invite to milkshake and french fry dinners. I pretend to spot Harry and William many times over, and Zach shakes his head every time, smiling and laughing. For a fleeting second, it feels like we're a family.

Which feels weird and squicky. They aren't my family. I don't want to adopt them or pretend they're mine. I'm honestly not even sure I'm truly *Daddy's friend*. I'm more like Lucy's friend and Daddy's frenemy.

His one-time enemy who he nearly kissed on the plane.

Who wanted to be kissed. Who still wants to be kissed.

Shake it off, Piper.

I tell myself I'm the cool aunt.

Just like I am with Paige's soon-to-be peanut.

That makes me feel less squicky.

Even though I do feel a little like I'm playing house when later we go for afternoon tea at a fancy shop. As the kids head to the bathroom to wash their hands, I spread my napkin on my lap. "Thanks for letting me tag along."

He shoots me a look like I'm crazy. "For *letting* you?"

"You're being all 'dad on vacation,' and I'm the interloper."

He reaches for my wrist. This is becoming a habit of his, one I don't want to discourage. "I invited you to spend the day with us. I wanted to do this with *you*." The emphasis is most definitely on *you*. I'm the direct object of his want in this sentence.

Am I in real life too?

My heart skips stupidly. "You did?"

"It was fun. Very *Forty-Eight Hours in London*."

"We could write a magazine article on how to do this city in two days."

"So far it's been good," he says, his voice a little rumbly. He looks down at my wrist in his hand.

A boldness sweeps over me, buoyed by need. "You seem to be holding my wrist often these days."

Please don't let him shoot me down.

He wiggles his eyebrows. "Guess that means you have nice wrists."

"Do I?"

He tightens his hold, squeezing, sending sparkle after sparkle of fireworks through me. "Yes, you do."

He peers in the direction of the kids, and they're not heading back yet, so he inches closer, whispering in my ear, "I'm glad you're having so much fun here."

I shiver. Visibly fucking shiver. "Are you?"

He smiles. "I'm having a blast."

His grin is different this time, like it's free of his usual wink and a nod. It's just an honest grin, an honest answer. And the look in his eyes, the expression on his face, melts another layer of ice inside me. I'm not sure I have any left to protect me from him.

But I need some.

I need something.

Because I'm not here to play house.

I'm not here on *holiday* with this handsome man and his kids, even though I've offered to take care of them while he golfs with the guys, and he said yes.

I'm here to be a good friend and to work, and once the tea ends, I dedicate myself to the Jessica cause nonstop, checking on the event, making last-minute plans, meeting up with the bride that evening and ensuring all is in place for her party tomorrow night.

Seeing her is my reminder. I need this job. I need it for myself and for my sister and for my friend. I don't have the time and space to let Zach Nolan deeper into my life. He won't stay; he won't stick. After all, love isn't a fairy tale. I should know. I've watched my mom seek it over and over, coming up short every time.

A man like Zach, he's already given his heart away, like my mom did with my dad.

It's best for me to be *Daddy's friend*, no euphemism implied. Simply his friend.

The next night, I get ready for the engagement party, grabbing my phone and my clutch.

When it's time to leave, I run into Zach in the elevator. He wears a dark-blue suit that matches his sapphire eyes so well that it takes my breath away.

"You look . . ." I can't even finish. I'm as speechless as he is handsome.

He gazes at me in my simple black dress and heels. *The wedding planner shall not wear bright colors.* "So do you."

As the elevator whisks us down, those flutters aren't from the drop, but from the fear.

The fear that something is happening between us and I can't stop it.

16

ZACH

Garbage day in Manhattan.

The musk of the men's locker room at the gym.

Cooked onions.

Clenching my fists, I do my best to imagine Piper smells like something other than an orange blossom, because her citrus scent is driving me wild.

Also, is this torture? I don't think she's smelled like this before. Or maybe I've never noticed.

As the black cab we share—why the hell did I think it was a good idea to share a cab with her?—plods through London's evening slog of traffic, we make small talk.

What the kids are doing tonight. I tell her I hired a local sitter through the hotel's nanny service and Louise is in the suite with them, reading books, playing board games, and ordering fish and chips, since they begged for an English supper.

Who's coming to the engagement party. Jessica's friends and colleagues here in London where she's been selling books like a bandit, and some of Charlie's new friends too, Piper informs me.

What we like most about London. The side streets and little lanes with bookshops and boutiques, she says.

Shopping. Kids. Chitchat.

The conversation steers me back to safer shores so I'm not lasering in on how much I want to bury my face in her neck, sniff her hair, and kiss the hell out of her.

"I could get lost in the bookshops here," she muses.

"I thought you'd say the jewels and palaces."

She shakes her head. "That's my dream side of London, and I love it. But when I'm traveling, I always like to picture myself living in places I visit, so I see myself in a little flat above a bookshop."

I laugh gently at the image. "And then you'd visit the bookshop every day and smell the pages of old books."

"I absolutely would. And you?"

Wait. Why am I laughing at her answer? She met her ex-husband in a bookshop. She fell for his artistic side. Perhaps that's her type. Maybe she wants to live above a bookshop and meet some *looks like James Bond, fancies himself a poet* type. I can picture it too perfectly: Daniel Craig acting all moody and broody as he convinces her to go for tea then a shag.

I hate him.

"And you?" she asks again, reminding me that I never answered her question.

What would I be doing in London?

Spying on Daniel Craig in the bookshop.

I square my shoulders. "Just running my international spy organization. I believe they call it MI6 on this side of the pond," I say, since I don't have an ounce of artist in me.

Her lips form an O. "Not chasing down the bad guys yourself?"

With a lopsided grin, I answer, "I'd have done that over lunch."

"Impressive," she says as the cab speeds up, rushing to beat the light.

As the driver swings onto the next block like he's operating a race car, Piper slides a few inches closer, her shoulder slamming into mine.

Great. Her orange scent drifts to my nose, and I fight not to dip my head and inhale the scent of her hair. To ask, *Is it your shampoo, your perfume, or your skin that smells so damn decadent? And can I take you back to your flat above the bookshop and find out?*

"You okay?" It comes out strangled. I feel strangled.

She nods, straightening. "That was a sharp turn."

"Just taking a detour," the driver calls out. "I'll have you there in a jiffy."

"Better to be early," Piper says, sliding away from me back to her spot.

I want to haul her back over here, thread my hands in her hair, and devour her lips. Let her straddle me. Forget the traffic and the driver. I want her on me, under me.

But as she adjusts the neckline of her dress, I grit my teeth and tell myself she's wearing that outfit for Jessica. For our friends. For her job.

She's not here for a tryst in a foreign country.

Nor am I.

I need to focus on my role. "Yes. I'm aiming to be an ideal best man, arriving early."

Recalibrating, I stare out the window as the car shimmies down a quieter street, passing streetlamps outside of quaint shops. "Looks like Diagon Alley," I say, since that's a safer topic.

She raises a brow. "Are you a Harry Potter aficionado?"

"If by 'aficionado' you mean did I take my kids on a Harry Potter walking tour of London today, complete with stopping by the spot outside Scotland Yard where the red phone booth would have been located, the one that zipped Harry into the Ministry of Magic, then the answer is yes."

"And did you pretend to dial MAGIC to be let in?"

I blow on my fingers. "That's six-two-four-four-two, if you didn't know."

"Oh, I know. What house are you in?"

"Slytherin. Obviously."

She smirks. "Me too."

"You? Slytherin?"

"What? I'm not conniving enough?"

"I don't know. Are you?"

"Maybe I am," she says, and it comes out flirty, sexy.

Or maybe that's where my mind is.

But that's exactly where it shouldn't be. I'm not Daniel Craig, but I am the perfect best man.

And I plan to stay far, far away from her bookshop.

* * *

The restaurant is beyond trendy. It's so swank, it's going to set a whole new standard for hip with its colorful cocktails and small plates. Jessica's friends are clever and interesting, sharing stories about living and working in this city, while poking fun at the bride and groom.

Throughout the evening, I'm zeroed in on Charlie and his new English buddies, as well as a few Americans working here who they've befriended.

I'm here for him, being the best fucking best man ever. He stood for me at my wedding more than a decade ago, and he didn't try to get with the maid of honor. I can do the same.

We make our way around the crowd, and I am the consummate best mate, poking fun when called for, talking him up at other times.

I don't look at Piper once.

Charlie introduces me to a bearded guy named Graham. One of Jessica's top clients, he's an outgoing and remarkably loud fellow who shares a story of the first time he hung out with Charlie.

"And then he asked me," Graham recounts, dipping into an American accent, "'*Are you a fan of Manchester United?*'"

Charlie shrugs amiably. "In my defense—"

Graham cuts him off with a cheery smile. "There is no defense. You think you're all fans of Manchester United. There are other teams, you know."

"But they're a good team," Charlie points out.

"Some of us like Arsenal," Graham says, tapping his

chest pointedly before he takes a drink and turns to me. "What about you? Favorite football team?"

I'd rather organize my utensil drawer than watch a soccer match. But that's not an acceptable answer this side of the pond, so I go for a diplomatic one. "I'm more of a Yankees man myself."

Graham furrows his brow. "The baseball team?"

"That's the one."

"You've got to have a football team, mate."

"The Giants, then, since we did beat Tom Brady twice."

Graham's expression turns aghast. "American football is dreadful. How do you even watch that? It's like rugby gone wrong."

"I'm starting to prefer English football," Charlie admits.

I stare daggers at my friend. "Charlie, you're a traitor. It's that simple. That's high treason. We're sending you to the Tower of London."

"Unless you stay here," Graham chimes in. "If we can convince you to move, there will be a stay of execution."

Hold the hell on.

Is Charlie relocating to another continent?

"I thought Jessica was coming back to New York. Are you and Jessica moving here?" My gut tightens at the thought. While I don't see Charlie often, I like the possibility that I *could* see him anytime. For basketball, for beer, for a board game with the kids. Charlie's been in New York since I graduated from law school and he from business school. He's my constant. I was friends with him before Anna, during Anna, and after Anna.

He's been the same, and I love it.

He smiles a little sheepishly. "I'm not actually sure. She has so much business here, and I can work from anywhere at the moment."

Graham jumps in. "You'll stay here. Mark my words. This city is addictive."

"It is," Charlie says, and my stomach churns. "But I think we'll live in both places. Split the time."

I breathe a sigh of relief. Correction: a half sigh, because he'll be half gone. But some of Charlie is better than none. "Good."

Charlie claps my back. "Aww, you'd miss me."

I scoff, lying through my teeth, "Not in the least."

His grin spreads. "Yup. When you deny, it's really a lie."

I laugh despite myself. I love this guy. I don't want to lose someone else, though I won't admit that now. "I wouldn't even notice you were gone."

"You'd notice, and you'd cry. Because you love me. It's that simple. You love me, and you'd be sad if I left. I know that's what you really meant."

"Asshole," I mutter.

"Wanker," Graham pipes in, and I'd really like to give him the side-eye for butting in. I'm having a moment with my best bud.

But I'm the *best* best man, so I pile on the groom. "*Arsehole.*"

There. Take that, bearded boy.

Graham laughs, a boisterous sound, then lifts his empty glass. "Now this—this is what's truly sad. Can we agree on that, lads?"

"That is a sorry sight," I say, and gesture to the bar.

He heads in the direction of a refill. Good riddance.

Gesturing to the crowd, Charlie lifts his chin. "What do you think? Of this whole thing?"

One quick look at my friend from college tells me everything. "That you're one happy bastard, and I'm thrilled that you're loving it here, and loving your life."

"And I'm glad you could make it, especially with the kids. Looking forward to golf tomorrow, and that's awesome of Piper to take care of my godchildren. Though what the hell were you thinking with that early tee time?"

"Tee time is always early. Plus, it's easy to be up at the crack of dawn."

He arches a skeptical brow. "You say that because you operate on kid time. I bet you're up at six every day."

"I've been operating on kid time for ten years."

"True," he admits. "And it's pretty damn impressive that we've stayed friends even as you went down the parenthood path."

"And you went down the tech bajillionaire route."

He scoffs. "Please. Multimillionaire. But we can toast to bajillions someday soon."

I raise my beer, and Charlie does the same with his. A waiter circles by, offering tuna carpaccio on a chip. We both snag one, then Jessica saunters over, slides an arm around Charlie's waist, and plants a kiss on his cheek. His expression shifts subtly, like he's more relaxed, happier when she's near.

Lucky son of a bitch.

I turn away, but Jessica clamps her hand on my arm. "Don't you slip off. I have more friends to introduce you to. Eliza's in the biz too. A lit agent who reps all these fabulous nonfiction books that you'd love. Stuff about urban legends and where they came from. Like *Mythbusters*. You'll love her."

She tugs me over to meet Eliza, who's chatting with Piper.

I brace myself for the scent impact. I've been avoiding Piper all night, hanging with the guys, making small talk, but now I'm within a five-foot radius of her. Maybe if I don't get closer, I won't be able to inhale her. If I don't smell her, or touch her, I won't want to take her to the imaginary flat above the bookshop.

Jessica makes introductions, and Piper's smile is radiant as everyone says hello. Her smile says she's happy to be spending time with her good friend. She's having a blast. She's in her element.

My element? It's back in the hotel with two rug rats. It's the courtroom. It's the gym. It's the couch with a book and a glass of scotch late at night. It's boxing gloves to fight like hell for my clients. It's math problems and *Goosebumps* and tae kwon do and Lucy's list of things she wants to do for the summer.

But I'm supposed to be more social, so I keep up the conversation, talking with Eliza about how the Tide Pod Challenge spread like wildfire. Soon, though, the conversation fades, and when she heads off to join some others, I'm left standing with Piper.

And wondering if she still smells as good as she did in the cab.

I glance around, doing my best to keep the conversation innocuous. "You pulled this off. This engagement party is everything Charlie and Jessica could want. It's classy and cool, elegant but modern. It's a perfect mix of new and old, of friends from college and friends from the last year."

"Thank you. That means a lot to me. And the bride and groom do seem quite happy," she says.

There's that word again.

Happy.

Charlie, Jessica, Piper.

Everyone is so goddamn happy. Even Graham. Eliza seems buoyant too.

They're playing their cards and drawing winning hands.

I don't know what's in my hand.

Or what I want to find when I turn over the cards.

All I know is that brand of happiness, the kind I see on their faces, has felt elusive. It's been so far out of reach for the last few years.

But lately, it's less so. It feels like it's peeking around corners, poking at me. And that's both a welcome and a terrifying thought.

I shake it off, concentrating on the here and now. "And are *you* happy with how everything came together?"

"I will be, once we make it through the last-minute addition to the agenda."

"And what is that? A pub quiz? Ride the London Eye? A Jack the Ripper tour?"

Like she has a secret, she shakes her head. "Nope. Clubbing."

Visions of sweaty bodies, blaring techno music, and neon-blue drinks fill my brain. "Did you just say 'clubbing'? As in, going to a nightclub?"

She laughs, waving toward the front door. "Down the block there's an ultra-cool club, where one of the city's best DJs spins tunes all night long. You should come."

Jessica and Charlie appear beside Piper. Charlie wiggles his eyebrows. "The nightclub scene here is top-notch."

I shake my head. "Love you, man, but I'm not a nightclub person."

"C'mon. It's fun." As Jessica pulls Piper away, Charlie lowers his voice. "Plus, Eliza says she thinks you're a *handsome bloke*. Her words."

I stare at him. "Do you really think I'm going to have a one-night stand while my kids are back at the hotel?"

"You have a sitter, man. Use that to your advantage." He winks.

"It's not going to happen." Though, truth be told, the hotel nanny service said Louise could stay well past midnight if needed. She told me herself that I needn't worry about her curfew. *I'm in graduate school for English literature, so feel free to stay out late,* she'd said.

Translation: she needs the money.

He claps my shoulder. "A night out could do you good."

I hold my arms out wide, gesturing to the club. "What's this? I'm out. Right now."

"You know what I mean." He nudges my arm. "I'm just trying to have your back."

"You're convinced that sex is going to cure me of whatever you think ails me."

"Sex cures everything, doesn't it?"

I laugh. "Wouldn't that be something." I take a beat, then turn more serious. "Listen, nothing ails me. I'm fine."

He furrows his brow. "I know that. I know you're good. I'm just trying to help you feel a little better."

"You're like a drug dealer for sex."

He snaps his fingers. "Yes! That's it. That'll be my next business venture."

"Oh, good. Because there's *nothing* at all like that in the marketplace."

His eyes twinkle with mischief. "Can you hear the music? Can you picture the British women dancing at the club? Bet they all want you."

"You are literally the world's worst pimp."

"I'm not trying to be a pimp." He puffs out his chest. "Wingman. Call me the world's best wingman."

"Thanks, Goose. But I'm not going to a club. Sorry if that makes me the world's worst best man, but I don't club, I don't need to get laid, and I also don't want a hookup in London."

My eyes catch on the far edge of the room where Piper and Jessica are laughing with some of Jessica's local friends.

And if I did hook up with someone, it would be with the brunette who smells like an orange, looks like the sexy girl next door, and treats my daughter like her best friend.

17

ZACH

When the party makes its way out of the restaurant en route to the club, I say my goodbyes on the sidewalk, telling Charlie I'll see him on the course bright and early, ready to destroy him.

"I'm prepared to be crushed."

"I'd crush all of you if I liked your brand of golf," Piper adds as she unzips her purse and slides on some lip gloss.

"What's your brand of golf?" Graham asks her curiously.

She mimes swinging a club. "Mini golf. I rule when it comes to obstacle courses with clowns, dinosaurs, and windmills. I played it in high school and college, and I won a ton of tournaments."

His eyebrows shoot into his hairline. "I had no idea that was a thing. How cool. I'd love to hear more about it."

Is he for real? He wants to hear about mini golf? I

mean, the game is fun, but could that be any more of a line?

She smiles at him, and I wish I could tell if it was a professional smile as a wedding planner or a friendly smile as the maid of honor or a flirty smile as a woman. "Consider yourself warned. I can talk mini golf all night long," she answers, and I grit my teeth, seething inside because I can't tell what kind of smile she's flashing his way. And I don't want her doing anything with him *all night long*, no matter what the nature of the challenge.

Graham steps closer to her. "Challenge received and accepted. We can chat at the club."

"Good luck talking over the music," I mutter, like the third wheel I've become.

"Good point," Graham says, smacking my shoulder, then turning his focus back to her. "Piper, I'll have to take you on a tour of London where it's not so noisy. See the little side streets. The shops only the locals know."

Great. Just great. I've unwittingly set them up. Why don't I just suggest he take her to a bookshop and seduce her senseless? *Here's the key to winning her, courtesy of the jackass who's heading home alone.*

She gestures down the block. "But for now, why don't we just go to the club? I need to be there for Jessica."

"The club it is," Graham says, sweeping out his arm as if he's a gallant Sir Walter Raleigh.

Briefly I consider jettisoning my rules about clubs. Protecting my turf. Tossing her over my shoulder and claiming *mine*.

But she's not mine.

I'm not hers.

And I have kids asleep back in Kensington. I have a nanny to pay gobs of pounds to.

That's my element. That's where I belong. I don't have my feet in this clubbing, partying, no-kids world. Hell, perhaps it's fitting that Charlie's going to be living here half the time. I'm the interloper in his world—mine is back in a hotel suite.

I wave goodbye, march up the block, and catch a cab once I'm away from all of them. As I buckle in, a text flashes at me from Louise, telling me the kids are sound asleep and have been for a few hours.

Sleep sounds . . . impossible.

I'm not the least bit tired, thanks to the time change. And I'm not the least bit relaxed, thanks to Graham and his fucking *I want to hear about mini golf* bit.

Wanker. Fucking wanker.

But he's a wanker with Piper at the club. He's likely slinking an arm around her waist, buying her a cocktail, telling her he'll take her to a quaint little bookshop tomorrow then go grab a spot of tea. Speaking in that accent that makes women drop their panties.

My muscles bunch as images keep relentlessly taunting me. Staring out the window, I have half a mind to stop the car and walk the rest of the way back to burn off this frustration.

But I need to do more than walk.

I text Louise that I'd love to hit the hotel gym, if she's still willing to stay. She says she'd be thrilled. When I reach the suite, I say a quick hello then stop in the kids'

adjoining room where I drop kisses onto their fore-
heads. I pause for a moment, savoring the quiet, the
sweet, sleepy faces. Neither one of my babies stirs, and
in moments like these, I'm home. Completely home.

"Love you," I whisper. "So much."

I change quickly in my room and tell Louise I'll be
back in an hour and a half. She waves me off. "Take
your time, Mr. Nolan. I'm going to pop open my laptop
and do some more work on my thesis. That's what I did
when your little darlings fell asleep. It's so much quieter
here than at my flat."

"Great. Good luck with it."

I head downstairs for a workout, where I crank up
the volume on my playlist and prepare to pound out
miles on the treadmill to AC/DC, since that's my mood
at the moment. I zoom in on the tunes, hoping they'll
erase whatever's happening at the club.

Soon enough, I'm in the zone, running in place, my
brain bathed in head-banging music. Eventually, I'm no
longer thinking of anything but the burn in my legs and
the pounding of my heart.

When I return, Louise is conked out on the couch,
her laptop open on the coffee table.

I scratch my jaw.

Do I wake her up? Let her snooze?

I turn down the volume on my phone so a sharp
alarm or loud ring doesn't wake the kids. I park my
hands on my hips, assessing the situation.

I can't sleep with the nanny on the couch. That's . . .
strange.

But I'm not sure it's my place to go rustle her either.

Anna would have done that. But it seems like something the mom would do, not the dad.

Deciding to go about my business and hope the ambient noise rouses Louise, I check on the kids once more, unzip my suitcase loudly to grab some lounge pants and a T-shirt, and then peer into the suite's living room again.

Louise is still snoozing.

Impressive.

And time for me to kick things up a notch.

Let's see if the noise of a shower does the trick.

Fifteen minutes later, I'm freshly cleaned, and she's deeper into the land of nod. She's tugged the blanket off the back of the sofa, and is snuggled under it, breathing steady and even.

Look, I know how to be loud. I know how to wake up anyone. But I don't know jack about Louise. I don't want to scare the hell out of her. Maybe she desperately needs her sleep. She did say it was quieter here than at her flat.

Still, I try.

"Louise," I whisper from a foot away.

She doesn't move.

I draw a deep breath, then gently shake her shoulder.

She flips over to her stomach, mumbling something that sounds like "I'll finish the Austen essay in the morning."

All right. Let's give it the old college try. Well, not *that*. The college try would have entailed dumping ice on a buddy or blasting a foghorn in his ear. Because, well, we were assholes.

One more nudge.

"Brontë. The Brontë essay," she mutters.

And I thought law school was brutal.

Bewildered, I grab the card key, snag my phone, and step into the hall to call my sister and ask her advice.

Before I can dial, I spot a notification. A text that arrived twenty minutes ago. From Piper.

My jaw tics. She better not be telling me she's having a great time with Graham, cheery old chap and fan of shitty sports.

Piper: Apparently, Jessica and Charlie can't club for long either!!! They're done, and I'm on my way back. LOL.

Her name on my phone makes my chest light up and pisses me off too. I reply.

Zach: Where's Graham?

Piper: I don't know!

Zach: He's not with you?

Piper: Let me look around and check. Hold on.

I sigh heavily. Doesn't she know I'm not in the mood? I tap a short message.

Zach: Piper . . .

Piper: Wait. I found him in the inside pocket of my purse.

Zach: Does that mean he's with you?

Piper: Yes, he's eating a cracker that was in my clutch. Hungry little guy.

Zach: Where are you for real?

Piper: What's got into your bonnet? Is this the inquisition? I'm in my room. Jessica and Charlie gave me a bottle of champagne, so I'm having a glass and watching *The Crown*. Anything else you want to know, counselor? Or has the cross-examination ended?

I drag a hand through my hair and slump against the wall. What the hell am I doing? I write to her.

Zach: The sitter fell asleep in my room. I'm standing in the hallway. I have no clue what to do. I can't sleep in the next room with the sitter on the couch.

Piper: You can't?

Zach: I can't.

Piper: So what then?

I sink down to the floor, parking myself on the

carpeted hallway, my phone clutched in my hand, her message blinking at me.

It's like a neon sign at the end of a road. Beckoning.

But what's my answer?

The chug of the elevator hits my ears, and I snap my gaze in its direction. A couple stumbles out, laughing, touching, heading to their room. The man slides his key card in the lock. The woman's arm is wrapped around him. In seconds, they're in the room, and the hall is empty again.

I lower my head, picturing what I want, what I don't want, what I might be able to have.

I send a text.

18

ZACH

Once you decide, you just go.

With the sent message to Louise on my phone—*I stepped out, but I'm in the hotel. Text or call when you wake up and I'll be right back*—I head upstairs, skipping the elevator, taking the steps two by two. I have energy to spare.

I reach her floor, find her room, and rap loudly on the door.

Stuffing my hands in my pockets, I wait. She doesn't answer right away. I shove a hand through my still-wet hair, glad I showered.

My stomach churns. With nerves? With anticipation? I'm not sure. Maybe it's with latent annoyance.

A clinking sound ends the silence. Metal against metal. The safety lock undone.

My pulse spikes. I'm on high alert.

The door creaks open an inch, then she yanks it open more.

"Hey?" It's more than a whisper. It's a curiosity. In

that one syllable she's asking why I'm here. Of course she's asking.

She's a woman asking an unspoken question after midnight.

I want to answer, but my throat is dry. She's not in her black dress anymore. My mind goes haywire as I drink in her attire.

Or, rather, the lack thereof.

A strappy black camisole clings to her chest and sleep shorts hug her hips. So much exposed skin. So much territory to explore, to taste.

Does she still smell like orange blossoms, or has it faded?

Desire rips through my body, white-hot, vibrating in every molecule. In every cell. I'm shaking with lust.

"Hey." I barely recognize my own voice. I barely know what to say. Or do.

But maybe she can read a million things into that one word.

Maybe she can translate what I've said into what I'm not saying.

You. I'm here for you.

To grab her and crush a kiss to her lips. To push her against the wall and strip her to nothing. To take her.

Because I want her so fucking much.

And it's more than a physical need.

It goes deeper, farther than I expected.

Seconds pass in silence, and I'm so parched I can't talk.

She puts me out of my misery. "I'm guessing you're dying to know who's sleeping with the prince?"

I blink. Is she speaking Turkish? "What?"

"*The Crown.* I presume you couldn't resist the idea of watching *The Crown* and having champagne."

She's right on one count. "Exactly," I say, staring at her face then letting my gaze travel up and down her body. I'm transparent. My thoughts are written in my eyes. "I couldn't resist."

Her breath seems to hitch. "Come in, then."

I cross the threshold, letting the door fall shut behind me.

Her room is smaller than mine, a room for one. The bed is made pristinely, the duvet a crisp white cover. Past the bed, a navy-blue couch sits against the wall, a coffee table in front of it.

Her suitcase is tucked neatly by the closet, unzipped but not open. On the nightstand is her phone and an e-reader. There are no outfits strewn everywhere, no cords to navigate around.

"You're neat," I remark.

Instantly, I want to smack myself upside the head. *You're neat? Jesus Christ, how long has it been, man, since you talked to a woman you wanted?*

But I know the answer to that. Too long.

"Confession: I make my bed in the morning."

"In a hotel?" Maybe she is speaking Turkish.

She nods sheepishly.

"You do know they have people who do that?"

With a shrug, she wanders to the couch and flops down. "I don't like messes. Don't like looking at them. They ruin my mojo."

She lifts her glass, her eyebrows rising too. An invitation.

Maybe she knows I'm a mess right now. Maybe she's trying to sort me out.

I follow her. Do I sit near the armrest? Or close to the middle? Why the hell am I stuck in this morass of indecision? I don't waffle. I don't hem and haw.

But tonight, evidently figuring out where to sit is hard.

I split the difference as she pours champagne into a bathroom glass.

I take it. "Nice flute."

She winks. "Only the classiest for me."

I raise my glass. "What are we toasting to?"

She tucks her feet underneath her. "You tell me, Zach."

And like that, the ball is in my court. She's asking me what's going on. Why I'm here. What I want.

To feel again.

Instead, I toast to the truth. "To Graham not being here."

Rolling her eyes, she clinks, and we drink. She's quiet, and I guess that means it's still my turn. And I still need to know if she's taking a tour with Graham.

"So, did he hit on you?"

She runs her finger along the rim of the glass. "Is that why you're here? To inquire about Graham's intentions? I thought it was to watch *The Crown*."

I glance at the screen. I bet that queen asked for what she wanted. My lips quirk up. "Never have I ever come here to watch *The Crown*."

Her eyes widen, and she stares pointedly at my glass. I don't take a drink.

She lifts a brow, her brown eyes twinkling with mischief, with a *so this is how it goes* kind of spark. "Never have I ever gone to a woman's room to inquire about a man I'm jealous of."

I laugh. Busted. I drink, and it tastes spectacular. The best swallow of champagne ever. It takes like the truth, like a weight lifting.

It tastes like a chance.

And it feels like fun, something I want more of, something I like a whole hell of a lot with her. So I keep it up.

"Never have I ever made plans with an English bloke to go on a tour of bookshops and other stupid shit."

She cracks up, clutching her glass resolutely. "Well played."

"So you're not going with him?"

"Did I not just answer that?"

"Did you want to?"

"I already said I'm not going with him. Why are you asking if I wanted to?"

"Because I want to know."

"Then shouldn't you ask your question in the form of the game?"

She keeps me on my toes. "You're right. I should."

I assemble the words carefully in my head first. "Never have I ever turned Graham down because I have zero, nada, zilch interest in him, rather than because it would be a bad idea to have a fling with him."

The look she gives me reminds me of a woman lazily

swinging in a hammock, biting into an apple, a satisfied grin on her face.

I wait several interminable seconds that last for hours.

She takes her time, quirking up her lips as if she's considering all facets of the question. A long sigh falls from her lips, then a hum. "Well, let's see . . ."

"Piper . . ."

"Let a woman answer."

I sweep my arm out. "The floor is yours."

She taps her bottom lip. "So you're asking if I'm attracted to Graham? And if it was difficult to turn him down?"

"Yes," I bite out.

She raises the glass halfway. "Let me think. Never have I ever turned Graham down . . ."

I groan.

And she finishes the thought. "Because I'm not attracted to him." She smirks, lifts the glass, and takes a fabulously large gulp. Her nose crinkles. "Ooh, that tickled." She sets down the glass, rubs her palms. "But now it's my turn."

"Bring it on," I say, more cocky than I expected. But then this is my turf. Back and forth. Tête-à-tête. We're in the ring boxing, and this is what we do.

She taps her chin. "What to ask, what to ask. . ."

I make a sound, like a ticking clock.

"Oh, hush. There's no time limit." She stares at the window, then at me, studying my face. She adjusts herself, sitting a little higher. My eyes stray to her chest, to her perky breasts, and I stifle a moan. Raising my gaze, I catalog her glossy lips, her soulful eyes, her simple elegance.

She inches a tad closer, as if she's about to taunt me.

Taunted is not what I feel.

Exponentially more aroused is more like it.

I'm not sure how that's possible, but there it is. It's happening. My skin sizzles as she moves nearer.

She speaks. "Never have I ever come to a woman's room after midnight for reasons other than champagne and Netflix."

That's so easy.

In fact, it's so easy, I make it clear. "Obviously, I'm not here for the bubbly or the show." I take a long drink, keeping my eyes on her the whole time.

When I lower my glass, I kick the game up a notch to the next level. "Never have I ever wanted this guy to come to my room."

Her lips part slightly. She says nothing. She raises her glass, takes a drink.

I'm so buzzed, and it's not from the liquor. I've barely had any. I'm tipsy on her. I'm intoxicated with anticipation. And I want to get drunk on this night, this woman, and all the possibilities.

She starts to speak, but I raise a hand, stopping her. "Let me go again."

"Okay." Her voice is scratchy, a little nervous.

But I need another turn. I'm the one who appeared at her door. I'm the one who needs to go first.

To show my hand.

I lift my glass, never taking my gaze from hers.

"Never have I ever wanted to kiss this woman on the plane, in the elevator, in the cab."

Her eyes spark, flecks of desire dancing across the irises.

I push on, hogging the turn, taking all the turns, because I have to. Because I'm a jack-in-the-box, wound so damn tight, and I have been for months. These last few days with her have been some of the best I've had in ages, and even though I shouldn't do this, even though I shouldn't be here, I am.

Ready for what comes next, damn the risks.

"Never have I ever wanted to know how you taste, if you smell as good when I kiss your skin as I imagine you do. Never have I ever come to your room after midnight because I couldn't get you out of my head."

She gasps, blinking, then a shudder seems to run through her. "Really?"

Nodding, I finish my glass and set it down. I take hers and put it on the table, then thread my hand in her hair. "Get your lips on mine. I need to taste you."

"Oh God," she whispers.

We crash into each other, two tigers fearlessly tumbling. I yank her close and claim her mouth, my thoughts going hazy as I kiss her deeply, and deeper still.

I'm not interested in soft, whispery kisses.

I'm hungry. I'm downright starved, and she's the only thing that can satisfy me.

She kisses exactly how I imagined, because, oh hell, have I ever imagined this. She's fiery and fierce, all heat and need. Her hands curl around my head, through my hair, and she kisses me hard—so damn hard it blurs out the world. It erases everything but this room, and her, and my aching desire to have her.

Dropping my hands, I grab her hips and tug her onto my lap so she's straddling me. In lounge pants and sleep shorts, little is left to the imagination. My intentions are wildly clear and incredibly loud.

She sinks down against my hard-on, and I groan, a sound that's equal parts relief and pent-up desire. I'm not satisfied, not in the least. I need so much more. I need more than this.

But I will take this gladly.

Oh so fucking gladly.

Grabbing her ass, I squeeze, moving her against my hard-as-stone dick.

She breaks the kiss, letting her head fall back, her hair spilling behind her. She lets out a carnal cry. A greedy *yes* that lasts for days.

My cock jerks against her as she rubs herself on me, her hips swiveling and grinding.

The sight of her like that, chasing her pleasure already, sets my chest to flames. I grab her face, pulling her back to my mouth. "Kiss me again. Kiss me while you ride me," I murmur.

She slams her lips to mine, and we kiss like the world is burning behind us, like it's spiraling away to ash and this is the last thing we'll do.

Our teeth click, and I love the roughness, love the sloppiness. My tongue skates over hers, and I bite her lip, nibbling, and she yelps, but then it turns into a long, lingering moan that lasts for fantastic lingering seconds. "*Zach.*"

My name on her lips is the sexiest thing I've ever heard. It unravels me. It unlocks me. I need to be inside her now.

I don't want her coming on my lap like we're in high school. I don't want child's play. I want the real thing. Her wetness against my hardness.

I break the kiss. "Bed. Now. I need to be inside you." Then reality slams into me. "Shit, fuck, hell."

Instantly, she stops moving. "What's wrong?"

"I don't have a condom. Do you? Wait. I bet the hotel does. I can call the concierge."

Even though the wait for him to bring one feels like it would be an eternity in hell.

A smile sneaks across her face. "I'm on protection, and I'm safe. Clean."

Ah, glorious words. Beautiful, glorious, incredible words. I can fuck her without barriers.

"Good. Because I hate condoms. Also, I'm safe too," I tell her.

She scoots off, and I stand, removing my shirt as I walk to the bed.

She stares at me. "Whoa."

I stop before I toss my shirt to the floor. "Whoa, what?"

"Your chest. Your abs. Your stomach. Can I just spend the night licking you?"

Laughing, I drop the shirt, step closer to her, and fiddle with the hem of her cami. "Love the sound of that. But no. I need to be inside you. Need to feel you." I lower my face to her neck, flicking my tongue up the column of her throat, inhaling her citrus scent—yes, it's everywhere, and it drives me even wilder than it did in the cab—as I make my way up to her ear. She trembles while I kiss her neck, nibble on her earlobe. "Need to fuck you, Piper. I need it so much."

"Me too." She runs her fingers up and down my chest. Tracing the grooves in my abs, she bites her lip, looking mesmerized.

I feel mesmerized.

By her. By this night. By her touch.

I haven't been touched in so long.

Haven't wanted it. Haven't craved it.

Till her.

Now all I want is this electricity, this crackling energy.

It flickers and sparks like a current that won't stop.

I pull off her cami, my hands cupping her breasts, kneading them, before my fingers travel down to her shorts and strip them off.

They fall to the floor, and she's naked and it's breathtaking.

"You're so damn sexy," I rasp as I tuck my thumbs in the waistband of my pants and push them down, my cock announcing how very happy it is to be free of clothes and standing in front of its goal.

She shakes her head. "No. You are."

I lift a brow. "You're gorgeous."

"Just fuck me," she says.

And I'm not going to deny either of us.

She falls down on the bed, scoots back to the pillows, and I crawl up, savoring every single second.

She settles and reaches down, making grabby hands. With a grin, I move closer so she can touch me like she wants.

Like I want.

She wraps a hand around me, and I'm lost. I'm simply lost in the extraordinary feel.

Her eyes float closed as she touches me, and mine do too. For a moment, maybe more, my mind goes blank. I give in to the sheer ecstasy, to the incredible feeling of intimacy.

Of hands exploring bodies.

Of desire playing the lead role.

Of being human once more.

Of being alive.

It's everything I didn't know I was missing. It's everything I now have to have.

Opening my eyes, I gently swat her hand away. "Spread your legs for me."

She lets her knees fall open, and heat blasts through me as I stare at her, so wet, so ready. I'm a supernova, and I'm not even inside her.

I have to warn her. As I settle between her legs, rubbing the head of my cock against her heat, I groan but still manage to get a word out. "Piper . . ."

She arches against me, pleading with her body. "Yes?"

She sounds as desperate as I feel.

"It's been a while," I say, my voice low, bare truth on my tongue. "A long while."

She pushes up on her elbows. Lifts a hand. Cups my cheek. "Then make it fast and good. Because I feel like I could come in seconds."

I push into her, my eyes rolling back in my head at that first decadent feel of her heat.

"That's . . ." I can't finish the sentence.

"Incredible," she murmurs, and I slide inside. All the way. I am engulfed in her, and it's spectacular.

A blast of pleasure shoots down my spine, a comet appearing from out of nowhere in the night sky.

"Need a moment," I grunt, bracing myself on my palms, looking away from her face.

"Take your time. I'll be here. Just begging to come."

She wriggles against me, and I laugh.

And that does the trick.

That's enough for me to return my focus to her. To direct all my attention on this woman beneath me, wanting me, needing me.

I'm a shark.

I'm tough as nails.

I'm made of steel.

I can hold off an orgasm to pleasure her first. You better believe I can.

I pace myself, going slow at first, taking my time as I listen to her cues, her sounds, her murmurs. She's not quiet. She's wonderfully noisy, her moans and groans a fantastic soundtrack.

As she lets out a series of *oh God, yes, like that,* it's not hard to discover her rhythm, because she knows what she wants. She knows what she needs. She tells me.

I shouldn't be surprised at all.

Piper has always spoken her mind.

I'm not shocked when she shifts a little, turning slightly to the side, and says, "One of us is going to need to play with my clit."

I smirk. "I volunteer as tribute."

"Good. Get tribute-ing."

Adjusting myself so my weight is on my left arm, I slide my other arm between us, running my thumb across the swollen rise of her clit.

Her reaction is instantaneous, making me feel like a king as she screams. "Yes. That. Oh God."

Her noises turn the dial in me up to ten, to one hundred, to a hundred million. But I grit my teeth, stroking her clit, fucking her hard, fighting off my own release.

Her hands travel down my back, sliding over my hot skin till she grabs my ass. Squeezing. Parting her legs. Wrapping them tighter around me. Making her intentions clear.

She intends to come and to come hard.

And I have one job: to finish the motherfucking job.

We are a blur of bodies, of skin, of sound. I stroke and thrust, and she rocks and grinds.

Pleasure curls inside me, lust threatening to overtake my brain, my entire being. But she's a merciful woman, and an honest one too. Because she's trembling, reaching the edge quickly, like she said she would.

Putting me out of my misery.

Her mouth forms an O, and then she's quiet. Blissfully silent before she announces to the whole hotel—no, make that this entire city—that she's coming.

With Superman-level strength, I stave off my own release for a few more seconds so I can watch her. So I can memorize how she looks as her eyes squeeze shut, her face tenses, and she shudders, writhing beneath me as my name and God's name fill my ears.

I let go at last as the orgasm wins the battle, and I happily surrender to it.

The world fades to black.

This. Yes. Everything.

A stark and terrifying awareness hits me. This feels like everything I didn't know I was missing.

19

PIPER

"Well, that was delightful."

He arches a brow. "Delightful? That was delightful?"

Sighing contentedly, I stretch my arms above my head and lift a brow. "What's wrong with delightful?"

He growls. "Delightful is for a stroll through a garden."

Remaining deadpan, I ask, "How would you describe it, then?"

"Epic. That was mind-blowingly epic."

Not gonna lie. Inside, I'm glowing at that description. But toying with him is too fun. "Epic? Do we still say 'epic'? I thought that was out of vogue."

He huffs, his nostrils flaring. "Woman, is now the time to debate trends in popular colloquialisms?"

"You mean, it's not the time when your machismo is at stake?" I can't resist.

He props himself up on his elbow. "I'm pretty sure no one says 'machismo' anymore."

I quirk up my lips. "I guess you're right. Machismo is for the history books."

He rolls his eyes. "All right, time to go." He pushes up, and I grab his arm—his toned, firm arm. He wasn't kidding when he said he spent time working out, and I'm not kidding when I say praise the Lord for his devotion to barbells—and flash him a smile. "Delightful was an understatement."

He stops, stares at me. "I thought so."

"Did you now?" I counter.

His eyes drift to my hand on his arm, then they roam up and down my naked body.

For a moment, it hits me—I'm naked with Zach Nolan. We're fire and ice. We've shot arrows and hissed at each other. We're champions in the sport of eye rolling and lobbing clever invectives.

I should be freaking out. I should be trying to wake myself from a dream, because no way do we screw in real life.

But this is real life, and real life is fabulous in this moment.

Especially as he eats me up with his eyes, making me shiver.

My response to his dirty gaze does not go unnoticed. He looks back at me with his standard intensity, speaking with his tough, no-nonsense tone. "I believe what you meant to say was . . . never have I ever come so hard. Is that right?"

I pretend to lift a glass and to down it. "That is exactly what I meant to say."

Yup, this is real. This is us. We still have our arrows

and quivers, only they've changed. They're not as barbed. They're fun and fiery.

He laughs, then runs a hand down my stomach. The feel of his touch turns me to jelly, and I was already a weak-kneed mess of hormones.

But when he swings his legs over the side of the bed and says, "Let me clean you up," I'm no longer a mess of lust.

I'm a puddle of swoon. It's embarrassing, completely embarrassing, how much the sweetness of the gesture hooks into my heart.

I should shove off the bed, wave a hand, and march to the bathroom to do it myself. But I don't. I lie here waiting, savoring the aftereffects that still radiate through my body, the lingering glow from the way he made me climb the mountain then soar off the other side. Who cares if "epic" is out of fashion? That was *epic*.

He returns with a warm washcloth, gently sliding it between my legs. I close my eyes, because the tenderness is nearly too much.

I don't know how to handle this Zach. This side of him is too endearing. Too wonderful. I could fall for this side of him. The passionate lover is a tender lover too.

And I know that because we're not fire and ice anymore, and we haven't been for a while. But I don't know what that makes us other than something else, something unnamed, maybe even unknown.

He returns to the bathroom then joins me again, stretched out in the bed.

"So. That was indeed delightful," he says dryly.

Yes. This. I can do *this*. I open my eyes and meet his gaze. There's that teasing glint in his blue eyes, there's the twinkle.

I understand what to do with this Zach so much more than the kind, gentle one.

"Fine," I grumble. "It was better than delightful. It was . . ." I pause, searching for another adjective to needle him with. "*Lovely*."

Laughing, he parks his hands behind his head. "Look, you can call it lovely. You can call it delightful. I'm just patting myself on the back for getting you there first. That was literally my only goal."

I flash back to those seconds before he entered me, when pure vulnerability crossed his eyes. When he said, *It's been a while*. In that phrase, I heard everything, understood everything. He hasn't been with anyone else since his wife died.

I'm his first.

Part of me doesn't know how to manage the weight of being his first after her, after a love like that, a life like that.

Another part of me is doing a hula dance. *Me*. He chose me. The everything fruit. The girl down the hall. The girl he spars with.

The vulnerable part of me is happy. Happier than I imagined I'd be. But trying to dig into why this delights me—yes, this knowledge is delightful—requires an excavation that isn't welcome.

This was sex, right?

An itch. We scratched it.

I keep the mood light, since he didn't come here for

a heavy talk, nor do I want one. "I'd say you achieved your goal. Also, you take direction extraordinarily well."

He blows on his fingernails. "Feel free to give me any more you like. For instance, *lick harder, suck my clit, lick my pussy, fuck me with your fingers.*"

My jaw drops at his unexpected dirty mouth. "Zach Nolan, you're filthy."

He shrugs unapologetically. "I'm just saying, I'm up for it. You saying any of the above. Me taking your direction."

I tremble, my body betraying me. I want to give him all those directions. I want him to take them to town and light me up again.

His eyes sparkle. "Seems you might like that too. Any of the above?"

I purse my lips. I don't know why I'm having such a hard time admitting that I want more. Maybe because I don't know what we're doing. I don't know what's changed. If this was a one-time thing, or if it could be something more.

I don't know what I want it to be.

But it can't be anything more, a voice reminds me.

My attention needs to be on my goals. My sister, her baby, my job, Jessica's wedding. I can't tango with Zach, because . . . what if it ends badly? I can't bring that kind of negative energy on Jessica.

And of course it would end badly. We are too much up in each other's business and lives. We have our friends and this wedding and—

"Hey, when I told you that you were sexy and

gorgeous, why did you say, 'No, you are'? It's like you were saying you weren't."

I cringe, wishing he'd forgotten that. Those types of compliments are hard for me to hear. I don't know how they can be true.

"I was just saying you were," I answer, aiming for misdirection. I'm a magician. Now you see it, now you don't.

He looks through the illusion, pushing on. "Don't you realize how gorgeous you are?"

I turn to face him, propping my head in my hand. Might as well level with him. "Look, thank you. But you don't need to say that to me to get me in bed again."

A laugh seems to burst from his throat. "What? Do you think it was a line the first time? Give me more credit."

I shake my head. "I'm not saying it was a line. I'm saying don't feel obligated."

"Like you thought I felt obligated after the dinner in New York? Why are you worried about obligations?"

Because I don't know how we could handle them. Because I don't want you to feel like I'm one of yours. Because I don't know how to manage my feelings if I am. Because a part of me wants to be your obligation.

But that's not the core issue.

I key in on the question, answering matter-of-factly because this is a black-and-white truth for me, a cornerstone of who I am, what I do. "I'm not gorgeous, and I know it. If anything, I'm cute. I'm not stunning. I'm not beautiful. I'm not even pretty."

"But . . ." he sputters.

I raise a hand to stop him. "And I'm a hundred percent okay with that. Truly, I am. I don't suffer from low self-esteem. My esteem is just fine. Trust me—I think I'm awesome, and I'm good with how I look."

He furrows his brow. "How you look? How do you think you look?"

"I'm not the pretty girl. I'm the friend. I'm the wing-woman. That's who I've been. I blend in with my straight nose and brown eyes and standard-issue hair. I'm cute. That's all. I'm fine with cute."

He inches closer, running a finger across my top lip. "With your pretty pink lips that drive me crazy when you slide gloss on them." His hand travels down to my breasts. "With these perky breasts and rosy nipples that fit just right in my hand and feel . . . spectacular."

I shiver from his touch.

He brushes his fingers over my hair. "With these strands I want to run my fingers through."

"Zach," I say, trying to shush him, but I'm blushing. I'm going soft—I've got a liquid center from his praise. "You don't have to say that."

He pushes up, straddles me, pins my arms by my sides. His eyes are a laser beam. "I don't have to *say* anything. I don't have to *do* anything. You know me well enough to know I would never say anything just to say it. So let me say this: you're fucking sexy. Deal with it. You dress in that leather skirt that shows off toned thighs and makes me think filthy thoughts. You wear heels, and I imagine those legs wrapped around my neck. You put on that orange lotion or potion or whatever it is, and I'm a lost cause. I'm a dog panting, begging for a treat."

"That's quite a list." My smile takes over my face and spreads through my whole being.

"You and your lists. See, you might think you're the wingwoman, but the wingwoman does something to me." He lowers his hips, pressing his cock against me, thick and hard. "You're gorgeous. I can't stop looking at you, and I want you again, Piper."

"I want you too," I whisper, and it feels like I've cracked open my chest, that I'm baring my naked soul by saying that.

Maybe I am.

His lips curve up, telling me that was the only response he wanted, and it eases the tension in my heart, the tight knot of worry.

He lowers his face near mine, as if he's about to kiss me, then dodges my mouth. Instead, he runs his nose along my neck, inhaling. A long, deliberate sniff. "Don't you realize that for the last few months, when I've looked at you, I've been undressing you?"

When a man you've sparred with whispers sweet dirty nothings, it's thoroughly disarming.

I have no barbs to toss back at him. Nor do I want to.

Still, I'm not entirely sure how to take all these compliments, other than with a quiet "Thank you."

But my body is sure. Tingles spread from my head to my toes, so I focus on the physical. I glance down, lowering my voice suggestively. "I'm still undressed."

"You are, and I'm not a one-and-done kind of man."

"So what else are you going to do?"

He silences me with a soft kiss. I nearly die from the tenderness, from the sweet, slow, and lazy way his tongue explores my mouth.

Then my neck, my breasts, my belly. He makes his way down my body, turning me to a boneless woman with every flick of his tongue, every press of his mouth, till he's there, right there, where I want him.

He groans as he tastes me.

I do too, my hips shooting up, and I zero in on the sensations—the toe-tingling, knee-melting sensations— as he goes down on me like he's kissing me. He's not one of those painters, the guys who work a straight line up and down, up and down. No, Zach is caressing me with his mouth, devouring me with his lips, and claiming me.

Pleasure coils in my body, tightening and circling, till it climbs higher and higher, and I'm close, so damn close.

Then the switch flips, and I'm falling, flying, coming undone.

The sheer bliss blots out my worries about what's next, where we go, what we do.

Until the morning, when he bolts out of bed, clutching his phone, cursing as he tugs on his pants, and says he has to go.

20

ZACH

My kids are pretty well-adjusted. They've dealt with some shit no kids should have to face, but they've come out on the other side. Lucy, being older, bore the brunt of Anna's illness and her death. But with honesty, love, and a father who was there for her every single day, every single night, she's made it through, and she's one hell of a happy, balanced child.

Henry's an easier one. He was five when he lost his mom. Grief for him was different. It was sharp and immediate and gone quickly. He probably doesn't remember many details about Anna. While snapshots of her might exist in his head, they're likely blurry and, frankly, fading fast.

But he knows me.

He's used to me.

I'm his person, his steady, his rock.

And every morning, the first thing he does when he gets out of bed is pee, brush his teeth, then give me a hug. "Good morning, Daddy," he'll say.

"Good morning, little man."

It's a routine, nothing special.

A completely average, everyday routine.

But it's his, and it's mine, and it's ours. We've done it for the last two years and never missed it once.

He's crying today.

I scoop him up into my arms the second I push open the door to the hotel room. Like a koala, he wraps his arms and legs around me, clinging fiercely.

A bright English voice floats over the sound of sniffles. "See? I told you Daddy would be back in a hurry. All better now, yeah?" Louise's cheery tone is a cover-up.

"I'm here," I whisper to Henry, patting his back, soothing his worried mind.

"He probably just couldn't sleep and was wandering the hallways," Louise offers, meeting my eyes and nodding. *Go with it*, they say. "I do that myself sometimes when I can't sleep. I roam and roam and roam."

She's a saint, and she deserves the biggest tip in the world as she paints over the cracks I sledgehammered into the night.

"I was," I lie, sludge in my chest, bile in my throat.

Henry sniffles. "When I couldn't find you, I was worried. You're always there."

"I'm here. I'll always be here," I tell him. It's a promise I can't entirely make, but I don't care. I have to believe it. I *do* believe it.

"I told you he'd be fine," Lucy pipes in as she wanders into the foyer from their room then throws her arms around my back.

"But I was scared. I didn't know where he was. I didn't know what happened," Henry says, then tucks his head in the crook of my neck and burrows, a scared little animal seeking refuge in his den. I'm his den, and he couldn't find his safety.

My heart craters, and it's entirely my fault. This is *not* a no-fault situation. There is one guilty party, and it's me.

Because I fell asleep in Piper's bed.

I left the volume down on my phone.

I missed three texts and a call from Louise.

And I missed several more from my son.

Henry: Where r u

Henry: i can't find u

Henry: r u ok

I ruffle his hair, trying to keep the mood light. "I'm fine. See? I'm fine. I couldn't sleep because of the jet lag, and I went to work out, and then I wandered around the hotel," I say, peeling off another layer of the lie.

And I sound like an idiot. Who wanders around a hotel because he can't sleep? Who strolls aimlessly down the corridors because of jet lag? It would be obvious to any adult what I've been up to, with my rumpled hair and morning breath. God, I probably have her scent on me. I probably smell like sex.

As these thoughts collide, a pit forms in my stomach. A fucking sinkhole, and it funnels all the good feelings from last night into it.

I've never thought a single parent should be hand-cuffed to his kids. No need to be a monk, or even be home every night. I completely believe single parents should be free to date. Moving on, finding romance, and falling in love again is normal and healthy. It's something I tell my clients, and I mean it. From the bottom of my black heart.

But if you're going to do those things, you have to do them the goddamn responsible way.

With a plan. With sitters or family booked for the night.

With your phone on.

With a return time.

With clear details shared with those who need it.

Me? I did none of that.

I thought with my dick and my emotions. My wound-up, pent-up, torqued-up jealousy over a guy Piper didn't even want to get with. That was what drove me.

I made irresponsible choices, and now here I am, doing something I despise.

Lying to my children.

"I'm sorry you were worried, little man. I wasn't thinking, and I'll do a better job next time," I say, because I can't reside in this sinkhole. I might not be able to tell the truth—they don't need the truth—but I can't live in the lie. I will do better. I will improve.

Henry jerks back and grins widely. "You're the best. I love you to New York and back."

I laugh and tug him in for one more hug, then set him down. "I love you to London and back."

He smiles at me. "Can I have scones for breakfast, and jam? That sounds good and I'm so, so, so hungry."

Just like that, he's moved on. He's over it.

He rubs his belly.

"Give me a couple minutes to pay Louise and brush my teeth, and then we can go downstairs."

Lucy claps. "I want to have tea with my breakfast scones."

"Then you shall have tea," Louise chimes in.

Yup. I'm nominating her for sainthood.

I pay her, brush my teeth, convince Lucy to read Henry a book for five minutes so I can take the fastest of fast showers, and ten minutes later, we're out the door.

Henry runs down the hall. "I want to press the elevator button."

"It's my turn," Lucy declares and rushes ahead of him.

All is well. All is forgiven.

But I don't know how to forgive myself.

I'm keeping secrets from them. They don't need to know who I'm sleeping with or if I'm sleeping with anyone. But they should at least know where I am. They shouldn't have to wake up and wonder where their father is.

We eat and drink tea, and when we're done, I get ready to meet the guys for golf and to hand off the kids to Piper.

As we planned, she waits in the lobby, a Mary Poppins grin on her face when she sees them. She only has eyes for Henry and Lucy. "Just you wait. I have so much fun in store for you."

She waves goodbye to me with barely a word.

Yeah, I'm an asshole.

It's official.

21

PIPER

I'm taking a trip through time.

As we wander down Cecil Court, it's as if I've stepped back into another century.

This entire alley is bursting with bookshops of all kinds, from those that sell stamps and antique maps to those that peddle secondhand, rare, or children's books, and even one that purports to sell psychic literature.

Can I find a book that'll predict what happens to a woman who sleeps with a man who then runs the next morning and can't even manage a single text saying a single word? Oh, wait. Who needs a book for that? I know the answer. Nothing will happen.

After all, it's been six hours since his bat-out-of-hell exodus.

And sure, I do understand your pants are on fire when you've overslept and your kids—I surmise—are calling or texting.

I get that completely.

But I've already shepherded them through a

morning at the park scampering up a climbing wall, down a slide, and up into the sky on swings. Incidentally, I am a rock star at pushing a seven-year-old on a swing.

Never have I ever heard a kid squeal so much as Henry did with his endless requests for again and again, and higher and higher.

I didn't stop.

There was no cell phone gazing for me at the park. No plopping down on a bench with my e-reader as they played. I was involved every second, and when we left, I checked my phone, figuring that's when a *"Last night was amazing, and let's talk later"* text would have arrived.

Something.

Anything.

Surely he could have texted me on the way to golf. Or maybe then once he arrived.

Nada.

Fine. In between holes?

No chance.

See, I don't think you're supposed to ignore a woman after you rock her world three times. I'm counting each orgasm because orgasms should always count. I'm deeming the first bang as one, that fantastic tongue-lashing as two, and then the flip-me-to-my-knees-and-drive-into-me-like-a-man-on-a-mission that he did after going downtown as three, especially since my last O was the hallelujah kind. We're talking the lasted-for-minutes variety of *oh God, oh God, oh yes, right there, God*.

Fine, maybe it was one minute, but it felt like I was

coming forever, and isn't that a delightful thing to experience?

Yes, *dee*-lightful.

Getting ignored? Not so much.

I don't believe in ignoring people.

And I won't ignore his children even mentally, so I shut the door on thoughts of Zach, devoting my energy to these two people who *do* know how to make a girl feel adored.

"Let's speak in English accents the rest of the day," Lucy announces as we stroll down the cobblestone street.

"Proper accents, and we must pretend we are royalty," I add.

"I want to be a prince," Henry says.

"In your accent," Lucy chides.

Taking direction well, Henry repeats in his best rendition of a little English boy as we wander down the street from centuries ago: "I want to be a prince."

"And now I declare we shall visit all the bookstores," Lucy says grandly.

Henry chuckles, chiming in as best he can. "I declare we shall read all the books."

Ah, is there anything as wonderful as a kid who's embraced the written word? They are both voracious readers, and that warms every inch of my soul.

"And I declare we shall sniff all the books too," I add as we amble past a store peddling antique maps. I make a note to return there after we reach our main destination.

"Smell them?" Henry asks in his regular voice. "Why would you smell a book, Piper? That's weird!"

"Have you ever smelled a book, Sir Henry?"

He crinkles his nose. "No."

"Lucy, your royal highness. Have you ever sniffed a book?"

Lucy twisted her lips, her forehead furrowing. "I think so . . . maybe in the library."

"'I think so' and 'maybe' aren't sufficient! We're taking a detour."

With an abrupt right turn, I guide them into one of the Victorian era shops with rare books. A man in a tweed vest and horn-rimmed glasses, who couldn't be anything but the proprietor of such a shop, greets us with a chipper, "Hello. How can I help you today?"

"Dear sir, my charges and I would be eminently grateful if you would let us sniff a few books. Would that be at all possible?"

He chuckles. "As you wish."

He directs us to the ones that smell the best—a shelf of first edition Agatha Christie hardcovers. Gently, like he's tending to a delicate bauble, he opens a book, holding it for us.

Henry goes first, taking a deep inhale.

Lucy's next.

When it's my turn, I draw a deep breath, savoring the smell of the pages, the delicious scent of paper and time.

When I straighten, the man says he has another one for us.

He totters over to a different section, locates a Virginia Woolf, and opens it for us.

"This one smells the best. Like words and ideas," he whispers as if sharing a secret, and I think I'm a little bit in love with him.

The kids bend forward, sniffing together. The image is so precious that my first instinct is to capture it. To remember this always. I grab my phone and snap a picture, knowing I'll cherish it—the looks on their faces, their sheer delight at the first time they've truly experienced the wondrous scent of an old book.

Figuring I should probably buy the thing as a thanks, I sneak a glance at the price, and my eyes bug out. With my heart beating fast, I scan the store. There has to be something cheaper than a thousand pounds as a way to show my gratitude.

My gaze lands on a pack of postcards by the register —Victorian era illustrations. Ah, that'll do.

I thank him profusely, and so do the kids.

"You're very polite," he says to Henry and Lucy with a bow of his head.

Henry lifts his chin. "Thank you, sir. My daddy says being polite is really important."

I smile despite my ire at Henry's father.

"It absolutely is," the man adds, then lowers his voice to a conspiratorial whisper. "Also, my brother owns the children's bookshop just across the lane. You should make sure to pop in."

"We will," Lucy adds, ever the little lady today.

I stuff the postcards in my purse as we exit, and when the kids scan the street and catch a glimpse of an

Alice in Wonderland book next to a stuffed bunny in the window, they take off running.

"Slow down in the store!" I shout.

Sheesh. I sound like their . . .

I stop myself.

I sound like an aunt.

That's who I am. I'm an aunt, a friend, that person you trust to watch your kids.

And yet, as I watch them disappear into the store, I feel like a bit of a trollop, and heavy shame takes over from anger to clobber me. I'm good enough to watch the kids, but not to text? I remember the panic and remorse in his eyes this morning. Is he ashamed of what we did? Does he feel guilty for sleeping with me?

My stomach roils when I realize the possible reason.

Is it because of Anna? Since I'm his first after her, does he feel like he's cheating?

But I catch hold of bits and pieces of things he's said —that he's moved on, that he's no longer in love with her. And then other things, like how he told me he's been wanting me for months.

My belly has the audacity to stop churning and instead . . . *flip*. It freaking flips with the memory of his dirty words, his ode to my body, his lust for me.

His avoidance today can't be guilt over her.

Is it guilt over the kids?

Is that why he's gone radio silent?

But maybe I'm being ridiculous. Maybe I'm expecting something when there's no real call for it.

And really, what's in a text anyway? Would Virginia Woolf have required a text?

I think not.

I raise my chin. Who cares about texts?

I'm a strong, independent woman. I don't need anything from a man. I certainly don't require a note waxing on and on about the epic bang.

Last night was last night. It was a moment in time, and it ended when it needed to end. Hell, maybe it ended at precisely the right moment, saving us from the awkwardness of *Where do we go from here?*

Clearly, we go down the road to Nowhere.

The man has made it clear he's not dating.

Like a blaze of sunshine illuminating a shadowed corner, I see what last night was.

I see it so damn clearly.

I time travel again to a month ago, to Charlie's "I have news" party, when Dina tapped Zach's hand and asked, *Are you on the dating circuit again?*

His answer was as clear as a four-carat diamond.

No.

The man didn't hedge; he didn't hesitate with his answer.

Holy smokes.

I've been foolishly clutching the notion that we might become a little something. Maybe see each other again. Maybe even, gasp, date.

Because . . . how the hell did this happen . . . I like Zach Nolan. Like a woman likes a man she doesn't just want to bang but wants to see.

Except he's not on the dating circuit.

And that means I need to let go of these blooming feelings.

I choose to. As I head into the store and watch his children tuck into books and scurry around shelves, I am opting to let go of that want.

To forget I had any wish for more.

It's best that I remain where I am. The one-time enemy, the maybe-now-and-then friend, the aunt character in this story.

I'm better off like this.

I'm happier this way.

Raising my chin, I declare myself resolved.

I hang last night in the closet like a coat I've put away. I tuck this morning and the afternoon onto a shelf.

I join Henry and Lucy, who've found a giant stuffed bunny to use as a chair. I settle in next to them and read paragraphs from Roald Dahl books they thrust at me, then Lewis Carroll and Brian Jacques. I read until Lucy gets up, pointing at a shelf on the other side of the store.

"Be right back." A minute later, she announces that she found a Nancy Drew.

"I didn't know you liked Nancy Drew."

She tucks a strand of hair behind her ear as she carries the book back to me. "I don't know if I like Nancy Drew either. But she's a girl detective, and I decided I should get to know her better. She's really one of the first heroines in modern literature for young girls."

Smiling, I lift a brow. "Someone knows her women's lit. Did you read that somewhere?"

A knowing grin spreads on her face, and for a split second, I see her father in that smile, that same wink and a nod that says, *I'm going to share something with you.* I feel a tug somewhere in my chest, tugging me toward him.

Another feeling to shake off.

All the way off.

"I was talking to Louise last night. She was telling me all about Jane Austen and Charlotte Brontë and the heroines they wrote."

"Then why aren't we getting Austen for you?"

Lucy rolls her blue eyes, and it happens again. That flash of her father. Have Lucy's eyes always been this blue? This cool?

"You have your father's eyes," I blurt out.

She runs a hand over her hair. "And my mom's hair and nose. She was really pretty."

"She was gorgeous," I say reflexively, because she was. Chestnut hair, big brown eyes, and a face that you couldn't look away from.

And maybe that's a thought I ought to shake away too.

Lucy flips open the hardcover. "Anyway, Louise read some Jane Austen to me, and I don't think I'm ready for that, but I think I'm ready for Nancy Drew. I want to read about girls doing cool things, like solving crimes and running countries and battling dragons."

I gesture to the books. "Then let's get you some. After all, you need to know all your predecessors so you're completely ready when you're cast in *Girl Power* and you win your Oscar."

"What's 'predecessor' mean?"

"Those who came before."

"Yes, I need to know my predecessors," she says.

I scoop up the books from her, ready to head to the counter, but she grabs my arm. "You don't have to buy them for me. I can bring my dad back here."

Their dad raised them to be polite. She knows it would be impolite if she didn't offer to have her father buy them.

But the thought of not purchasing these books for her feels terribly wrong. The thought of leaving it to Zach feels worse. I'm getting her these books, because this isn't about Zach.

This moment is about this girl. This outspoken, curious, creative, wide-eyed girl who's trying to discover who she is.

I'm not her mother, and I don't want to play house and pretend to be one for her. What I am is her friend, and I'm not going to miss this chance to lead her down the path to becoming a strong woman someday.

"I insist. Girl power, right?" I bring them to the counter as Henry skips over, offering up *Lyle, Lyle, Crocodile*.

As I prepare to pay, I spot a book of letters written by kids. Lucy will love that. She's in another section of the store now, so I add it to the pile, along with a journal that has a saying on the front that I know she will love.

Afterward, we stroll to the other shops on Cecil Court, where I stop in the one with antique maps, picking up one of Tahiti for my friend Sloane since that's where she and her husband went on their honeymoon, and at another store, I buy a Winnie the Pooh antique print that I'll give to Paige for the baby's room once that little peanut is safely in her arms.

Then I take Lucy and Henry to the London Transport Museum where they clamber onto buses, trains, trams, and subway cars. Henry is a speed demon, climbing up and down everything as I snap photos.

Soon enough, Henry is exhausted, yawning like he simply can't stop. It makes sense. It's three in the afternoon and we've been going nonstop since eight.

On the way back to the hotel, my phone lights up with a text from Zach.

For a sliver of a moment, I want it to be full of sweet words and invitations and offers to see me again. I want him to tell me he can't get me out of his mind and that he's ready to be on the dating circuit again, with me, only with me.

But Virginia Woolf wouldn't require that, nor do I.

I slide it open.

Zach: We're on time and on our way back. I promise I won't be late. I promise I'll be back exactly when I said I would. Also, I can't thank you enough for today . . .

My heart softens, turning to pudding. The poor man. I can read between the lines, and he clearly feels awful over what happened this morning. He's probably been beating himself up all day long. He likely still feels terrible for having slept in my room and missed whatever was going on with his kids—they probably sent him texts asking where he was. He has obligations, and he screwed them up this morning.

And yet, I'm not going to let myself become one of those obligations.

I can't ask him to take on any more. His plate is full. It would be rude. It would be wrong.

Once we're inside, I carry a tired Henry through the lobby and to the elevator, heading for my room. Zach should be here in five minutes to pick them up.

Lucy scampers down the hall ahead of me, then spins around, a curious glint in her eyes. "Do you wander the halls at night when you can't sleep?"

"Why would I do that?"

"That's what my daddy did last night. He couldn't sleep, so he wandered the halls."

I raise a brow. "Is that so?"

"Yes. Isn't that silly?"

She turns and runs the rest of the way to my room.

I'm not insulted he made up a tale for the kids. But I am several more degrees of resolute. That story underscores what last night was—a one-time thing. An incredible interlude of an evening that required a lie to return to reality in the morning.

And I will keep doing the same, letting it exist as a sidebar rather than a scene that needs an encore. Because an encore would require another lie, and Zach Nolan is not a liar.

Nor am I.

As soon as I set Henry down to open the door, the seven-year-old perks up, darting into my room as if he's discovered an underground cave full of wonders.

"Wow. Your room is different. Your couch is over there." He points, and my gaze swings to the couch.

To where it all began.

Never have I ever started to fall for your father on that couch.

But I don't let myself take an imaginary drink, because I refuse to fall for him.

* * *

Zach swings by at four on the dot to pick them up.

I don't let on that my emotions rode the roller coaster two dozen times today.

Nor do I reveal that I'm thinking of him naked.

Because I'm not. I'm not thinking of how he looked when he shed those lounge pants, or when he climbed over me, and definitely not when he spread my legs and entered me.

But hell . . .

I am.

Tingles spread down my chest, and I do my best to ignore them, especially when the kids throw themselves at him in a fit of hugs and *Hi, Daddy*'s.

Yes, that's who he is. Not my lover. Just their father.

I fasten on a professional smile like I would with a client who needed my calm, centered side.

"How was golf?"

"Charlie won."

I shoot a knowing grin.

See? I can do this. I can play the last-night-didn't-exist game. "Did he really win, or did you let him?"

"I never let people win. I was . . . *tired*." He says that last word like we have a secret.

But I'm not sure we do.

He crouches down and looks Lucy in the eye. "Can you take Henry back to the room? I'll be there in five minutes, I swear."

"Of course." She turns to me and offers a salute. "Girl power."

I salute her back. "Girl power. But don't forget your books." I add in a stage whisper, "There might be extras in there for you too. A few goodies."

Her face lights up as she grabs the bag then takes off, little brother in tow, big sister handling the task as capably as Nancy Drew.

Zach stands, raking one hand through his hair. That thick hair I had my hands in.

Shake it off.

"Thank you again, Piper. That was so helpful."

"It was my pleasure," I say, keeping it cool.

He's quiet, as if he's thinking. "Listen, about last night . . ."

Tension speeds through my bones at a lightning pace. Tension mixed with fear. Fear of rejection. Because nothing delightful has ever started with that word: *Listen*.

"I don't think I handled any of it well. I don't know how to do this. I need to figure out what—"

Oh, hell no.

I won't let him have the last word. Not after I thera-pied the ever-loving heck out of myself today. Not after

I sorted out my messy stew of emotions all while watching his kids like Piper Freaking Poppins.

I lift a stop-sign hand. "Yes, about last night. It was a one-time thing. You're not dating. I get it. It's probably best that it shouldn't happen again, don't you think? After all, I don't want you to have to make up tales like wandering the halls and whatnot." My tone is bright with cheer. I am the queen of lighthearted, letting him off easy.

He blinks, like I've splashed water on him. "What?"

"Well, that's what you were going to say, right?"

He shakes his head. "I was coming here to talk to you. I figured talking was better than texting."

"It generally is," I say, as if I hadn't longed for a text. Because really, who longs for texts? Not this girl. I can rewrite the story of my feelings, edit out any hankering for a text.

"I just wanted to apologize for how I left this morning," he says. "That's what I wanted to tell you."

Ah, the apology. He came to offer one, like the polite man he is.

I wave it off. "We are all good." I affect a yawn. "Listen, I'm exhausted. I need to take a nap before I catch my flight."

His eyes fill with surprise. "Are you leaving tonight?"

"Yes. I have brides to tend to in New York. Katya and I need to finalize her dress, and Sierra wants to look at venues, and Aisha is insisting I join her for a cake tasting. And I'm not about to turn that down."

"So we'll talk in New York, then? I'm staying another day."

"Oh, sure. Naturally."

Easy breezy.

Look how it's done.

He takes a deep breath. "Listen," he says, and there's that word again. That word that signals backpedaling, apologies, the beginning of what you don't want to hear. "I felt terrible this morning. I was irresponsible. It was a careless thing to do. Just to fall asleep with the volume off on my phone."

"So we won't do it again. We won't spend the night together. That's the easiest way to avoid irresponsibility."

His brow creases. "Wait. Is that what you want?"

What do I want?

What I want is so much more than I can ever get from him. He's a magnet, pulling me to him. That's what he's been doing these last weeks—luring me in, making me want him.

And when I want him like this, I feel vulnerable, too vulnerable. Especially with a man I don't think can give as much of himself as I know I'll eventually want.

Hell, I don't think he can give me *any* of what I want.

Because I don't want *just sex*.

I don't want to bang him again for fun.

I want more of him, and he's simply not available. He's off the dating circuit, and I don't want to hop on the booty-call merry-go-round.

He's not equipped to handle more, and I'm not prepared to be hurt when I don't get it. But for better or worse, we're in each other's lives, and I'd rather we be civil. Keeping my voice light and even, I answer, "What I want is a great experience for our friends. I want Charlie and Jessica to have the best wedding possible. I want it to go off without a hitch."

He nods, absorbing my comments, digesting them, it seems. "And it'll go off without a hitch if *that*"—he waves to the room, the scene of the crime—"doesn't happen again."

I plaster on another smile. "Don't you think?"

His eyes lock on mine, as if he's trying to find the perfect answer in them. He takes his time, a long time. Then he nods. "Sure."

"Why don't we focus on our friends? And on us being friends?"

"Okay." His voice is flat.

Mine is upbeat as I make my case. "Since it seems we're finally starting to get along. Besides, what else would we be now but friends?"

"Yeah. I don't know," he says, sounding thoroughly confused.

That's the issue. He doesn't know what we'd be.

And I do.

Because something became painfully clear to me this morning when I was out with his daughter and son.

If he'd been there, I'd have fallen harder for him. I'd have craved even more of him. And I can't let that happen, because I'm not going to be able to have him that way.

One more yawn for show, and I shut the door on everything I want.

* * *

Later that night, when I'm safely buckled into my seat on the plane next to a harried businessman barking last-minute orders to an underling on the phone, I send the photo of the kids to Zach.

Piper: Took this today. Thought you'd like it.

He replies instantly.

Zach: I love it.

I power down as the plane takes off, flying far away from him and that one night when, for a moment, everything fell into place.

A few nights later, Lucy is wide awake at midnight.

I stop by her room in our apartment. Her nightstand light illuminates her hair, tucked into a braid. She's on her stomach, propped on her elbows, furiously writing in one of her journals.

Like father, like daughter. I've been up late since we returned from London, tackling unfinished work and briefs once the kids go to bed.

I lean against the doorframe. "Can't sleep?"

She flips over and slams the journal shut. On the front of the silver notebook are the words *She wasn't looking for a knight. She was looking for a sword.*

"I'm still on London time," she remarks.

I point to the notebook. "Secret letters?"

She clutches it to her chest, whispering, "Yes."

"Pumpkin, I'm not going to look at your secret letters," I say, stepping into her room and sitting at the foot of the bed.

"I know. I just . . ."

I pat her leg. "It's private. I get it."

"But I want to show you one someday soon, like I told you, like I put on my list," she adds quickly.

"Whenever you're ready." My eyes drift to her notebook. "New journal?"

She smiles brightly. "Piper got it for me in London. In the same bookshop where I got the Nancy Drew book. She bought me a book of letters too. I sent her a thank-you note, like you taught me to do."

A pang sharpens in my chest. I haven't seen Piper since I returned. She's mostly been out of the office, I suspect, and I've been busy.

Correction: I've been keeping myself busy. Because I am genuinely buried in work, and also because I don't know what to say if I see her.

So I've packed my nine-to-five schedule with meetings, lunches, appointments, and work, work, work.

It's easier this way.

"That was nice of her," I say, my throat tightening. "And good of you to send her a thanks. That's important."

"She's really into girl power too."

"Why does that not surprise me?" I say with a sliver of a smile.

Lucy sighs dramatically. "Fine. Since you asked, I was writing a letter to myself."

I didn't ask, but I love that she offered. "I bet the recipient will enjoy it."

She sits up higher, clasping the notebook tighter. "I wrote about the trip. I wrote a letter to myself so I don't forget how much fun it was and all the cool things we did."

God, I love this kid. I love her so damn much. My heart grows three sizes as she tells me more about her letter.

"I wrote about the crown jewels and afternoon tea. Also, Dad, tea tastes gross. Why do adults like tea?"

"Probably because we're always tired and need the caffeine hit."

"I don't like tea. It tastes boring. But I wrote about Louise. She's super cool too, and I bet she'll be in *Girl Power*."

"Wait. I thought you were *into* girl power. Now you're saying someone's going to be in it?" I furrow my brow.

"*Girl Power* is the movie I'm going to star in someday." She taps her pen against her lip. "Or maybe I'll direct it." Her eyes turn the size of pizza pies. "Wait! What if I produce it? I could be the executive producer."

"Any or all of those would be fantastic. But is this your way of telling me you want to be an actress?"

She laughs, shaking her head. "No. I like being me. But sometimes, I like to imagine all the things I might do when I'm older. Anyway, I wrote about the bookstores and the old books and how good they smelled."

The pang deepens, digging sharply into my chest. To think I was stupidly jealous that Piper was going to tour bookshops with Graham, and instead she took my children and sent me a photo. More proof that I'm not ready to date again. I don't know what the hell to do with that kind of gesture. Since she sent the picture, hell, since I stood in the doorway of her hotel room, I've been wondering where I'd gone wrong.

The answer? I likely went wrong everywhere.

I shove the thought aside as Lucy continues, "Have you ever smelled an old book?"

An image of the law school library comes to mind. "Definitely, but I don't think I was as enamored of the scent of torts and statutes as you are of old books."

"What are those?"

"Boring law stuff," I say dramatically. "Sort of like tea. Go on."

"Anyway, the point of the letter is I felt like I was having all these new experiences. That's what I like to do. I like trying new things and doing new things. Like mini golf and reading about detectives, and maybe I can try to learn French. That's how I can figure out what I want to do someday."

I tap the notebook. "Then you need to keep all your letters safe and sound. Because someday, you'll be looking at them again, reading them. Someday, your older self will look back and embrace the advice and the memories."

"I will. And don't be offended that I don't let you read them. Someday I will. They're just personal."

I hold up my hands. "They're yours, pumpkin. I don't want to invade your privacy. But I do have one question."

"Yes?"

"Are you ever going to try to go to sleep tonight?"

She laughs. "It's five in the morning in London. Also, check this out." She grabs her *Dream Big* notebook and flips it open to her summer list. "I marked off three items."

She flips open the page titled *Things I Want to Do This Summer.*

"We went to London, I ate a sundae with all the toppings, and I stayed up past midnight."

I scan the three remaining items. "Now, you just need to share something hard, swim with turtles, and snorkel. I sense a water theme."

"That's because I might want to be a marine biologist. That's another thing I want to try. But I don't think I can do those in New York though."

"Unless you want to snorkel in the Hudson?"

Her nose crinkles. "Gross."

"I can think of few things grosser than snorkeling in the Hudson."

"Maybe we can go someplace where snorkeling is better . . .?" She gives me puppy-dog eyes.

"Are you angling for me to take you on another trip?"

She smiles like she's oh so innocent. "What a great idea, Dad! Look at all the pages left to fill. That's a lot of experiences. That's what life is all about." She takes a beat, like she's prepping herself. "That's what Mom said to me: 'Do everything. Try everything. Be unafraid.'"

A lump knots in my throat.

But it's not from missing Anna. I've learned how to move on. Hour by hour, day by day, week by week. Time is the greatest friend grief could ever ask for. The months and the years ably do their job, lessening it, then lovingly untying the hold it has on you.

This feeling strangling me? It's because Lucy is following this great advice. Following it to the letter. She's bold and unafraid. I'm so damn proud of my daughter.

And, admittedly, a little jealous.

I open my arms for a hug. "Have I ever told you how amazing you are?"

She snuggles into my arms. "Every day, but I like hearing it because I think you're awesome too."

When she lets go, scooting back on her bed, she shoots me a serious gaze. "You should write a letter. If there's anything you want to tell yourself, write it down." She beckons me closer once again, like she wants to share a secret. "Sometimes, letters are even better than lists."

I gasp in an exaggerated fashion. "There's something better than a list? Blasphemy."

"What's 'blasphemy'?"

"It's when you say or do something that goes against the core of what you believe."

Her eyes narrow quizzically. "I believe in lists and letters."

"Of course you do. I'm just teasing. Now try to go to bed. You have a full day of ridiculous, insane, awesome fun at summer camp tomorrow. Miranda is going to pick you and Henry up at the end of the day, and then take you to Emmy's house. I'll get you from there because I have a late appointment with a client."

"Be a shark, Daddy."

I make a snapping sound like a great white's teeth. "I promise."

She yawns and tells her Haven smart home device to "Turn off Agatha Christie."

"Agatha Christie?" I ask as the light dims. "You named your lamp Agatha Christie?"

"It's one of the books we checked out in the rare bookshop. It was cool."

"Of course."

I leave, feeling Piper's presence.

She's everywhere.

Notebooks and names of smart home devices. Girl power and lists.

It's not even intentional. It's not like she left a pair of gloves behind on a date so I'd have to call her.

She's left imprints on my kid just by being herself.

I retreat to my bedroom, scrub a hand across the back of my neck, then grab clothes for bed.

After I brush my teeth and flop down on the mattress, I park my hands behind my head and follow my daughter's advice.

Dear Zach from a couple days ago in London,

You should have done a lot of things differently.

Me

* * *

The next day I mumble a hello to Piper when I walk past her office, but she's on the phone, talking coolly and calmly to someone about an arrangement of cabbage and chrysanthemums.

She shoots me a smile, then rolls her eyes as she points at the phone, as if to say she's stuck on a call.

But what would I say if she wasn't?

How about them cabbages?

How the fuck does anyone attempt dating anymore? I can't even manage a conversation with a woman I slept with.

I spend the afternoon burying myself in Taylor's case, the perfect way to occupy my brain with something that's not Piper, especially when I meet up with my client at a coffee shop to review the status of her divorce filing.

Taylor drags a hand through her hair. "So this is what it comes down to? Six years of marriage and he's trying to pull this?" Her eyes are hard, her jaw tight. "I can't take it anymore. I can't take another late-night call or early morning text where he tells me what he's going to try to take from me."

I draw a deep inhale. She needs to make the next choice on her own, free from my desire—my goddamn natural instinct—to knock her ex down to his knees. "What do you want to do? It's up to you."

She purses her lips, breathes through her nose, then answers like she's underlining each word. "I want him to leave me alone. I want him to stop calling me. I want him out of my life. And I don't want him to touch my restaurant ever."

A small grin tugs at my lips. "Say the word."

Her eyes darken. "Play hardball, Zach. Can you play hardball with him? I can't risk losing my business."

I rub my palms together. "That's my sport." I'm fully fueled, ready for battle.

When I leave, I call her soon-to-be ex-husband's lawyer and let him know exactly what he can do with his client's requests and precisely what will happen if his client sends so much as a text message asking what's on the menu at her restaurant ever again. "Do you understand me?"

"I had no idea he was still doing that," the man says, sounding as if he's been caught off guard.

"The other week, I called politely and asked it to stop. Now I don't feel such a need to be polite. Get a leash on your client. Tell him this is being settled between you and me, or we will go to court, and I will not back down."

"I'll talk to him."

"Yes, you do that. Do that when I hang up. Is that clear?"

"I-I will."

"Do not ever have him call her with these spurious threats again. He's not touching her business, he's not touching a single dime from her restaurant, and I only want to hear from you. I do not want him to call her again till this is done, and even then, I see no reason why he ever should. Is that absolutely, completely, without question clear?"

He takes a long, nervous beat before he says again that he'll talk to his client.

I remind him how it will end up if he doesn't sort this out.

When I hang up, a wave of satisfaction rolls over me. At times like this, I'm the warrior. I'm the dragon slayer. I'm righting the wrongs.

I can handle anything, anyone, any argument. Bring it on. I only wish I knew one-tenth as well how to handle this uncharted territory of falling for a woman.

The scent of well-seasoned vegetables greets me when Emmy answers the door.

"Mmm. Smells incredible."

She waves me in. "Tastes even better. I made a spicy dish for us, and a totally bland, boring one for the kids."

I look around her spacious pad on the Upper West Side. "Speaking of the kids, where are they?"

"Jamie took them to the park," she says, naming her oldest, who's sixteen.

"Where's Jenna?" That's her fourteen-year-old.

"Piano lesson. And Greg is on his way home." Her husband.

My stomach rumbles. "How far away is he?"

She rolls her eyes and grabs some plates. "He's on Wall Street. It'll be a while. I'll feed you first."

"Best sister ever."

"Only sister ever."

"True. Caught me on a technicality," I say, rolling up my sleeves and washing my hands.

She nods to an open bottle of wine. "Want a glass?"

"Sure. I'm not driving tonight," I joke, since I rarely drive, seeing as we live in the city.

She pours, then serves us both, and we sit at the island counter. My sister has always been a good cook, so I groan in pleasure at the first bite. "This is amazing."

"Tell me about Piper."

I choke on a forkful of rice. A hard cough racks my body. "What?" The question comes out strangled.

Emmy sighs heavily, shaking her head as she takes a bite. "Serve it up. Give me the deets."

"Hello? Give me the Heimlich," I say roughly, since I'm still choking on surprise.

She waves me off. "You'll be fine."

My coughing settles, and I take another drink of the wine. "Good wine. What's the vintage?" Maybe the distraction ploy will work.

Her eyes are vipers, her fangs out. "Seriously? Just tell me. I know I'm onto something."

I dodge to the right. "Why are you asking?"

"The kids can't stop talking about her. Piper this, Piper that."

I shrug it off. "We're part of the same group from college. It makes sense we'd spend time together. Plus, the kids know her from after school at the office. So when she offered to look after them on golf day on the trip, I jumped at the chance for some tee time with the guys."

Emmy nods as if she's taking it all in. "The old college crew. Right."

Ah, I sense an escape route and open the hatch and dive down. "Yep, exactly." I take another bite, murmuring my appreciation, hoping that does the trick.

"And did you need alone time wandering down the halls at the hotel one night too?"

My shoulders tense. She should have been a lawyer. Oh wait, she is. We are peas in a pod.

I try to make light of it, because I've never been able to get away with anything, thanks to Lucy and Henry blabbing about my habits. "Couldn't sleep and the sitter conked out in the room. I tried to call and ask your advice, and then decided to just walk around."

One highly skeptical brow rises up to her hairline. "To Piper's room?"

I scoff. "No."

She folds her arms across her chest. "Bullshit."

I sigh. "Why are you asking?"

"Because I think there's something going on and, judging from your extreme levels of broodiness the last few days, I'm guessing it's not quite going how you want."

I shrug and throw in the towel. "It's not going." My voice is heavy, giving away everything I tried to keep inside. Opposing counsel won this round, it seems.

Emmy downshifts to gentle, setting a hand on my arm. "Well, have you told her how you feel?"

"What do you mean, how I feel?" Now my sister's speaking Turkish.

"You clearly feel something for her. Maybe try letting her know."

I open my mouth to peel off a round of reasons why I shouldn't: she only wants to be friends, we need to focus on Jessica and Charlie, I have kids, I don't know if I can give her everything she deserves, and I don't know if she wants what I can give.

My sister seems to sense the direction of my protests.

She squeezes my arm. "What can it hurt to try?"

I spend the rest of the night telling myself she's wrong—the part of me that wonders if she's actually onto something.

23

PIPER

Baby clothes. A sea of pink and yellow, blue and peach, and sweetness as far as the eye can see. So many awesome little adorable things that I must buy. Cute little T-shirts with sassy sayings, adorable onesies with giraffes on them, and jammies with cartoonish panda bears.

I grab one, then another, then one more.

Wait.

Look at all those blankets.

Swaddling blankets. Nap blankets. Sleep blankets.

How can one baby need so many blankets? I have no idea, but the possibility that my niece-to-be might is thrilling.

Grabbing my phone in the middle of the department store, I call Paige. It's ten thirty in the morning, but she answers right away.

"Hey, everything okay? I have two minutes before a conference call with the superintendent," she says.

"I love it when you talk fancy administrator

language to me." I run my hand over a soft robin's-egg-blue fleece as I return to business. "First, is everything okay with your baby mama?"

"Yes. Stacy's doing well. Just a few more weeks now. But there hasn't been any more drama, just updates on the baby. She's the size of a honeydew melon and the length of a head of romaine lettuce."

I make a mental note to run that past Bud Rose as a possible centerpiece, then dive into why I called. "Second, how many blankets does the lettuce-length, melon-size baby need? Five? Seven? Ten? I mean, she might need a lot of blankets."

Paige laughs. "I don't know. Maybe one or two?"

I scoff as I thumb through a pile of the softest pink blankies, including one with—eek!—bunnies. Sweet, precious bunnies. "That doesn't sound right. I'm getting her ten. Love you. 'Kay, thanks, bye."

"Don't jinx us," I hear her say as the call ends, and I scoop up five, six, make that seven blankets and bring them to the register.

As I leave, I pat myself on the back—both for stopping at seven and for having successfully avoided thinking of Zach and all that went wrong in London.

Well, until he popped into my head just now.

* * *

Strong fingers dig into my scalp, and I groan obscenely in pleasure. I'm not even remotely embarrassed at the sounds coming out of my mouth. There is little that feels as good as a shampoo.

This is better than a soak in the tub. More heavenly than lying on a beach.

"You're so good at this, you should do it for a living," I tease.

Adrien chuckles as he massages the shampoo throughout my hair. "I'll take that under advisement. See if I can make it as a stylist in New York."

"You never know. You might have enough talent." I open my eyes to shoot him a knowing grin. "You do know that's how I found you years ago? Women everywhere were whispering about your shampoos and blowouts. They called them orgasmic."

He shimmies his shoulders as he works his magic. "I'm not too shabby, it seems."

"They were all gabbing about you. I'm not kidding. You were the talk of the whisper network. *There's this stylist in the east Sixties who gives the best blowouts.*"

We both laugh at the sound of that.

"Well, the boys do say that about me too."

I snicker, giving him a wink. "Why am I not surprised?"

He waggles his hips as he kneads in the shampoo. "When you got it, flaunt it. I'm enjoying my singleness, thank you very much. Now, tell me more about London."

I keep my cool, answering lightly, "London was great."

That's all I want to say. He already asked me how London was, and I said it was fantastic. No need to say more.

I settle deeper into the leather seat, savoring the feel,

craving the distraction. All of this—the shampoo, the conversation—it diverts my thoughts from that night and Zach. I don't want to spend so much brain power on someone I can't have, so I search for other topics, settling on a safe but amusing one. "Did I ever tell you the story of how I started my first business?"

"As a wedding planner?" he asks as he rinses the shampoo.

"No. As an entrepreneur. When I was in high school, I bought a bag of Blow Pops every day from the local drugstore for two dollars. Before homeroom, I'd usually sold them all—twenty-five lollipops at twenty-five cents a pop for a little more than six dollars per bag. Made four dollars profit. Used it for lunch money. So yes, my first job was earning lunch money selling Blow Pops," I say with a naughty twinkle in my eye.

"It's hard to say that without it sounding dirty, isn't it?"

"But I was *sooo* innocent."

"And now? You're not so innocent, Blow Pop girl."

I tut. "Please. I'm a good girl."

He pours conditioner into my hair, working it through. "I'm not so sure about that. You have that look about you."

"What look?"

He stops, walks around me, and peers at my face. His silvery eyes seem to read me like a crystal ball.

"What's wrong?"

He shakes his head. "Why don't you tell me what's really on your mind, love?"

"What do you mean? I'm telling you."

He rolls those metallic irises and heaves a dramatic sigh. "Piper Radcliffe, I have known you for more than a decade. I've seen you fall in love, get married, get divorced—"

"Shhh."

He waves a hand. "No one is here. And I've seen you date men you like and men you might love. And there is one thing all those ups and downs have taught me about you."

"What's that?" I ask cautiously.

He returns to my hair, the maestro resuming his podium before the symphony. "It's that you *love* to ramble and share tales of days gone by when you don't want to tell me what's really going on."

I scoff. "I tell you everything."

He arches a brow, staring down at me from a strange, inverted vantage point. He's a cat, and he won't lose this staring contest.

"Why don't you tell me, then, what happened in London that has you dodging the question *How was London?*"

"This is not fair," I say with a huff.

"Life's not fair, but what is it about my question?"

"Because you have my hair in your hands and you're demanding stuff of me."

He laughs as he finishes with the conditioner. "Ah, so there is stuff to tell."

"Please. You know your mind-reading skills are spot on. Of course there's stuff."

"So tell, tell, tell. I want to know."

I draw a deep breath then blurt it all out. "I slept

with Zach. It was amazing. The next morning when his kids called, he took off like he was doing the hundred-meter dash then kind of ignored me all day, but whatever. I got over that. And when he wanted to talk that night, I let him down easy for both of us. He doesn't want to date, he's said as much many times, so I said let's be friends. And now everything is back to normal."

I slap on a cheery grin.

Adrien lifts a brow. "I think that was mostly the truth except for the bald-faced lie at the end. Nothing is back to normal. You don't sleep with someone you've fired missiles at for years and then go back to normal. How is it, truly, between you two?"

"I've been busy," I say, glad my schedule has been packed. "Fittings with Katya and so on, and when I saw him the other day, it was cordial."

"And how does that make you feel?"

I look up at my friend, and for the first time in days, something unknots and lets relief flood in. I haven't whispered a word of our night to anyone, not my sister, and clearly not Jessica. But telling Adrien feels like I'm untying a shoe that's too tight.

Wanting Zach is a gnawing ache I've clutched and kept secret. But talking is a balm, a salve to the wound.

"Sad," I say softly. "It makes me sad."

He finishes the rinse, drapes a towel around my neck, and offers a hand. He tugs me up from the chair, parks his hands on my shoulders, and stares fiercely at me. "So what are we going to do about that?"

"I don't know. He's not on the dating circuit. I can't

change that. All I can change is what I do. And I need to keep moving forward."

"Or maybe you need to tell him you want to have hot hotel sex with him again, then order room service after, and have him take you to the movies the next day."

I laugh at his way with words. "Why, yes, I'll order that up from the kitchen now."

"Fantastic. It'll arrive at your room in thirty-five minutes." He escorts me to his booth and combs out my wet hair. "Or . . . you could ask him to dinner and see what happens."

I shudder.

"Oh, please. Don't be such a princess."

"I have nothing against asking a man out. I just don't want to be rejected."

"No one does. Fear of rejection is part of being human. So is facing that fear and vaulting over it."

I swallow thickly, considering. "You want me to ask him to dinner?"

He smiles at me in the mirror, nodding exaggerat-edly. "I do. Stylist's orders.'"

My stomach twists. "What if he says no?"

"If he says no, I will give you a free orgasmic shampoo and blowout."

It's not a bad consolation prize. "That's tempting."

"Of course it is. Now, tell me what he was like under those delicious clothes of his."

I don't tell all—I'm a lady, of course—but I give enough tidbits for Adrien to whistle in appreciation.

Which is only right. Zach deserves whistles, cheers, and ovations for the magic he performs in the sheets.

* * *

When I leave, I head to meet Jessica for lunch as planned, since she's back in New York, working in her office here for a few days. As I walk up Madison Avenue, I run through my call list, chatting with Bud Rose, with Jonathan at the Luxe, and with concierges across town.

Anything to keep my mind off Adrien's advice.

His sage advice?

His insane advice?

Which adjective applies?

I don't know. All I know is I haven't felt this kind of longing, this kind of ache in my heart since I met Jensen.

I switch off the faucet of thoughts, choosing instead to admire the chichi shops and cute boutiques, the florist on the corner with the display of cornflowers and daffodils, all while savoring the June sunshine that warms my shoulders.

Yes, I'll just focus on the weather.

So much easier that way.

When I arrive at the café to discuss the next set of pre-wedding fiestas, Jessica has already snagged an outdoor table. Sporting big sunglasses and a huge grin, she pops up when she sees me and throws her arms around me.

"So good to see you." She holds me tight, like we haven't been together in ages.

I hug her back, curious. "Good to see you too. But what's with the exuberant welcome? I saw you last week. Not that I don't love seeing you. But you seem particularly peppy."

She gestures to the seat across from her, and I grab it, dropping my purse on the empty chair.

Her brown eyes sparkle with a festiveness I haven't seen on anyone in a long time, and she seems to be positively bursting with news. "Piper," she whispers giddily.

"Yes?" I say, a little cautious, but excited too, because her enthusiasm is infectious.

"You remember my plan to do a few pre-wedding parties? London and here?"

"Sure, of course."

"We need to skip the New York one. Can we move up the wedding?"

"It's your wedding, sweetie. We can do whatever you like."

She claps twice. "Thank God. Because I want to switch it to next month."

And a skywriter wings her message across the clear blue canvas of day.

"You're pregnant?"

"Yes!"

24

PIPER

Six weeks pregnant.

Anguilla.

A July wedding.

I repeat those three key facts as I tuck into work at my office later that afternoon.

Because . . . hello???

I have to plan a summer wedding in a fancy tropical locale in a mere four weeks. Jessica doesn't want to be huge, as she put it, for her wedding.

I reassured her that she probably wouldn't show at ten weeks and likely not even till five months, but she was having none of that.

Her parents are conservative, so it's better off this way, she'd said.

I'm not so sure they'll be fooled when she pops out a baby less than seven months after the wedding, but who am I to argue?

Especially with a preggers lady.

Sheesh.

Bridezillas are easy as pie next to that.

Here I am at my desk, diving into a veritable four-week all-nighter as I take a crash course in pulling off a destination wedding in one month. One mere month. So much to do. So damn much to figure out. I barely have time to think about anything else, let alone to marinate on Adrien's advice about Zach.

Dinner? It's going to take all my Super Wedding Planner Strength to squeeze a meal in at all in the next four weeks.

I spend the afternoon researching the ideal venue in Anguilla, making calls to my contacts in New York to ask for referrals. I lob in a quick call to Jason, just in case he knows anyone.

"Bloke expert, at your service," he says when he answers.

I smile. "I need your expertise, but the best man, not the bloke, part."

"Let me switch hats." I can hear him pretend to put down the phone, then bring it back to his ear. "All right, best man extraordinaire here. How may I assist you?"

"Any chance you know anyone in Anguilla? My client wants a wedding there next month."

"Someone has a bun in the oven," he says, singsong.

"That obvious?"

"As lipstick on a collar."

I sigh. "I know. Now I need to pull off the impossible."

"But that's what you do. This is a chance for you to show your mettle."

"I take it that's a no, you don't have any tips for Anguilla?"

"Sorry. I haven't made it there yet. But a lad can dream."

I shift gears. "Tell me more about your dreams. How is the pursuit of your lady love going?"

He chuckles like he finds the situation thoroughly amusing when he says, "She hates me."

"Sounds perfect for you, then."

"Indeed."

We chat more about his dilemma, then I hang up and cuddle up with Google for the next few hours.

I learn that they need to be in Anguilla forty-hours before they tie the knot. Easy enough. I learn the cost of a marriage license. And I find a great room rate at a hotel for about twenty people, which is the number Charlie Warbucks wants to send to the island.

But finding a wedding spot is a wee bit harder.

After several exhausting phone calls, I'm a teeny bit closer, but only in the sense that I've been told ten times, "We'll check our calendars and get back to you."

I drop my forehead on my neat desk—there's barely anything on it except a laptop and a mug—and mutter against the wood, "Who do you have to screw around here to get a wedding venue in Anguilla?"

"I know someone."

I startle, lifting my face. Zach stands in the doorway, doing that tie thing. God, why does he have to look so damn sexy smoothing his green tie? His emerald-green silk tie that I want to grab to yank him to me, then hike a leg around his hip and kiss the hell out of him.

"You know someone who'll trade sexual favors for a wedding venue?" I ask.

He laughs, leaning against the doorframe. "If you're particularly keen on trading a BJ for a spot on the beach, I suppose that could be arranged. But I don't think it's required."

I laugh. "My days of selling Blow Pops are over."

His brow creases. "Blow Pops? Those gum-filled lollipops?"

I tell him the story of my first real gig, and he laughs. "I bet you drove all the boys crazy when you licked the sour apple ones."

"How did you know I liked sour apple?"

"Good guess?"

"Fine. I liked sour apple. But seriously, who do you know in Anguilla?"

"Taylor's sister. She's one of my clients. I basically got her dickhead husband's lawyer to curl up in a ball, quivering like an elephant does when it sees a mouse, after I told him how things were going to work." Zach blows on his fingernails, pride practically wafting off him.

"Congrats." Now that I understand him better—his motivation—that seems less like seeing who lands bloodier punches in the ring, and more like fighting for someone who needs a knight with a sword. "That's great."

He lifts a hand and pats his own back. This Zach is the one I'm used to. The man who stood in my doorway in London seems long gone.

But something is different about this Zach too. He's

not needling me. He's not shooting arrows. Does that mean he's lost all interest? Will he turn me down if I ask him out for soup and crackers?

My chest tightens, and nerves scurry up and down my arms. I don't know what he'll do or say. That's the issue. The hairy, thorny, scary issue.

But that's why asking someone out is taking a chance. It's stepping off a cliff without a safety net.

He tips his forehead in the direction of his office. "Want me to ask her if she can grease any wheels?"

"That would be great."

"Give me five."

Five minutes later he returns, handing me a sheet of paper with a number and a name on it. "Chellize at the Heyward Grand Ocean Suites says to give her a call in an hour."

Gratitude and glee are like silver and gold flowing through my veins. "Thank you. Thank you so much." The enormity of how much he's just helped me has me riding a rush of endorphins that makes me brave enough to try laying a bridge to asking him to dinner. "Also, this is nice," I say, pointing from him to me.

"Nice?" The word comes out like he's drunk acid. "This is *nice*?"

Quickly, I explain, "Getting along like this. I'm glad we can."

But my throat is clogged with too much anxiety to say what I truly want.

Have dinner with me.

Have a drink with me.

Take me out.

"It's nice?" He steps closer to my desk.

"Yes. Nice. Us talking like this is nice." Why is molasses coating my tongue? Years and years of arguing with this man have made the fear of rejection strong in me.

His eyes narrow. "You like being friends?"

My stomach swoops with worry. Oh God, is he setting me up? Is he prepping for a dig? Have we gone back to fists up, guns ready, dueling officemates?

"I like getting along with you," I say, choosing honesty, even though it's gut-wrenching. This is like turning my heart inside out and hoping it still beats properly.

"You do?"

"I do." My voice wobbles. I don't know what he's getting at, why he's firing all these questions my way.

He comes around my desk and sits on the corner, closer still. I can smell him. Like cedar and sex and the man I want to lick.

"Listen . . ."

That word pierces me, making me crumble. That's the word he used in London. Is he going to let me down again?

"I'm listening." My tone is even, giving away nothing, as I don my armor once more.

His eyes meet mine, and he holds my gaze. "I don't think I said everything that needed saying in London."

Tension flares inside me, chased by a dash of hope. "You didn't?"

"First, I should have said something to you the next day, and I didn't."

I hold up a hand, grabbing his, absolving him. "Don't think twice about it. Don't apologize. We're good on that."

"But I should have said something. Should have reached out to you sooner. I'm new to all this and figuring it out."

"It's fine," I say, reassuring him. "I swear it's fine."

"Good." He looks down at my hand, then back into my eyes. "But you need to know, I'm still replaying that night. It's on a loop in my head, I swear."

I'm warm all over. Please, please, please let him feel the same. "Is that so?"

"I can't stop thinking about you," he says, not looking away.

My skin tingles. "Your mind must be an interesting place."

His eyes darken. "Very interesting."

For a second, I fear he wants only a rebound screw. But it's time to vault past fear. I can't take it anymore, this not knowing. I draw a deep breath and step off the cliff. "Have dinner with me," I blurt out.

Scrubbing a hand across his jaw, he groans low and growly. Maybe in frustration? I tense for a second.

"You don't want to?" I ask, quieter.

He stares at me, his eyes intense. "Oh, I absolutely want to. But I was planning on asking you. And you beat me to it."

My lips curve in a wicked grin. "Guess you need to be faster, then," I taunt.

He arches a brow. "Do I now?"

He moves off my desk, plants his hands on the arms of my chair, and stares at me. I heat up like a star.

He leans in close, his face near mine, his voice demanding. "Go out with me."

I can't stop grinning. "Yes."

"Good. Because I want to see you again. I want to take you out. I want to date you. I don't *just* want to fuck you."

I'm buzzing with happiness. "It's the same for me."

He clasps my jaw, holding me tight. "But right now, I'd really like to fuck you."

The way he says those words sends heat to my core. A pulse beats between my legs. I grab for his tie, but this time he *is* faster. He stands, lifts a hand, and slowly, deliberately unknots it, loosening it. Zach like this, in his tailored slacks and crisp shirt, his green silk tie slightly undone, poised to take me, is the sexiest thing I've ever seen.

He leans over, running his nose along my neck, setting me to flames. "Just like I remembered. Just like I think about every goddamn night."

"Every night, you say?"

"Every night. Every morning. You're in my head and under my skin."

I'm on fire. "Please," I beg.

He pulls back and smirks. "Since you asked for it."

He claims my mouth. He owns me. Owns my lips. Owns this kiss. He kisses like a man who won't be denied. Like he came in here with one intention: to have me.

It's a dominating kiss. A kiss he controls as he holds

my jaw, angles my face, and devours my lips. It's a kiss that won't stop at kissing, that can only be a prelude to fucking.

He's hard and ruthless, and I swear it's like he's making up for the way we've both been lost since we returned.

I don't feel lost anymore.

I don't know where we're going. But I feel found.

The only issue is my door's wide open. I slide a hand up his chest and push him away.

"Door," I pant.

He stands, walks around my desk, and closes it. Locks it shut.

He returns to me, moves my laptop to the side of the desk, then sets me on the wood. Exactly where I want to be right now.

25

ZACH

This is so much better.

This is light years better than the alternative—the alternative of having said nothing, having done nothing.

Because I spoke my mind, I get to have *this*. I get to have *her* the way I want her: craving me as intensely as I crave her.

With her legs spread, her palms digging into the edge of the desk, she's ready, and once I unzip my pants, I slide inside her.

Sparks rain down my body, crackling across my skin as I close my eyes. An obliterating wave of pleasure rolls through me. It's instant and electric, and fucking fantastic the way it knocks down everything in its path but my desire.

"You feel amazing," I groan, opening my eyes again.

As she curls her hands around my shoulders, she draws a shaky breath. I don't know her noises yet, but I want to. I'm not sure if I was too fast, if she needs it slower to start or something else. I meet her gaze. "You good?"

She nods. "So good."

I'm learning her cues, learning *her*. I want to know everything. "How do you like it? Fast? Hard? Rough? A lot of dirty talk? Tender and gentle?"

"All of the above, depending on my mood."

I kiss her roughly, quickly. "Good. Same."

"Right now, though, I want to feel like you can't get me out of your head."

I groan from the sheer sexiness, the utter confidence of her words. "Right now, I can't fuck you any other way." I slide my hand down her back, cupping the top of her ass and yanking her closer as I drive deeper into her in one swift move. I shudder once I'm all the way in, and she trembles, and it's the perfect symphony of sensations: her reaction, my reaction, *our* pleasure.

We're in sync once again. Maybe in a whole new way.

Everything feels so fantastically dirty and so perfectly right at the same time. She wraps her legs around my hips, hooking her heeled feet over my ass, urging me on as she arches into me.

I stroke into her, hard, deep, as I bury my face in her neck, getting drunk on her scent. Oranges again, and it drives me insane. My nerve endings come alive, and my mind unravels as I growl, "You smell so fucking good, feel so fucking incredible."

She lifts her face up and nibbles on my earlobe. I shudder, loving the rough side of her. "Do that again," I tell her.

She obliges, biting this time, whispering, "I like biting you."

"I love it when you do."

She travels down my neck, sucking on my jaw, dragging her teeth over my skin.

I'm wild inside, wild from this. "You drive me so crazy."

"Same. I'm so turned on."

"Then let's get you coming on my cock."

She whispers in a broken pant, "It's been a week, and I want you. It'll be fast."

I laugh lightly as I thrust into her, loving the way she talks to me. Talks *back* to me.

It comes as no surprise that she gives as good as she gets.

There is no need to linger. This is an afternoon quickie, not an afternoon delight where I can savor every second, every touch.

The deliveryman might knock, my assistant might come looking for me, the phone could ring. I need to move us around the bases and get the woman tagging home.

I squeeze the side of her ass tighter, and she responds with a luxurious gasp, letting me know she likes my hands on her, likes what I have to give.

She tightens around me, her body gripping me. Lust ricochets through me, running rampant in all the thoroughfares in my body. With each thrust, with every single grunt and moan, the pleasure builds and coils.

I don't want to think, but one thought won't be still. And it's not about my dick. It's not about how immensely good fucking her feels. It's about how much I need *this*. Not sex in general, but sex with her. I need *this* intimacy. I need her in my arms.

I need . . . the word brands itself into my brain.

I set it free.

Grabbing her ass tighter as I drive deeper, I whisper, "I need you, Piper. Need you so much."

Something heavy inside me becomes lighter. Telling her frees something that weighed me down, that I was so used to, didn't even know was sinking me.

Her lips dust over my jaw. "Need this too. Need you too."

I'm even lighter now at hearing her words. I'm letting go of old hurts, saying goodbye to a persistent ache that doesn't need a home inside me anymore.

I shake off the emotions, homing in on the physical. I meet her gaze, slide one hand between her legs, and rub my finger against the delicious rise of her clit. She lets out the sexiest groan I've ever heard in my life, then gives me a dirty, sexy smile.

Her mouth parts in an O, her back bows, and she's crying out, reaching the edge. Her sounds are so spectacular, so mind-bendingly good that they're rattling loose the pleasure inside me. They're pushing my own orgasm to break free.

I don't want anyone in the hallway to hear her. "You're so fucking loud, and I love it. But I don't want anyone else to hear you." I clasp my hand to her mouth, and her eyes squeeze shut. She bites my palm as she shudders and then lets go, her moans stifled as she comes hard on me.

That's all I need. Because all I need is her.

Pleasure bursts inside me, my brain going blank, my mind nothing but white-hot electricity as my body thanks me for having come down to her office and talked to her.

I barely understand what's happening, but I also understand it so fully, so deeply. It's terrifying, and it's wonderful at the same damn time.

* * *

After we straighten up, she settles on her pink couch, all glossy eyes and tousled hair. She eyes her desk. "Never have I ever had sex on a desk."

Smiling, I sit next to her, running a hand over her hair. "Never have I ever had sex on a desk either."

We both grin. Her eyes are twinkling, and I bet mine are too. She arches a brow. "Really?"

I stare sternly at her. "I just gave you the Never Have I Ever promise. That's like a blood oath." Then I soften. "This is a first for me."

She nibbles on the corner of her lips, and she looks younger in that instant, delighted almost. Like a light illuminating a darkened room, I understand why. She wants to have some of my firsts. Even if it's sex on a desk.

And I'm learning I want to give them to her. I search in my mental files, hunting madly for another one, for something else that can be only ours. I find it, and a smile tugs at my lips. "This is going to sound kind of crazy, but would you want to do something super ridiculous like go play shuffleboard with me?"

She cracks up. A deep belly laugh.

"Okay, so that's a no."

She sets a hand on my leg. "Should I get my cheaters out? We can go in the Buick. Maybe have an early-bird special for dinner."

"See if I ask you out again."

Another laugh rumbles from her chest. "I think it sounds great. I'm presuming you mean in lieu of dinner."

"I don't know that I'm having dinner with you now. Mocking me and all." I cross my arms in faux indignation.

She grabs at them, batting her eyes. "Please, please forgive me for teasing you about shuffleboard. I think it sounds great. Even though I grew up in Florida, I've actually never played, and I heard there's a new place in Brooklyn."

"I've never played either. That's why I suggested it."

She freezes and then a smile spreads across her face. "I definitely want to play, then." She leans in and brushes her lips over mine. "Thank you."

She doesn't say why she's thanking me.

But I know, and she knows, and I'm glad we don't have to explain why we both want to find some firsts for us. There's a shorthand to Piper and me, and it's not simply from having run in the same circles. It's because we connect. She's emotionally astute too. She picks up on cues without needing anything spelled out. She *gets* what she's dealing with.

I have baggage. Hell, I am the baggage. But she doesn't seem to mind, and she doesn't seem to need to poke at the rips and the tears in the luggage. She accepts that I've come to her *after* I've been around the block.

She accepts, and she doesn't try to turn me inside out on a mad hunt for every little difference, every possible comparison.

I'm so damn grateful.

I take her hand, threading my fingers through hers, looking down at how our joined hands look. They fit. They look right.

I raise my gaze. "I don't know when I can go. I have to get a sitter. I have to do things the right way this time."

"Of course you do. I totally understand."

"I'm pretty sure my sister will watch them. She knows about you."

Piper grins, a confident look in her brown eyes. "So she knows how awesome I am?"

"Exactly. She knows you're awesome. I told her how I *feel* about you," I say, and that word—*feel*—should weigh a ton. But it doesn't. I'm not afraid of how I feel for her anymore. I'm only afraid, I suppose, of messing it up. This is a brand-new path for me, and I'm driving in the dark without headlights.

"How *do* you feel?" she asks, her tone a little nervous.

Shrugging, I smirk. "Oh, you know. I think you're . . . *delightful.*"

She swats my elbow, and I catch her hand, hauling her in for a kiss. A fierce kiss that says how I feel. Roughly, I answer, "You know how I feel."

"Do I?" Her voice is gentle.

I press my forehead against hers, searching for words that capture this wild mix of emotions claiming the real estate in my heart. "I want to know you, Piper. I want to understand who you are. And I want to spend more time with you, both in clothes and getting you out of them."

She shudders against me, looping her hands around my neck. "I like you in and out of your birthday suit too," she says, then whispers in a smoky, sexy voice, "And I like it when you bite me too. Makes me feel marked."

If ever there was an invitation, that's it. Curling a hand around the back of her head, I draw her close and nip her neck.

She groans, a sound that turns me on.

What a shock.

But I still want to talk to her, so I pull back, lifting an eyebrow. "And the rest of what I said?"

She smiles, looking coy. But her answer is all pure, honest emotion. "Yes. Yes to everything. Also, I think I love your sister."

"You would like her. She's very straightforward. I just have to check with her on her schedule, but I think she'll be willing, and then we can go out on a date." I laugh at that last word.

She stares quizzically at me. "Why are you laughing about asking me out on a date?"

"Because I never thought I would."

"I never thought you would either. I thought you hated me."

"I thought you hated me," I counter. "But I've been wanting you for some time now. I just didn't think we'd get past the way we used to be with each other."

"I'm happy to keep finding ways to get in digs at you."

"I bet you are. But listen, here's the other thing," I say, and she tenses when I say the word *listen*. I make a note of that. Maybe *listen* isn't the best way to start a conversation. "I can't say anything to my kids yet."

Her expression turns serious as she nods her agreement. "Of course. It's too early."

"And I don't know when I'll be able to. This is all new to me. And honestly, it's not like I've googled how to date after . . . how to date as a single parent," I say, finding the right words.

"It must be hard."

"I'm not sure how to make it all work. I don't know when I'm supposed to tell them. Plus, you're already in our lives, and my daughter thinks you're a rock star."

"I pretty much am," she says, in that confident tone that I love.

"You are. And she adores you."

"I adore her," she says, soft and earnest this time.

"So I don't want to mess with that. Or confuse her, or confuse Henry. Do you know what I mean?"

She squeezes my hand, as if she's giving me some of her certainty. "Absolutely."

"And I'm not saying I expect you to bend to my schedule and my family and my needs—"

She places her hand on my chest, smoothing it across my shirt. "I'm actually okay bending to your needs. You have kids. You have a family. They're important. They're the most important people in your life. But I do think since we're taking it slow, and keeping it kind of quiet, that we should keep it on the down low when it comes to Charlie and Jessica."

I nod. "Definitely. They have a lot on their plate."

"I don't want Jessica to worry about what this means or doesn't mean. And I don't want her to think we're stealing the limelight."

She's right. It makes perfect sense to keep this close to the vest. "I agree. So no kids, and no Charlie and Jessica. Sounds doable."

She smiles. "Definitely. And look, I don't want you to worry that I'm this super-needy girl who expects you to ignore your kids and schedule me first. I have a rich and happy life, and I have lots of friends and family of my own too. But don't ignore me again. Just send a text, okay?"

"I promise."

"Good. And please know that I completely understand you're not the twenty-eight-year-old investment banker from Morgan Stanley who only has a houseplant to take care of in his loft in Tribeca."

I arch a brow. "He has a houseplant? This Morgan Stanley banker?"

She snaps her fingers. "You're right. It's a plastic houseplant. But it's so realistic-looking."

I laugh then return to the conversation. "Anyway, all I'm saying is I don't know how to do this. Mostly what I want right now is to not have any more conversations in doorways of hotels where I let you slip through my fingers."

She trembles and nods. "Same here."

"I want to try this." I point from her to me. "Whatever *this* is."

"I want *this* too."

That heaviness that's been in me, it sheds a few more pounds. Maybe it was a darkness. I've always had a little bit of a darkness and anger inside me, probably because of how my parents' marriage ended.

During the last few years, the darkness changed shape. It doubled down due to a change in my life that I never expected.

But then, being with Piper is a change I didn't expect either.

And I like it.

I like this change so damn much.

I'm not going to analyze it six ways to Sunday. I'm not going to turn it inside out and upside down and make comparisons that don't need to be made. She's not Anna, and Anna's not Piper, and that's fine by me.

This woman is the one with me now, and that's all I can think of.

The present.

It's a gift, and one I want to keep opening over and over.

I'm okay with that. In fact, I'm good with it. I want this present so badly, and I want to see what kind of future it brings.

Somehow, I've been given another chance. Another chance at happiness.

And I want to discover how that happiness looks and works with the woman next to me.

The woman I'm falling for.

I don't say any of that out loud. It'll come when the time is right.

Instead, I loop a hand through her hair and pull her close, bringing my lips to hers once more.

When I break the kiss, she breathes out hard. "Wow."

Maybe she can understand everything unspoken.

"Zach, I'm really looking forward to shuffleboard."

Yeah, I think she might know how I feel. And I'm good with that. I'm good with wherever we're going.

She points at the door. "But now you have to go. I have to call Chellize at the Heyward Grand Ocean Suites."

"Go work your magic."

That evening she texts, telling me she secured the venue, and she's so grateful that she wants to give me a thank you blow job.

I'm so damn tempted to find a sitter and take her up on her offer.

But I don't. I send her an eggplant emoticon and the words *Rain check is mandatory.*

26

ZACH

"Where are you going tonight?"

Ah, that's the question.

The inevitable question that I knew was coming from the peanut gallery.

But this time, I'm armed with the truth.

Well, most of it.

Tonight, I've shepherded Henry and Lucy along like a drill sergeant, reminding them to gather bags and books and phones and earbuds.

Lucy's question clangs in my head, echoing. As I steel myself to serve up some of the details, the tension in me ratchets up, even though I'm being honest. "I'm going to play shuffleboard. With your friend Piper."

She stops mid backpack-grab. Spins around. Lifts a brow. "You're playing shuffleboard? With Piper? What's shuffleboard?"

I breathe a ten-story-tall sigh of relief, choosing to answer what's behind door number three. "It's a game.

An outdoor game, where you push weighted discs down an outdoor court. Except we're playing indoors."

Her nose crinkles. "That sounds weird."

I laugh, grateful for the game analysis rather than the date one. "Maybe to you."

She pats my arm. "You have fun playing your weird game." She returns to her bed, grabbing her earbuds and jamming them into the front pouch of her backpack.

I relax, but only a little. Because the truth is Piper and I are going to Brooklyn to play, then to drinks, and then to her place.

The kids are spending the night at my sister's.

They probably think I'll be here, in the only home they've ever known. But nope. This place will be empty. Daddy gets a sleepover too.

"That's cool that you and Piper are hanging out," Lucy says breezily, then offers me *please, pretty please* eyes. "But why can't I come along? I guess I don't mind a weird game if I can play with Piper."

I gulp. Yup. It was too easy. Like I could actually get off scot-free.

I tug Lucy in for a nuzzle. "Because your aunt wants to see you. You have no idea how much Emmy is looking forward to having you over tonight. And your cousins are dying to see you too. Don't you want to hang out with your cousins?"

Lucy seems to consider that then shrugs happily. "You're right. I'm excited to see Jamie and Jenna. Jenna said she wants to show me a new Instagram baking show she found. So that sounds like fun."

"And Jamie has all sorts of games picked out too.

And she wants to make waffles with you in the morning. And don't forget how much you like making waffles." I poke Lucy's sides, tickling her, desperate to distract the inquisition.

"But are hers as good as yours?" Lucy counters.

"Well, that would be impossible."

She laughs. "True."

"But try to enjoy them anyway."

She sighs dramatically. "I'll do my very best."

"Also, Daddy wants to sleep in," Henry proclaims as he shows up in Lucy's doorway. "We should let him sleep in tomorrow all by himself." Henry turns around to face me. "I will give you a morning hug when I see you at Emmy's tomorrow."

I cringe inside. This is tougher than I thought.

I resolve to work on my parent-navigates-dating-his-daughter's-favorite-person skills as I gather the kids and head out of the apartment.

Lucy and Henry are ten feet ahead of me, darting down the hall, and I follow—then stop in my tracks when my gaze snags on my wedding photo. It's been here so long, but it feels like I'm really noticing this picture for the first time in months. I step toward it, scanning the image, faded from sun and light and time.

Mostly from time.

But I can see how happy I was as I looked into Anna's eyes, seeing forever.

Feeling forever.

She gazes back at me the same damn way.

In an instant, our marriage unfolds like a flip book. A honeymoon in Paris, our first apartment in Hell's

Kitchen. The nights out and the nights in. The way she laughed at her friends' jokes, at my jokes. She was one of the most upbeat people I've ever known, one of the happiest. When she found out she was pregnant with Lucy, six months after we walked down the aisle, she was a ray of sunshine, and so was I. We wanted the baby so badly, even though we were young.

Her first pregnancy was remarkably easy, and we strolled through Target, registering for things we were convinced we simply had to have to be parents.

We moved into this place, then Lucy showed up, and my life truly changed. Late nights, early mornings, hardly any time for each other. Anna and I argued every now and then over who should clean the kitchen and the bathroom, but never over whose turn it was to take care of the baby. We were a team, and when Henry came into our lives, we were the consummate upper-middle-class Manhattan parents, somehow balancing jobs and kids and sitters and classes and weekend activities.

Until Anna got sick.

And everything changed once again.

As I stare at me in my tux, her in her dress, I see it all, remembering mundane details, like how she took her coffee, and forgetting others, like the smell of her hair. Recalling her telling me a funny story about a coworker eating cake from the break room fridge, then barely able to remember what her favorite Ed Sheeran song was, the one she said made her heart ache and long for me at the same time. Was it "Photograph" or "Thinking Out Loud"?

She's becoming faded around the edges too, and maybe this is how it's supposed to be more than two years later.

Maybe I'm supposed to stand here with the pieces of memory falling through my fingers as life goes on.

And maybe I don't need to have this photo front and center anymore.

It feels both right and wrong.

"Be right there," I call out to the kids, then take the picture and take it to my room, setting it on the bureau. It's not standing, and it's not face down, but face up. Later, I'll figure out where to put it, but it no longer needs to be in the living room.

I'm not one to talk to ghosts. I've never spoken to Anna's picture. But tonight, I tap the frame and whisper, "I know you'd be okay with this."

She didn't have to grant me permission, but she did anyway near the end, wagging a finger at me, issuing her final instructions. "You better fall in love again."

At the time, I just shook my head. That's what you do when your wife is dying.

"I mean it, Zach. You better. You really better." She'd reached for me, stroked my hair. "Not for me. For you."

I don't know that it was her dying wish, but whether it was or wasn't, I have a pretty good feeling it's coming true.

* * *

Once I arrive at Emmy's, my sister's kids take over as little teenage parents.

I let out a long sigh, glad I made it uptown without any further questions from the jury. Emmy pats my shoulder, sensing my relief. "Easier said than done?"

"I think I botched the whole thing," I say out of earshot of the kids as I tell her what Lucy said about shuffleboard and me going out with her friend.

She offers a small smile. "Sounds like you did fine, actually. You told the truth, and that's good, but you didn't tell them stuff they don't need to know. Now, stop beating yourself up and go enjoy the first date you've had in ages."

I rub my palm over the back of my neck. "You think I did okay?"

"More than okay." She shoos me out the door. "The clock is ticking. Go, go."

A little later, I push open the door to the shuffleboard club in Brooklyn and find Piper at the counter, checking in. She's wearing jeans and a tight black T-shirt, and all thoughts of whether I was a super dad or a just-okay dad vanish because, holy hell, I pulled this off.

And I'm going to enjoy the hell out of my night.

For me.

I'm going to enjoy every single second of falling in love.

27

PIPER

With the wooden pole, I shove the disc down the court, scoring again. "And another game goes to the brunette."

Zach laughs, shaking his head. "You didn't tell me you were a secret shuffleboard expert."

I feign surprise. "Oh, I didn't? So sorry."

"You've played before, haven't you?"

I hold up my free hand, taking an oath. "I swear I haven't. It's the Florida girl in me, I suspect. I'm just naturally good at party sports. I'd probably kill it at mah-jongg, bridge, and boccie ball too. And look, if you want to be crushed harder than this, we can play mini golf." I offer a big smile because, honestly, whipping his cute butt on a mini golf course would be a ton of fun.

"No way. I am not letting you destroy me at that."

"Too tough on your male ego?"

He nods without hesitation. "Um. Yeah."

"One more round?"

"I can't seem to deny you, so the answer is yes, even

though you've been killing me." As we set up for the next round, he nudges me. "So, Miss Florida girl, do you ever go back there?"

I tense, thinking of my mom, of our last phone call when she went on and on about Trevor. Or Travis. Or Trey. "My mom keeps asking me to come back. She wants me to meet her new boyfriend."

"You don't want to?"

"What's the point? It won't last. She thinks he's the one, but she always thinks the new guy is the one, and he never is."

"And you don't think she'll ever meet someone she truly falls for again?"

I go first, sending the disc along the floor. "If I were a betting woman, I'd say no."

He frowns. "That sucks."

"She doesn't really have the best track record. So what should I do? Go down there, meet him, act like she'll keep him? And then in a year, he's gone too, because that's how it goes with her."

"But what if?" he presses, setting up for his turn.

I lift a brow skeptically. "What if he's the one for her? I don't buy it. She met the one, she loved the one, she won't let go of the one. She still has my dad's picture up in her home."

He tenses, his next word coming out like it has potholes in it. "Where?"

"In the living room. Like a shrine. She justified it because it's of the four of us. But I can't imagine how her boyfriends feel."

"Should be someplace else. Not the living room, for sure." He sends the disc down the court, scoring.

I give him an approving nod, then return to the topic. "Exactly. A wall in the hall, for instance."

"You really think she's still in love with your dad?"

"No. But," I say, sadness coloring my tone, "I do think she's hung up on what she had. I think she's trying to recreate that magic, that once-in-a-lifetime love, and she's falling short each time."

He hums thoughtfully. "I feel bad for her, then."

I spin around, surprised. "You do?"

"Best thing she can do for herself, for her sanity, for her own soul is to learn to move on."

That buoys me—his strength, his solid footing. Even though we're not at that stage yet, he seems healthy, and that's a damn good thing.

Maybe that's why I don't want to linger on my mom.

I wave a hand before I set up for my turn. "I don't want to talk about her. Let's talk about something happier. Like, my sister's baby should be here in a few weeks," I say, updating him as I play, since he knows already about Paige's adoption plans. "And my living room has become a home to her wardrobe for the first fourteen years of her life, with an extra chair just for all her blankets."

He stares at me, hands wrapped around the pole, his expression deadpan. "So you're just completely forgetting about this kid's teenage needs. Way to go, Piper."

I sigh dramatically. "I know, I'm the worst. So thoughtless for not yet prepping clothes for the teenage years. But I'll get there. I just have more blankets to buy first. I bought seven the other day. I might need to shop for three more."

"Of course. You need to make it an even ten," he says, deadly serious.

I nod, patting his chest. "You get me."

Laughing, he sets the pole on the floor, grabs my hand, and tugs me close. "I do. And let me tell you, that baby is going to be one lucky kid to have you for an aunt."

I raise my chin proudly. "The Aunt Society already gave me World's Best Aunt award. They said no one else would even hold a candle, so they were giving it to me preemptively."

"You're great with kids. My daughter thinks you're the best. I told her I was playing shuffleboard with you tonight, and she actually said to me, 'You're going out with *my* friend?'"

I smile big and wide. "I love that she thinks of me that way."

"Me too."

My smile falters because the way Lucy feels for me, and the way I feel for her, is also one of the challenges I face in this burgeoning romance with her father. Lucy is perhaps the biggest hurdle. I love being a part of her life, and she evidently adores being in mine. What would happen, though, if this tender new thing with Zach fell to pieces? What if we hurt each other, break each other's hearts? I would want to remain Lucy's friend, but could we?

I have no idea. I detest the thought of being out of her life. I want to fight like hell to keep her in mine.

He tucks a strand of my hair behind my ear. "One more thing, though, about your mom. If you ever wanted to see her, I'd go with you."

I nearly stumble, shocked from his comment. "To see my mom?" I want to make sure I understand.

"If you wanted to. If it was important to you."

I swallow, a lump tightening in my throat.

Something hasn't just changed with Zach.

Something has seismically shifted in him.

He's not the man he was ten years ago. Or ten months ago, or even ten weeks ago. Sure, I can see on the surface he's still strong, sarcastic, and smart. But now I see inside him. Because he's let me, and what I see is so much more than I ever expected.

What I see is beautiful.

And it floors me.

I'm unprepared for the wave of emotions that roll through me from his offer, stirring something I haven't felt in years.

Something I've only truly felt once before.

I silence all the feeling with a kiss, whispering a "Thank you" against his lips, wondering how on earth I'm going to handle the fall.

* * *

Later, we stumble into my place, kissing and touching. Unable to stop. Unwilling to.

I want to go all night.

We find our way to the bedroom, and clothes fly off.

I fall down on my bed, and he climbs over me, his blue eyes dark as a lake, his intent fierce.

He claims my lips once more, then in a heartbeat, he flops down on his back, grabs my hips, and pulls me up, murmuring dirty words, telling me to fuck his face.

He's filthy and hungry, and I love it. I love the rawness, the realness. I ride him, gripping the headboard, doing as asked, and finding my release in minutes.

Once I do, he flips me over to all fours and slides into me. Pleasure consumes my body as he drives into me the way I want. Hard, powerfully, wiping away the day, the worries, all the what-ifs.

He's biting my neck, my shoulder, like I asked for the other day in the office. Giving me what gets me going until I come hard.

But he doesn't follow me there.

Instead, he pulls me closer, raising me up, wrapping his arms around my chest. Kissing my neck, running his nose through my hair.

Slowing down.

Inhaling me.

Touching me everywhere.

And I shudder again, and again, because everything feels too good to be true. He runs a hand down my belly, sliding it between my legs, then he lowers us to the bed so we're both on our sides, and he fucks me slowly and wonderfully.

It's like he's luxuriating in me. In this time. In our chance. In everything that's happening tonight.

Soon he's whispering my name. Growling it.

Grunting it. I urge him on, wanting his release, craving it.

When he comes inside me, he says my name like it's a jewel in his mouth. Like I've become something precious to him.

And I'm pretty sure he's become that to me too.

No, I'm certain.

* * *

The next morning, I make him breakfast. Eggs and potatoes and toast. He devours my cooking, and I love seeing him at my kitchen counter, in my home. As we eat, he asks more about my sister, and I tell him about Paige and Lisa, and how I was one of two maids of honor at their ceremony. I grab the photo of my sister's wedding from the coffee table and show it to him.

He wiggles a brow as he taps my face in the frame. "For the record, if I were at that wedding, I'd have tried to bang this maid of honor."

I stage-whisper, "For the record, you've banged her already. A few times."

"And every single time was epic," he says, setting down his fork as if to punctuate his point. Then he kisses my cheek. "Because it's with you."

I shiver from head to toe as that deep, sexy voice fills my senses. *Because it's with you.*

We're so close to something.

So close to becoming so much more.

When he cleans up, doing the dishes and putting

them in the rack, my heart flutters. The man can screw and the man can clean.

Yes, I'm officially floating.

He hangs the towel on a hook, then cups my cheeks and gives me the most wondrous goodbye kiss. Who is this man? This romantic, passionate, can't-stop-touching-me man? He's both the same guy I've always known, and a complete upgrade now that I'm seeing all the other sides.

And I want to keep learning everything about him.

Because I'm doing more than floating.

I'm falling.

Falling so deeply in love that I don't know who's going to catch me.

Or if I'll have to catch myself.

When his phone alarm beeps, his official reminder, he heads for the door. With one hand on the knob, he says, "Have lunch with me some day this week, okay? We'll slip out of the office. And I'll find another time for us to have a night together."

"Of course."

He leaves, and I shut the door then sigh happily.

I picture him heading uptown, picking up the kids, spending the day in Central Park with them as he said he planned to do.

A part of me wishes I were with them.

But I have plenty to do here.

I wander through my apartment and settle in at the couch, where I pick up my latest to-do list. I have a few wedding errands to run today, some calls to make and emails to return.

I'm a busy lady, and I dive into the emails first.

But when I'm done, I stare out the window, craving the sunshine then instantly picturing Zach under this great big sky, playing with the children.

For a second, I want to be there.

Or elsewhere.

If he were a regular single guy, no kids, no complications, he could see a movie with me, wander around the city, enjoy the sunshine.

Then I reprimand myself. I'm lucky to have some alone time to relax, set my own pace. I don't need to spend every second with a new beau.

Besides, this gives me a chance to see a friend.

I text Sloane and ask what she's up to. She's heading out to a cafe with her husband, and our friend Haven, and instructs me to join them.

I haven't seen them in a while, and it's an order, so I go.

I find the trio in the Village, at a sidewalk café on Jane Street, laughing. Malone swipes something off Sloane's lips, and she sticks out her tongue. Then she leans in for a kiss.

They're so in love, it's sickening—in the good kind of way.

Haven meets my gaze and rolls her eyes. "These two," she says, pointing her thumb at the lovebirds.

"I know, right?" I say to her. "Will you two ever stop with the PDA?" I tease the couple when I reach them.

Malone looks up at me, a twinkle in his dark-blue eyes. He pretends to consider my question. "Never."

He pats the chair they saved for me, and I plunk my butt down.

Haven gives me a quick hug, and Sloane does the same, then asks if I want anything. I pat my belly. "Still stuffed. I'll just grab a carrot chia seed smoothie."

Haven stares intently, her dark eyes studying me. "What have you done with our friend Piper?"

"Kidding. Iced coffee. Obviously."

Haven flags the waitress and asks for the drink. When she's done, she turns back to me. "Did you have a wild Saturday night?"

A knowing grin spreads on my face. "Maybe a little."

"Tell us everything." Haven sets her chin in her hand, waiting.

"Don't leave out a single salacious detail," Sloane adds.

I give them the basics, grateful that I can share with this crew.

"He sounds great," Haven says, flicking some strands of brown hair off her shoulder.

"And I definitely thought he was a cutie when I met him the other month," Sloane seconds. Then her face lights up. "Malone is singing at the Lucky Spot next weekend. You should bring Zach and come see him with me."

"You should. I have some new tunes," Malone chimes in.

"Maybe. He'd have to get a sitter. But I can ask. I like the Lucky Spot. Is it the Midtown one?"

Sloane shakes her head. "No, the new Chelsea one."

I've been to the Chelsea location. It's cool. It's also a

popular place with Dina and Freddie and Steve and the whole crew from college.

Jessica and Charlie too.

If I go with Zach, what if someone sees us? Are we keeping it a secret from all of them too?

I smile and say maybe.

The rest of the day feels like a big maybe.

28

ZACH

I'm sweating like I stepped out of the sauna. New York in July is punishing. My T-shirt sticks to me. "Are you sure Anguilla isn't going to be like this in a few weeks?"

Charlie smacks me on the back as we wrap up our game of basketball on the outdoor court then head into the gym. "C'mon. Anguilla is way better than New York. It's in the nineties here and balls-hot. Anguilla is eighties with a nice breeze."

"News flash: eighties is still hot."

"Then you better grow a pair of unsweaty balls."

"Jackass," I mutter.

"Ooh, is it tough for you that I beat you at basketball today?"

"Miracles do happen." I wipe the sweat from my brow with my sweaty T-shirt. "There better be a perfect ocean breeze."

"Don't get your jockstrap in a twist. Besides, that's why the groom and best man are wearing shorts."

That is some of the best news ever. "I cannot thank you enough for the no-tux rule."

He pats his chest. "That was my idea. Plus, the ceremony is at sunset. The weather there is perfect when the sun sets on the beach."

I roll my eyes. "Have you become a wedding planner? You sound like one."

He wiggles his eyebrows. "Speaking of wedding planners, anything going on with you and the wedding planner?"

Surprised, I scoff, since it's easier than looking at him. "Why would you ask me that question?"

He shrugs casually. "When I took the kids to the bookstore the other day, Lucy mentioned you'd been playing shuffleboard with Piper. I didn't know you guys were so into parlor games."

I clear my throat, doing my best to be honest with my buddy. "Seeing as we're best man and maid of honor, we thought we'd meet up, learn to play nice, and discuss some secret none-of-your-business wedding stuff."

What else can I say? The rest is on the tip of my tongue, but I don't want to take away from his moment. This is their time. Plus, it's best for the kids right now if Piper and I are on the down low. They're my priority. They lost their mother and came out the other side still healthy, still happy, still awesome. I need to be certain, to be sure. I don't want to rock their boat if I don't have to, or challenge their emotional fortitude till the time is right.

I'm not going to tell my best bud, especially since Charlie can't keep a secret for love nor money.

Honestly, though, I'd love to smack him on the back and say, *Yeah, something is going on with the wedding planner. I'm in love with her. How about them apples?*

I smile at the thought of Charlie's reaction. The guy would be ecstatic. He wants me to have this.

But like I learned in London, you have to do things in the right order. Tell people at the right time.

This is not that time.

29

PIPER

We don't go to the Lucky Spot to hear Malone sing. I'd like to say it's because it doesn't work out with a sitter, but the truth is—between God, me, and the lamppost—I don't invite Zach. I don't really know how we're supposed to act around friends of ours.

But I know one thing. A down-the-hall-from-each-other romance has its perks.

The first time we go out to lunch, our date is the stuff that movie romances are made of. We eat at a quiet café off the beaten path in the Village, and we talk about little things and big things over hummus and pitas. We trade stories from when we were younger and stories from the last few years too. He tells me about his toughest client, and I tell him about my most perplexing —the one who wanted to walk into her wedding on water. He asks where I most want to go in the world.

"*Everywhere.* I'm not picky. I am voracious. But I'll start with Italy."

"Italy is great. Lucy loved Rome and Venice."

I roll my eyes. "Your kids have traveled more than I have."

"They do seem to get around," he deadpans.

"You've always taken them to lots of places?"

"I want them to experience the world. I want them to understand what a great big place it is."

"I'd just like to experience Tuscany."

He takes a drink of his iced tea. "I bet Tuscany is nice."

"You've never been?"

He shakes his head, and I make a mental note to steal him away to Tuscany someday where he can be all mine, only mine.

We do lunch again the next day and the next.

The best part of these trysts? Well, besides getting to know him more?

The office sex.

On a Friday afternoon after sandwiches, we slip into his quiet office, since his assistant is out.

He sits down in the chair, I tell him to unzip his pants, and I treat him to a world-class blow job. He tastes good, he smells good, and he makes the most fantastic sounds. Groans and grunts and rasps and growls. It's all so masculine, so carnal. His sounds get me going—they drive me on. His hands do too. They twine in my hair, tangling up in it, tugging me close as he finishes.

In fact, this becomes such a wonderful *dessert* to our lunches that we do it again the next week. Lunch becomes our thing.

We sneak away for midday meals, even though it's

not truly sneaking. But it feels a little bit that way. Sometimes they last an hour, sometimes they're thirty minutes, and inevitably, they end on his desk, in his chair, on my desk, in my chair, or on the couch. One time, they end up against the door of my office with his hand over my mouth and me biting down hard on his thumb so no one hears me.

The next day, we go for takeout and pop into a secondhand bookshop. He pulls me down an aisle and kisses me hard by Greek history, then presses his teeth against my collarbone, leaving what I can tell will be a faint imprint.

"There. I want that to be your memory of being kissed in a bookstore," he says.

"You really do love marking your territory."

"I really do. So much that I'll mark you again."

I don't say no to that. I like being marked by him. I like being his.

* * *

The next day, I meet Jessica for her final fitting. As we walk to the bridal shop, I update her on the quickie wedding plans, since everything is coming together for her nuptials. But as I tell her about the reception food, she clutches her stomach and nearly doubles over. I reach for her arm. "It sounds that bad?"

She rises, straightening, shaking her head. "The summer, the heat," she moans, then she stares at me with wide imploring eyes. "I don't want to have morning sickness when I walk down the aisle. Can you please make that go away too?" She presses her palms together in prayer. "Pretty please, with sugar on top, world's greatest wedding planner?"

I laugh, wrap my arm around her, and guide her down the street and into the cool air conditioning of the dress shop. "I'm good, but no one is that good. That said, I will do everything I can to make sure you have crackers and whatever sort of anti–morning sickness potions and voodoo mixers and elixirs there are."

She throws her arms around me, and a little tear rolls down her cheek. "Thank you. I'm so damn emotional. I'm the poster child for a pregnant woman."

"You *are* a pregnant woman, so that's a very good thing."

She heads into the dressing room for her fitting and I sit on a plush dove-gray chair waiting to give the final verdict on her dress. She calls out from the dressing room, "I wanted to tell you—Graham is coming to the wedding."

He's Charlie's good friend, so that makes sense. "That's great. Do you need me to plan a role for him or something?"

She chuckles softly. "No, silly. I was just thinking that maybe I could try to get you two together again."

My shoulders tighten.

I've been able to tell her about others, even Jensen. She knew how I felt when I met him. She knew, too, how I felt when we unraveled.

This is the moment where I should be able to tell her about Zach, to share that I'm seeing someone. That I've fallen hard for someone. That I'm wildly, insanely in love with a guy I never expected.

Instead, this is the moment when I have to swallow whole that bubble of happiness, that effervescent, floaty, electric feeling you get when you can finally tell your good friend.

How I want to have that with Jessica. I want to blurt out my true heart and have her throw her arms around me and say, *I'm so happy for you.*

But Zach and I are a secret.

Are we a dirty secret?

I cringe inside, then shake off the unpleasant feeling.

That's not what we are. We're simply two smart adults taking it slow because there's so much at stake.

First and always foremost are the kids. You can't just parachute down and say *ta-da, we're dating, hope it works out* to any young children, let alone a pair who lost their mother. Besides, who knows where things will be with Zach in another few weeks?

A flash of memory crosses my eyes.

White lace, pearls, a giddy grin as she tried on a dress. Was it my mom's third, or her fourth, that I'm remembering?

This memory isn't random.

It's because I'm in a bridal shop, a place where I was practically raised. Ever the bridesmaid, helping my mother down the aisle as she sought love again and again and again.

She never loved anyone like my dad. My stomach twists in a painful knot. Would it be like that with Zach?

Would I be my mother's husbands? Always second best to the one he truly loved?

That's reason enough to keep this romance inside me.

Just in case.

I answer her, wholly truthful, "Thank you, but I didn't really have any spark or chemistry with Graham."

"Too bad."

The door cracks open with a squeak. She steps out. I stand and gasp. She looks stunning in a summer wedding dress, casual and perfect for a beach ceremony.

Jessica giggles, and this is one of the few times a grown woman can giggle and not seem completely silly. "Does it look good?"

"You look absolutely incredible. We're talking better than Meghan and better than Kate."

She waves a hand. "No one's better than Meghan or Kate."

"I don't know, sweetheart," I say to her. "You're pretty damn close."

I walk over to her, put my hands on her shoulders, and spin her in front of the mirror. "You look radiant."

"I feel radiant. It's crazy. But it's awesome too."

She returns to the dressing room, but with one hand on the knob, she stops and looks at me. "But is there anyone you feel that kind of spark with? Like you did with . . ." She lets her voice trail off, but I know she's speaking of the man I said *I do* to years ago.

My gut clenches. I'm dying to tell her the truth about Zach, but now isn't the time.

I deflect airily. "Someday, I'm sure. After all, aren't

we always searching for sparks? I'm glad you found yours."

"I've definitely found sparks."

I've found them too. But do sparks like this suffice? Are feelings this strong ever enough to overcome the hurts of the past and the hurdles of the present?

Jessica shuts the door, and my shoulders sag with the weight of all new worries.

30

PIPER

I'm on pins and needles for twenty-four hours.

I'm nothing but nerves frayed thin, unraveling as I wait for good news.

It comes on the Monday afternoon before the wedding, when Paige calls. Through tears of joy she blurts out that she's going home from the hospital with her baby girl.

I scream. It is an epic shout of happiness.

No, happiness isn't a strong enough word. This is elation. It's glee, bliss, and delight all stirred up together in the most wonderful cocktail, and I drink it down in one gulp as I hang up the phone.

There's a knock on my door, and Lucy pops in. It must be after camp for her. "Are you okay?"

I squeal again, clasping her shoulders. "That was a happy scream. My sister and her wife just went home from the hospital with their baby girl."

Lucy jumps up and down. I grab my purse, slinging

it on my shoulder and glancing at my watch. "I'm going to see them now at their house."

Lucy's eyes go wide. "Can I go with you?"

"Of course." I'd say yes to anything right now. *Can you take me horseback riding down Fifth Avenue?* Absolutely. *Can I adopt a Chihuahua puppy?* Let's do it. "But ask your father first."

Lucy rushes down the hallway into his office, and a minute later, Zach steps into the hall, a smile on his face. "Baby is healthy? Birth parents signed the consent? Everything's a go?"

"Everything is fantastic, and yes, both parents signed the consent. We're going to meet the baby. Lucy wants to come. Is that okay?"

"It's great."

I shoo Lucy along. "Let's go, let's go. I have a niece to meet."

She stuffs her phone in her yoga pants pocket and declares, "Ready, Freddy."

"Do you want to go with us?" I ask Zach curiously. He likes kids. He seems excited. Maybe I should bring him?

"I would love to, but I have a call with a client. I can't wait to see pictures, though. Will you send me pictures later?"

"I will."

* * *

An hour later, I'm holding my niece for the first time. "She is gorgeous and perfect," I tell her moms.

Lucy pipes in, "Can I hold the baby? I used to hold my brother when he was little, and I'm really, really good at it."

Paige nods, patting the cushion on the couch. "Of course you can."

Gently, I pass Lucy the baby, and she sits with her. She looks like the most well-trained, well-behaved older sister ever. My heart climbs up my throat, thumping loudly as I gaze at the two girls, a decade apart. Neither one shares my blood, but I've come to love the older one, and I'm in insta-love with the new little lady.

And that seems the right path for both. Both girls have claimed a piece of me, and I don't want to let either one go.

With emotions swelling inside me like a high tide, I take a few pictures as Lucy rocks the baby, singing "Hush, Little Baby, Don't You Cry." Once again, I tear up. Paige and Lisa do too.

"How do you know that song?" I ask her.

"I used to sing it to my brother," Lucy says matter-of-factly. "Like I said, I'm a really good babysitter. I can babysit for her. Wait, what's her name?"

Lisa clears her throat. "We're naming her Katherine."

"Beautiful," I say.

Lisa continues. "Katherine Piper Radcliffe-Foster."

I freeze.

And for the fiftieth time in as many minutes, I'm in tears.

"We wouldn't have her without you," Lisa adds. "We're so grateful."

I'm speechless. I don't know what to say, or how to even attempt to speak.

When we leave later that evening, Lucy takes my hand. "Can we visit her again soon?"

I say yes.

All I want is to do that again with this little girl.

And all I want is to do it again with this little girl and her father.

Especially when I show him the pictures when I bring Lucy back to his office. We're shoulder to shoulder, and Lucy's in front of him, leaning back against his chest, Henry parked in the desk chair drawing dinosaurs, as I flip through photos on my phone.

Zach takes his time with each picture, studying them, pointing out little details like the baby's fingers and her thick hair as he hums, ahhs, and murmurs, and I fall a thousand times deeper. I don't know that I want to have my own kids. I'm not even sure parenthood is in the cards for me, but the reminder that this man is such a family guy is a ray of sunshine in my soul. It says something about who he is, his values, his goals.

Being the best dad he can be has always been his top priority, and that is mega sexy.

"I'm definitely going to start outsourcing you, Lucy," he says, tousling her hair.

"What's outsourcing?"

"It means I'm going to rent you out to families who need sitters. You can finally start earning your keep, now that I know you're a sitter extraordinaire."

She giggles. "Fine. I'll do it because then I can make

enough money to adopt a rescue kitten. I wrote a list of everything kittens need."

She has a *plan* for a rescue kitten? And a list? May God have mercy on my soul because, like that, I'm falling harder for her too.

That's the problem.

This ten-year-old child has become the biggest hurdle, it seems, between having it all with her father and having only some of him.

Soon, soon, something has to give. There's nothing I want more than to make it all work.

31

ZACH

I have a doctorate in law, but after the last month, I'd like to submit my candidacy for an advanced degree in calendar engineering.

A Master of Science in Time Management, if you will. I've become brilliant at making the most of every unaccounted-for slot in my calendar to see Piper, take her out to lunch, shoehorn in dinner, or spend the night with her. And I'm still firing on all cylinders at work, looking out for clients like Taylor as we finalize her divorce, and kicking ass as a dad.

I'm juggling parenting, career, and new romance like a goddamn circus clown superstar.

Something, incidentally, I never thought I'd compare myself to. But it feels fitting—I'm doing life better than Bozo.

And tonight, this unclaimed hour in my schedule when it turned out Miranda wanted to take both kids to a festival in Chinatown, belongs to Piper and me.

I don't know how I'll get any alone time with her in

Anguilla, so I'm drinking it up now. I'm imbibing it, devouring as much time with her as I can.

We're in her apartment, with the early evening sun shining brightly through the bedroom window as she arches beneath me.

Her legs are wrapped around me as I move in her, slowly and luxuriously, taking our time.

She threads her fingers through my hair, meeting my gaze for a moment. The look in her brown eyes is wondrous and vulnerable. Then she closes them and lets out the most delicious moan. Soon she lifts her hips faster, grips me tighter. She's getting closer, racing toward the edge of pleasure, toward the endgame of desire, so I rock deeper, giving her what I know she needs to find her release, to fly down the other side of bliss.

When she's there, she says my name in a plaintive whisper, and something breaks inside me. Something breaks beautifully as I follow her.

It's not the awareness of how I'm feeling. I'm not a stupid guy. I'm smart, and I've known for weeks what's been happening.

Instead, it's the acceptance of it. The surrender to it.

To falling ridiculously in love again.

After, as I run my hands through her hair, I sigh, whispering, "What are you doing to me?"

"I don't know. What *am* I doing to you?" She drags her nails down my chest playfully.

I stroke my thumb along her jaw and give her all my truths. "You make me feel so many things. You make me feel everything. For the longest time, I never thought I would feel this way again."

She trembles, and her eyes flash with the same surrender that's inside me. "How do you feel?"

I don't look away. I can't. "I would hope it's patently obvious that I'm in love with you. But just in case, let me say it." I cup her cheeks. "I'm in love with you, and I love you madly, Piper Radcliffe."

A gorgeous smile takes over her face, bigger and wider than I've ever seen, more luminous than any other that's graced her lips. "I'm not going to say I had a feeling you were, but I had a feeling you were."

I laugh and tickle her hip, loving that she still finds ways to tease me and needle me. Her expression turns serious. "I'm wildly in love with you, Zach Nolan."

When you open your whole damaged heart that's not so broken anymore—in fact, it's not broken at all, and it's definitely not made of iron or of ice—the only thing to do is kiss.

We kiss for minutes, gorgeous, passionate minutes that threaten to spill into an endless night in bed together if I don't go.

But the clock is ticking, and I need to leave.

I need to figure out what to say to Henry and Lucy. I need to tell them the right way because the last time I felt this way for someone, she left our lives far too soon. My natural instinct is to protect them, to protect them ruthlessly like a shark, like a tiger, like a papa bear, from any other hurt.

Oh, if I could only protect them from hurt for the rest of their lives, I'd do it in a heartbeat.

But I'll never be able to, so all I can do is make sure I'm not the one inflicting the wounds.

I get dressed. "I'll get things sorted out, Piper. We'll figure it out soon. I can't wait much longer. I promise."

Sitting, she runs a hand down my arm. "I know. I'm not worried. I'm not worried about a damned thing."

32

PIPER

That's the truth.

I'm not worried.

I was before in the bridal shop, when I thought about my mom.

But now, alone with my thoughts, they don't scare me anymore.

Dressed in a T-shirt and yoga pants, I pour myself a glass of water, replaying the night, trying to figure out what changed.

As I down a thirsty gulp, I'm struck with a thought. An amazing, beautiful thought. One that surprises me but delights me too. There was no earth-shattering change. No aha spotlight from above.

Just acceptance.

And mine is this: I'm not my mother, and I'm not her husbands.

I believe great love comes around more than once in a lifetime, and you have to grab it, hold it, and treat it like the precious gift it is.

For a while, I stressed that I might be the first of many for Zach, like my mom's half dozen were for her.

I'm refusing to worry about that any longer.

Not at all.

Not one bit.

Because tonight with him felt like a defiance of second best. We thumbed our noses against the idea that new love never compares.

Second chances rock.

And I'm loving mine, and his.

There are no guarantees, no promises. But I'm embracing this chance with him, and he's embracing it too.

I refuse to compare him to my past, or myself to his.

He loves me for me.

With that thought—that wondrous thought— pressing against my mind, I decide to go to an evening spin class. I lace up my sneakers and head for the door. But first, my body reminds me that chocolate would be nice.

I riffle around in the cupboards, unearth a dark chocolate bar, and break off a square. As I chew, it hits me. I always get these chocolate cravings when I'm about to get my period.

I look at the calendar on my phone, counting back to my last one.

It should arrive soon. Maybe even tonight.

Only, it doesn't.

33

ZACH

I inhale the sea-salt air, drink in the tropical breeze. The sun beats down blissfully on my shoulders. "Fine. I'll admit it. You were right." I gesture to the wide-open waters; the calm, cool, placid Caribbean ocean in all its aquamarine glory; the blue skies stretching as far as the eye can see. "It's mildly pleasant here, I suppose."

Charlie snorts, leaning back against the railing on the boat, catching rays too as we bob near the sandy shore of a small snorkeling island. "It's not pleasant. It's paradise. I might move here."

The hotel's snorkeling instructor guides the kids in the nearby waters. I'm snorkeled out after three hours logged already today.

Plus, the concrete jungle of Manhattan offers little opportunity to relax and soak up the rays. Suits do nothing for my vitamin D levels, so I'm doubling down now. I'd like to say I avoid the sun like the plague, wearing big straw hats and swim shirts, but a man has to have some vices.

The sun is my drug.

I can't resist it, and I must have my fix.

But Lucy made me wear sunscreen this morning. Lucy's vigilant with sunscreen.

I'm confident Anna left that in a set of instructions for her daughter. It's a damn good rule, along with the others she passed on to Lucy.

Eat your vegetables, but make room for ice cream; always wear sunscreen; and don't forget to chase your dreams and tell the people you love that you love them.

Pretty damn good advice.

So it's SPF 50 slathered all over me. I turn to Charlie. "Hey, are you guys still moving to London?"

Charlie shakes his head. "Nope. Jessica wants to be near family and her family's in New York."

I shoot him the side-eye. "Thanks, asshole. For letting me know."

He arches a brow above his shades. "You could have asked me sooner. Also, isn't that what I just did? Like right now? I let you know."

I smile inside.

I am immensely happy. Life is insanely good. Charlie will stay in the city, my kids are fantastic, and Piper is one of the most awesome things to ever happen to me. Who expected that twist in the story? But there it is. Her and me, and soon we'll be able to *come out*.

I wish we were able to be open about it here. To walk around this island exploring it together.

I flash back over the last few days here, as the group of us trekked through limestone caves and swam with turtles, tagging them for a conservation group and giving Lucy another item to check off her list. What would that have been like if we weren't on the down low? A hand held here, a touch there, a kiss on the cheek now and then.

I picture Piper as she made her way through the caves yesterday, chipper and cheery as always.

Too cheery?

Maybe it's wedding planner stress. Everyone else is enjoying the tropical escape, and she's likely mired in worries like *What if the centerpieces don't arrive on time?* or *Will the cake melt in the sun?*

But then, she's never given off the worrying vibe.

She's the consummate pro, pulling off her job like an unshakeable quarterback in the huddle.

As soon as that thought touches down, something stirs in me.

I'm not always the most sensitive guy. But over the years, I've become more astute at reading women. Sometimes when they're too bright and shiny, it means something has gone dark inside. Something is nagging at them.

I make a note to find her later at the rehearsal dinner and ask how she's doing, discover if something truly is wrong.

For now, I return my focus to the groom. "I couldn't be happier that you're staying in New York," I tell Charlie, because there's something that feels remarkably good about letting the people in your life know that you want them in your life. Especially this guy. He's pushed and prodded me and done everything he can to help me be happy again. Even if I never went out with whoever he tried to set me up with, knowing that he gave more than a couple flying fucks matters deeply. "And in case I haven't said it, I do appreciate all the ways that you have given me a hard time for the last few years. You might not realize it, but it's made a difference."

He arches a brow. "Something you want to tell me?"

I laugh. "I'm just saying thanks. That's all."

"And you're welcome." He leans a little closer. "Also, not to further spoil my own news, but I'm going to ask you to be godfather to my kid. Don't let on to Jessica. She's a vault when she has to be, and she rides me for not being one, so keep this on the down low. I'm not actually supposed to tell you we want you to be the godfather until she's eight months pregnant, not two-and-a-half months, but—"

"But you're shit at keeping secrets?"

He shrugs helplessly, his eyes crinkling at the corners. "You know me so well."

"Thank you. I'd be honored. And I know I've said it before, but congrats again on joining the six a.m. club."

"But I'm going to enjoy the next several months of not waking up early."

A spray of water lands on my chest, my face, my arms. I turn to see my two favorite people climbing up the ladder and onto the boat, splashing me as they go.

I'm ready to jump in and splash back when Henry shouts, "Daddy, I saw a huge shark!"

I stand at attention, scanning the seas instantly. "Where? Is everyone okay?"

Henry laughs, his hand on his little belly.

Lucy chimes in, "JK."

My heart rate has spiked to one thousand miles a minute, and it doesn't calm down right away. "Don't scare me."

Lucy points at me, laughing. "You're the shark. You always say you're the shark."

Charlie glances at me, chuckling. "They got your goat."

She sure did. I haul my girl in for a hug, then hand her a towel. Grabbing another one, I dry Henry's hair a little bit, and soon we motor to the hotel's beach then head inside the resort.

We retreat to our rooms to get ready for an early rehearsal dinner. Once she's showered and dressed in a peach sundress, Lucy informs me she needs a purse tonight. I don't think she's used a purse before. But she's ten, so maybe now is when girls start.

"Did you bring one? Or do you need to make a quick trip to the hotel's sundry shop?"

She rolls her eyes. "Of course I brought one, Dad. I need someplace for my stuff." She darts into her adjoining room and returns a minute later with a tiny light-blue purse slung across her chest. It looks empty, but far be it from me to question the ways of women and accessories.

She grabs Henry's hand, declaring she's ready to tackle youngest bridesmaid duties at dinner.

At the restaurant, Jessica asks Lucy if she can sit next to Charlie's five-year-old niece. Lucy says yes and proceeds to grab the crayons and help blonde-haired Becca draw on the paper tablecloth throughout dinner. They illustrate an entire barnyard full of animals, while

I keep hunting for a chance to check in on Piper, who's busier than St. Peter on a bad day.

When dinner is through, and guests mill about dancing to island music and waiting patiently for dessert, Lucy pulls me aside to a corner of the restaurant's wide-open deck. The look in her blue eyes is resolute. "Remember my summer list?"

I bend lower, so we're at the same level. "How could I forget?"

"I've done almost everything on it."

"London, sundaes, snorkeling, turtles, mini golf, and being a night owl. Check, check, check, check, check, check."

She offers the start of a smile. "But there was something on it I wasn't sure if I was ready for."

"I remember. '*Share something that's hard to share.*'"

She takes a breath. "I think I'm ready."

"Bring it on."

"You know how I've been studying all sorts of letters?"

"Sure."

"I like to look letters up online, and I want to tell you why I've been studying them," she says, lifting her chin like she's hunting for her own confidence. "I've been doing it because . . . have you ever heard of those *you may want to marry my husband* letters?"

Furrowing my brow, I try to process where she might be going. I'm only vaguely familiar with the concept from the *New York Times* essay section. "A little bit. Tell me more?"

She takes a deep breath as if she's steeling herself.

"There was an article a couple years ago. One of my friends' moms mentioned it then. This woman who was really sick wrote a letter, and it was published in the newspaper, and it said, '*You may want to marry my husband.*'"

Every muscle in me tenses. A couple years ago.

Before Anna died.

Is this the letter Lucy's been holding on to? Her words from the start of the summer echo sharply in my mind. *It's just a letter. I'll share with you soon. When it's right. I've had one for a while that I want to show you.*

A strange and thoroughly unexpected dose of fear runs through me. I don't know that I can handle it if Anna gave one to Lucy for some reason, maybe for safe-keeping until she thought I was ready.

Because . . . I don't want to face a ghost.

I said goodbye to the ghost.

I've grieved for the ghost, and I've let her go.

I swallow past the Sahara Desert in my throat. "I know what you mean."

She sighs heavily, relieved. "Oh good. That makes things easier. I was waiting for—"

Jessica pops over, pointing to Lucy. "There you are!"

A second later, a blonde Tasmanian devil nearly tackles Lucy, grabbing her hand and shouting in glee, "Ice cream time!"

Ice cream—the universal trump card.

Lucy tells me we'll talk later, then darts off with Jessica, Henry, and Becca to the ice cream table.

Later.

We'll finish talking about this letter later.

A letter that has churned up the sand on the seafloor.

But I have to let it go for now, because I see the wedding planner marching the other way, toward the hall. She glances back briefly, and I detect that look again, that too-bright look in her eyes.

She's never like this. Something is off. I dismiss thoughts of letters I maybe don't want to read.

This is my present. This is what I need to read—this woman.

She leaves the restaurant, and I follow her.

34

PIPER

This is not okay.

I don't do this.

I don't escape to the bathroom.

But I'm a spring, bubbling up, overflowing with emotion, and I won't let on in front of the bride.

I rush into a stall and close the door.

When I'm done, I exit and exhale a wobbly breath. I wash my hands, scrubbing them, then splash cold water on my face. I take another breath, another yoga mantra I pluck from thin air since I'm no yogini. I press my hands against the sink, needing support, needing balance.

Maybe I should do a freaking tree pose. Better yet, I'll be a flamingo.

Still, I'm shaking. Do flamingos shake?

I close my eyes, trying to find my center. Or is it a chakra?

"Are you okay?"

The voice carries across the small restroom.

I snap open my eyes, stare at my reflection and his, and finally, *finally*, breathe again. I meet Zach's gaze in the glass. Concern is written across his forehead.

I point to the door. "Can you lock it?"

"Of course." He does as I ask, then walks over to me at the sink, clasping my shoulders fiercely, spinning me around. His lips are a ruler. His jaw is set. "What's going on, Piper? Are you okay?"

I purse my lips, nodding. "I just got my period."

He smiles faintly, a question mark in his grin. "That's a good thing?"

I nod, relief flooding my veins. "But I didn't get it on time. I'm three days late. I was supposed to get it in New York. It showed up a few minutes ago, and I'd been freaking out, and I was so scared that I couldn't even handle the idea of taking a pregnancy test in case it was positive. I didn't know what I'd do. And I'd finally pep-talked myself into buying one tonight if I didn't get it. But I did, and I'm so relieved." I draw a deep breath, desperately needing air as the worries, the what-ifs, the what-does-this-mean all spill free in a tumble of words. My voice is two sizes too small, and I sound like a twenty-something, but I *need* to talk. "For the last few days, all I could think about is what-if, what-if, what-if. What if I'm pregnant? I know we were safe, but things happen."

He nods, running his hand down my arm as if patiently waiting for me to talk more. And I do talk. It's all I do, because it's all I've *not* done the last few days. "The whole time I kept thinking, *What if I am?* What happens? I don't even know if I want to be a parent, but what happens? We haven't told your kids, and I feel like I'm breaking their trust. What if they saw us together? What if we were"—I flap my hands—"caught by them? That's so wrong. I'm breaking Lucy's trust. She's a friend, and she trusts me. And I can't pretend I don't have feelings for you. There's so much at stake, and what if we had done something so stupid . . ."

A fresh round of tears stops the words.

He steps closer, strokes my hair, and wraps his arms around me. His voice is low, but strong, so strong. "We would have figured it out."

I raise my face. "But how? How would we have figured it out?"

"I don't know. But I assume we'd have talked about it. We'd have sat down like adults. Because here's the thing: I love you." His tone is so fierce, so protective, like he's holding me up with it.

I can see why his clients need only him. He's a warrior, a shield, the one you want guarding your blind side.

"Because know this." His gaze never leaves mine. "Whatever happens to you, it happens to me now. Okay?"

I nod, my shoulders relaxing a tiny bit.

"I'm in this with you. We're in this together. We'll figure it all out together. I don't do things halfway, Piper. I don't love halfway. I don't care halfway. I'm all in. I love you completely, and I want to take care of you completely."

My heart. My God, I don't think there's room in my chest for it. It's overgrown its home. It needs a new house, one where light floods in because all the doors are open.

I wrap my arms around his waist, accepting his love, his need to care. It floods me, flowing through every cell, like liquid gold filling me up. "I want that."

"But do you want to have more kids?" He stops himself, laughing. "I don't know why I said it like that. More kids." He drags a hand through his hair, brow furrowing. "But I guess sometimes I feel like . . ."

He doesn't finish, but I know what he's trying to say. *Like his kids are mine.* "I understand. Sometimes you feel like . . ."

I trail off too, because I don't want to be so presumptuous as to voice it. But we both feel it.

He points to the door. "There's no more waiting for the right moment. I'm going to tell Lucy tonight. Because, let's be frank, Henry's pretty chill about everything."

I laugh. "He is pretty chill."

"But Lucy loves you. And I have to be honest. We can't wait for the next thing to happen. God forbid, what if something happens to you and Lucy wants to know why I'm sad that you broke a nail?"

I shoot him a quizzical look. "Please tell me you're not going to be upset if I break a nail."

He cups my cheek, strokes my jaw, and presses a soft kiss to my forehead, whispering, "You know what I'm saying."

"I do."

"It's not your nail I'm worried about."

I press a hand to his heart. "I don't worry about your

nails either. But I'm just so relieved, Zach." I need him to know where I stand. "I'm relieved because I'm not ready. I'm relieved because I don't know that I'm ever going to be ready. And I don't even know if you want more kids. Do you want more kids?"

A grin tugs at his lips. "I'm open to whatever happens with you."

A lump forms in my throat, pushing its way higher. "You are?"

His small grin transforms into a huge smile. "Whatever happens, I'm down with it. I am a lucky man, Piper. I have two healthy, amazing children. I have great memories that aren't shackling me or stopping me from moving forward, and I have you, an incredible woman in front of me, who I adore and want to keep adoring and loving for as long as you'll let me."

I scoff. "Let you! Let you? That's what I want too."

"That's my point." He gestures from me to him. "Don't you see? In a lot of ways, I have more than I ever expected. If you told me that you wanted to have a kid, I'd say, 'Let's go for it.' If you told me you don't ever want to, I'm cool with that too. Honestly, the only thing I don't want is for you to be sixty and tell me you're pregnant."

I laugh deeply. "I feel like that's probably not going to happen."

"Good. Because when you're sixty, we should be in Tuscany. Or here, snorkeling. Or just having a drink in Manhattan, looking back on the past twenty-five years. And laughing." He cups my face. "The thing I want most is for you to be sixty and still be with me."

There's nothing more I can say to that. Tears fall, and he kisses one cheek, then the other, then my lips, and it's the softest, most loving kiss I've ever felt in my life. I feel it in my mind, in my soul.

When he breaks it, he smiles widely. "You taste salty and sweet."

"Isn't that kind of how I am?"

He runs a thumb over my bottom lip. "That's exactly how you are."

I rise on tiptoe and brush my lips against his, whispering, "You're going to be so hot at sixty-two."

"Same to you. At sixty."

He drops his hand, threads it through mine, and tips his forehead toward the door. "Let me go wrangle the youngest bridesmaid away from the dessert table for a minute."

When we leave the restroom, the youngest bridesmaid is waiting for us, clutching her purse and a pale-blue envelope.

35

ZACH

Nerves crawl up my skin.

I can't do this now. If that's what I think it is, I won't do it now.

"Lucy," I say, a gentle warning.

She stares at me fiercely, her voice filled with fire. "Dad."

Holy shit.

She's my daughter through and through. She gestures to a rattan couch in the open-air hallway, pointing to the tropical-themed pillows on it. "I want to share this. Now is the right time."

I try again, because negotiation is not a one-and-done thing. "It's late. You can show me in the room."

She shakes her head. "It's for both of you."

Piper's brow knits, but she says nothing.

"Lucy, some things are private," I say. "Besides, I'd like to talk to you first."

The hallway is quiet, and she hops on the couch. "We can talk here."

She's so damn determined.

I sit next to her, and Piper takes the other side.

Lucy serves first, beating me like a horse out of the gate. She thrusts the letter out, but not to me.

To Piper.

The woman I love takes it, asking me with her eyes if she should wait.

I turn to Lucy, clasping her shoulder. She's the kid. I'm the parent. There is a right order to the universe. "Lucy, you seem pretty determined, but so am I. I need you to know that I'm in love with Piper, and we want to be together."

All the stars in the universe twinkle in her eyes. "Read it," she tells Piper, and I brace myself.

Have you ever read one of those you may want to marry my husband *letters?*

Scrubbing a hand across my jaw, I take a deep, fueling breath.

Waiting for Piper to read those words.

Words Anna wrote?

Words Anna left with Lucy for the next person?

Piper opens the envelope, unfolds a letter, and parts her lips, reading, "*You may want to marry my father.*"

I blink, snap my gaze to my daughter.

Her grin stretches to the edge of the galaxy.

Piper continues.

"*I've been working on this letter for a while, because there's so much to say. I could write a book! He deserves a book. But let me start with the basics.*"

The letter isn't from beyond.

It's from here. This is what she's been wanting to

share all along: her very own letter. I listen, waiting for more.

"*My dad is awesome. But don't just take my word for it. Let me share my list.*

"*One: He makes amazing waffles. With strawberries! And whipped cream. They are so delicious. I know what you're thinking. That's no big deal. But they are a big deal. They're so good, and the best part is he reads to us after he makes us waffles on weekend mornings. He reads* Goosebumps *to me, and* Clifford the Big Red Dog *to my brother, and I love to read too, so I'm reading* Harry Potter *to Henry because I'm awesome at reading. Girl power!*

"*Two: Also, speaking of girl power, my dad is great with girls. Like me. He let me polish his toenails a candy pink when I was six, and he let my friend Hannah and me put wigs on him at the party store last year. And he can braid my hair. My mom liked him a lot. Ha. It was way more than like. She loved him. Because he's so cool.*

"*Three: He's good with boys too. You should see him take care of my little brother. Henry is adorable and so chatty, and sometimes he's like a little koala, but my dad lets Henry cling to him when he needs to, and he always gives him good morning hugs and kisses and hellos. That's another thing!*

"*Four: I see him every day. I see him in the morning and at night and after school. He takes me to gymnastics and to art, and he goes to all my parent-teacher conferences, even the ones with Miss Jodie, who smells like onions and talks about the Revolutionary War without mentioning Hamilton, which is a super-boring way to discuss the war.*

"*Five: Plus, he listens when I talk. I like to talk to him about things that scare me, and things I hope will happen or worry will happen, and all my dreams for what I want to do someday. He doesn't push either. He wants me to tell him when I want to and how I want to. He respects my boundaries. He taught me that word.*

"*He teaches me lots of words, and then I get to use them in letters like this, so that's six.*

"*And this is seven: He teaches me lots of things. Like how important it is to tell people you love that you love them. He probably thinks that came from my mom, and yes, she told me to do that too. But he also says it. And he always tells me he loves me. And I don't forget it. I can't! His love is as big as the ocean. As deep as a canyon. As wide as the sky.*

"*Eight: He also gives great hugs.*

"*That's why you may want to marry my father. But you better love him as much as I do! Yours truly, his daughter, Lucy.*"

Lucy bounces, a bundle of energy, of anticipation. In her eyes, I can see a four-letter word.

Hope.

I'm not sure I can speak without breaking. Instead, I lean on the last few lines.

I reach for my girl, scoop her up, and hold her tight. Closing my eyes, I inhale her sweet daughter smell, and I let the emotions flood my soul, like a tsunami crashing over me. "I love you so much."

She nuzzles closer. "I love you too, but this isn't about you and me."

I chuckle through the lump in my throat, swallowing it back down as I open my eyes. "It's not?"

Lucy shakes her head. "It's about Piper. Well, I didn't

know it at the time. I wrote it a year ago, and I've been waiting to share it. It seems like the right time."

I look to Piper.

Her eyes are wet, rimmed with tears. The woman who was once my enemy, who seemed my opposite, who's become not only my lover, but my love, gazes at us with so much more than I ever expected I'd have again.

"She's awesome," I say softly, tenderly.

"I know!" Lucy declares. "You should marry her." She jerks her gaze to Piper. "And you should marry my dad."

"I probably should," I say, answering first, because that's not only the right order of the universe, it's also the truth. How could it be anything but? I told Piper I want to be with her when I'm sixty, and I don't mean as my booty call or a plus-one.

I want all of her for all of me.

I reach for Piper's hand. "What do you think, Piper?"

Her grin is nearly as big as Lucy's. "You probably should, but let's get the other couple down the aisle first."

Lucy clambers off my lap, drapes one arm around me and one around Piper, and sighs happily. "I wanted to share something hard, but it wasn't that hard. It was just right."

Just right.

That sounds exactly like what my life has become.

36

PIPER

The fiery orange sunset splatters itself across the horizon, painting the sky in brushstrokes of burnished gold and splashy fuchsia.

A white runner lines the sand on the way to the ocean, and twenty-two chairs are placed evenly on each side, with coral hibiscus bouquets arranged artfully on the top of each seat.

It's simple, but elegant.

Pretty, but not showy.

Just like the bride.

Who's indeed radiant as I wait with her on the edge of the sugar-soft crystals of sand.

The music is soft. Only a solo violinist plays as Lucy takes the first steps down the aisle in a pale-yellow sundress.

She reminds me of me at that age. But she also doesn't remind me of me. Because I know she won't become a perma-member of a parent's wedding party. Her father isn't the multi-marrying type.

How can I be sure?

Some things you just know.

I squeeze Jessica's hand, then I take my turn, walking down the aisle as both the wedding planner and the maid of honor.

I flash back to one of the first times I played double-duty in the bridal party and behind the scenes, for Sasha's wedding. That was the night I ran into Zach at the bar, more than a decade ago, when he placed a bet on the marriage. The wager ticked me off then, but it gives me an idea now.

I tuck that bet into my bouquet and walk toward the groom and the best man. Damn, the best man looks good in shorts and a white linen shirt.

I shoot him a small secret grin when I reach the end of the runner, taking my spot across from him. He smiles back at me, and when our gazes lock briefly, I feel sparks and desire, love and hope.

All in one person, all in one look.

Yes, I do love weddings something fierce.

They bring out all the emotions.

The good ones.

The music shifts, and all eyes turn to the bride heading down the aisle as the sun gently glides behind the sea.

Charlie's eyes brighten, shining with happiness. That's the way a man should look at the woman he's promising his forever to. The joy in Jessica's eyes is everything a groom could ever want.

As they pledge to love each other for the rest of their lives, Zach lifts a brow at me, sneaking a peek.

It's enough to send shivers down my spine. Shivers of happiness, of the start of our own happily ever after.

That's another thing I just know.

I zoom in on the bride, because if I keep staring at the best man like I want to eat him up, everyone at the whole damn wedding will know we're a thing.

Not just his kids, and let's be honest, the over/under on them spilling the beans soon isn't in our favor. Henry was indeed chill about us being a couple when we told him last night. He said, "Cool!" then he asked if I could read *Harry Potter and the Prisoner of Azkaban* because his sister had started the series, but he preferred my version of an English accent.

And I read him the first chapter in my best posh tone.

He promptly fell asleep.

I don't know if that meant I flubbed it, or he was zonked.

I left their suite, kissing Zach chastely on the cheek.

Maybe tonight there will be unchaste kisses.

A woman can dream.

* * *

Zach doesn't need to clear his throat or tap a champagne glass. His voice is that commanding. His presence is too, when he stands for the toast. "Anyone want to hear all of Charlie's dirtiest secrets from college? Wait. Scratch that. How about his investment tips and insider insight into the hottest new companies to make you a gazillion bucks?"

The attendees laugh and cheer their yeses.

Zach strides in front of the head table. "Yeah, me too. Charlie, time to share. Serve it up, man." Charlie laughs, and Zach claps his friend's shoulder. "But seriously, though, this man has already shared so much. Let's give a big round of thanks to the man and woman who flew us to this gorgeous island, put us up, and entertained us, both in the Caribbean and in London."

Everyone claps, and Charlie and Jessica bow their heads. "We are the lucky ones because you're all here," Charlie says.

Zach lifts his glass. "We are all indeed the lucky ones, to be surrounded by friends and family. Let's raise a glass to that: To being here. To love. To finding that special someone."

His eyes meet mine, and he holds my gaze as he takes a drink.

A little later, as the kids boogie and the newlywed couple dances at the reception, with waves gently lapping the shore mere feet away, I make my way to the best man at the bar, ordering a scotch.

I opt for wine, then tip my forehead toward the couple. "What's the over/under?"

He laughs, dragging a hand through his hair. He takes a deep breath then stares at Jessica and Charlie, studying them from a distance. "Judging from the way he looks at her like she's the center of his world and how she smiles at him like he's the key to her happiness, I'd say it's a can't-lose bet. Also, have I mentioned they only have eyes for each other?"

I tap my chin, as if in thought. "Why, yes, you did say that."

"It's a good sign," he adds, deadpan.

"Are you trying to tell me something?"

He inches closer. "Woman, when it comes to betting on me, you better be all in because that's where I am."

I laugh so hard I nearly snort. "Good. Because I never want to use your professional services."

He wiggles his eyebrows. "You can use my other ones."

"And what are those?"

His answer comes in a smoky whisper. "The ones where I make you come over and over."

Tingles spread over my arms. "You are cocky."

"Just confident."

"It's been a while though. At least a few days," I tease. "Are you sure you can still get me there?"

"Is that a challenge?"

"What else would it be?"

But before he can flirt back, Charlie and Jessica swing by. The bride shoots us an overly exhausted look. "Are you guys *finally* going to come out of the closet?"

"What do you mean?" I scoff, trying to play it cool.

Charlie pats Zach's back. "Don't play coy. It's about time. I've been suspecting you two for months."

"We both have," Jessica adds.

My jaw drops, but I say nothing.

Jessica points at me. "That's cute that you act surprised."

I still can't speak.

"It's so obvious. '*Shuffleboard*'?" She sketches air

quotes. "Secret wedding stuff? I mean, it's admirable and smart, and I get it. But we aren't fooled."

"I wanted to focus on you," I say, trying to regain my footing.

She squeezes my arm. "And I love you for it, but really, I'm all good. And you two should go get a room."

I protest with "It's your reception."

Jessica casts a glance at the dance floor. "And my wedding planner and good friend handled it so well that everything is going perfectly. We'll watch your kids for half an hour. Go."

"Seriously?"

"The pheromones radiating off you guys are too much to take," Charlie says dryly.

"Also, we need more than thirty minutes," Zach adds.

Charlie laughs. "Doubtful."

But you don't look a gift horse in the mouth. When we're alone, I remind him, "You do know I have a visitor. That means it's time for that mandatory rain check."

His smile is devilish. "Like I said, life is insanely good."

And it is for me too, when I'm on my knees in my room a few minutes later, taking him in my mouth and bringing him to the brink of ecstasy.

His sounds thrill me. His hands in my hair turn me on too much. Most of all, the way he groans my name when he gives in to all the pleasure feels like one more promise between us.

A promise of intimacy, of love, of openness.

When I look up at him, his blue eyes are hazy and so

damn happy. "And you're getting a rain check too. I can't wait to return the favor."

Yeah, we love each other a whole helluva lot, it seems.

So much for frenemies.

37

PIPER

A few days after we return to Manhattan, I meet one of my favorite men outside the Lucky Spot in Chelsea.

He's gorgeous, friendly, and funny, and I've had him in my life for quite some time. I'm glad I convinced Adrien to meet me here for a drink tonight.

After he strides up to me, he kisses me on each cheek. "I told you so," he declares.

I gesture to the bar. "You sure did tell me so. Why do you have to be so wise?"

He shrugs then winks. "It comes with the territory." He opens the door and holds it for me.

"The territory of being a hair maestro?"

He laughs as we head inside and grab two stools at the bar. "Is that what I am now, a hair maestro?"

"You are the god of all updos. The master of locks. The magician of beauty."

He snaps his fingers. "I'm putting that on my new business cards."

We order wine, and he turns to me, lifts a brow, and

rubs his palms. "Okay, hold nothing back. I want to know exactly how right I was about every little thing."

I lean my head back, laughing. "Is there anything better than a good *I told you so?*"

"No. There isn't. Serve it up, love."

The wine arrives, we toast, and I tell him about Anguilla.

"Sometimes you need a tropical location to set the truth free," he muses.

"Stylist logic?"

"But of course." He raises his glass once again and takes a drink. "And I'm not surprised you're so fabulously in love. I did know it would happen." He reaches into the pocket of his jeans and produces a lollipop. Sour apple. He sets it on the bar. "I knew it was true love once you mentioned Blow Pops."

I crack up, dropping my face into my hand. "I cannot believe you brought a Blow Pop, and I definitely can't believe a Blow Pop story was the tip-off."

"It was patently obvious when you rambled about Blow Pops that he was the real thing."

I look up, more serious now. "He's definitely the real thing."

"Plus, you had this glow about you. I call it the love glow."

"And what does the love glow look like?"

He peers at me with narrowed eyes, as if he's appraising me. "Rosy cheeks, a woozy grin, and a certain dewy look in your eyes."

I stare into his gray eyes. "Speaking of, you look different. Are you love-glowing and not telling me?"

He touches his own cheek and answers playfully. "Do I look like I'm glowing?"

"Tell me, tell me. Did you meet someone?"

He's coy as he answers. "Maybe I did."

I punch his arm. "I thought you were into playing the field?"

"We all are till we meet that special someone."

"And you like this guy?"

He sighs dreamily, then tells me about Carlos, and how his new beau is sexy and funny—and devoted, it seems. "There are never any guarantees, but I think he might be my second chance."

I'll drink to that.

A few minutes later, Zach heads into the bar, walking straight over to us. He wraps an arm around me and drops a possessive kiss to my lips, then extends a hand to Adrien, introducing himself.

Soon it's time for Malone's set, so we make our way to the lounge section, snagging chairs and sitting with Dina, Heather, Charlie, Jessica, Steven, and Jason and Sloane. Friends from college, friends from Manhattan.

They all know. We're out in the open, and it's awesome.

One glance around, and I'm grinning.

A while ago, I didn't even invite Zach here. Now he's with me, arm draped around my shoulder, so clearly mine and I'm so clearly his.

The lights dim and the music begins.

He takes my hand, and when the set ends, he whispers in my ear, "Time for your rain check."

38

ZACH

One of the great things about not keeping a secret is, well, you don't have to keep a secret.

That means I don't have to remember incredibly clever cover-ups, like claiming I wandered down the halls in a hotel in the middle of the night

After the music fades at the Lucky Spot, I check in with my sister, who laughs and tells me never to check in again when she has the kids, since all is fabulous.

"Fair enough," I say, then the Lyft arrives and it takes us to Piper's home.

Do I feel guilty about not being with the kids tonight? Hell no. I want this time with my woman. It makes me a happier person.

And I am a very happy man when Piper unlocks the door to her apartment as I kiss the back of her neck, my hands roaming up and down her sides, her little murmurs and moans driving me on.

She tries to swat me away, saying, "You're so voracious. Let me get us into the apartment."

"Yes, I am voracious. And I make no bones about that."

She pushes open the door, and once it shuts behind us, I grab her hands and raise her arms above her head. I kiss her neck and travel up to her ear, nipping it as she murmurs the whole way. "You don't even want to make it to the bedroom?"

"Bedroom, couch, counter. I'm good with any and all of it."

She hums as if she's thinking.

I stop the kisses, tapping her temple. "What's going on up there?"

"I was just thinking that we never truly had angry sex."

I raise a brow. "Is that something you want?"

"Supposedly, it's really hot if you hate each other and then screw."

I laugh. "Happy to role-play. You want to go back to how we were?"

She adopts a more serious expression, narrowing her eyes as if she's firing bullets at me. "And is that what you think is going to get me into bed?"

I dive right into the routine. "You know you've been wanting me. I see how you stare at me at the office."

She scoffs as she walks down the hall. "I've never even given a thought to the way you look naked."

"And yet your body says otherwise."

She stops in the bedroom doorway, glancing back. "And what do you think my body is saying to you?"

My gaze travels up and down her sexy frame. "That

you want me to strip off all your clothes and fuck you hard and senseless."

She trembles as if on cue, but it's not acting—it's real. Taking a step closer, I grab her hair and kiss her neck hard. She shivers. I slide my hand down her body, between her legs. "And if I touch you right here, would I find out that you hate me or that you want me?"

With a shuddering breath, she answers, "Want, need, love."

The game is over, the roles shed.

We're us again, wanting and needing.

And giving.

In several seconds, she's flat on her back on the bed, clothes off.

I pepper kisses down her belly then back up, lavishing attention on her breasts. She pants and moans and gets me so damn turned on that I can't wait much longer.

I spread her legs, and my face is between her thighs. She tastes like heaven, and I don't know who's more aroused, her or me.

This is where I want to be. Consuming her. Driving her wild. Giving her all the pleasure she deserves till she's crying out in a glorious soundtrack of bliss.

As her noises ebb, I move to my back, grab her hips, and guide her onto me. She sinks down, gasping as she takes me in.

Pleasure jolts through my body, and I slide a hand up her stomach, savoring the soft feel of her skin. "Want to watch you. Want to watch you chase your pleasure again."

"If you insist."

"I absolutely do," I say, thrusting up into her.

As her eyes squeeze shut, she lowers herself to my chest. She brings her mouth to my ear. "Fuck me and love me," she whispers.

And I've never been more turned on. Threading my hands in her hair, I pull tighter, harder. I bring her over the edge again, joining her on the other side of bliss.

Once she comes down, I stroke her hair. "Do me a favor, will you?"

"Maybe. Depends what it is," she teases.

"Remember our bet at the wedding last week?"

"Of course."

"Don't bet against us."

A smile is my reward as she says, "Never will I ever bet against us."

The next morning after we shower, I get dressed then ask what she's up to today.

"I'm heading to the park to meet my sister and the baby."

It seems so obvious. Why didn't I think of it sooner? "Do you want to go together?"

She smiles, soft and pretty. "Together?"

I roll my eyes. "Woman, we're together. You're going to see your sister's baby. I can meet my kids there. Let's go together. Let's be there together."

The smile that spreads across her face is magnificent. "That sounds lovely."

At the park, she holds the baby and chats with her sister as Lucy clambers up and down the climbing wall and Henry shows off all his new slide maneuvers. When Lucy scampers down for the five hundredth time, she bolts over to Piper and Paige. "Is it my turn?"

Paige hands her the baby, and Lucy coos and sings to her.

I observe them from a few feet away as Paige turns to Lucy. "Did we ever tell you our theory about the princesses?"

"I want to hear," Lucy says. So do I.

Piper laughs. "Here is what we think about The Little Mermaid."

After she shares her theory, Lucy nods thoughtfully. "She should have written him a letter. Letters can solve a lot of problems."

Yes, they can.

* * *

A few weeks later, the scent of waffles fills my apartment and Lucy stands by my side, chopping the tops off fresh strawberries. "I decided it was time for me to start helping you. I want to learn to cook now. You're a pretty good cook, aren't you?"

I pat her head and return to making the waffles. "Lucy, I'm pretty awesome at everything."

She leans her head against my arm for a moment. "You are. But I think you're really good at these waffles, and I'm really hungry."

"Then let's finish them. After all, it will be Piper's

first time having my extraordinary Sunday morning waffles. She's on her way."

"And we want to make sure they're amazing so she keeps coming back."

"We definitely want to make sure she keeps coming back."

Piper arrives shortly for our family breakfast date. At the counter, she takes a forkful and moans in culinary pleasure. "You're right, Lucy. These are absolutely the best."

When we're done, Lucy stares at me with big pleading eyes. "Can we please go shopping now, Daddy? I've been waiting so long."

Henry slumps onto the couch. "What am I supposed to do when you shop?"

"You're going to come along and be a most excellent companion," I tell him. "Besides, I just like it when you hang out with me."

Henry smiles. "I like that too."

He is indeed great company as I take the women on a very special shopping trip.

EPILOGUE

Piper

Once upon a time, there was a woman who wanted to go to Tuscany. But she wasn't willing to stow away in a bride's suitcase to reach her destination. For even though she was practical, she was first and foremost a romantic.

Luckily, a guy she loved told her he was taking her there for her birthday.

It's my birthday and the plane that'll take my man and me to Italy taxis on the runway. "Do you think the kids are okay?"

Zach laughs. "They're fine. My sister knows how to take care of kids."

"I know, but it's their first time without you."

"Without us," he corrects.

Summer has rolled into fall, so with the kids in school, this is a good time to get away.

He runs a finger down my nose. "Stop worrying."

"I'll do my best, but I promise nothing."

"So feisty."

"Same could be said of you."

An hour later, we're zooming across the ocean at thirty-five thousand feet as the lights dim and attendants treat us like royalty, having just served sundaes.

"Can you just do me a favor and always buy me first-class tickets? 'Kay, thanks, bye."

Laughing, he takes my hand. "I can promise you that, but I have to warn you, this might be your favorite flight of all."

"Why's that?"

He reaches into his pocket and takes out a velvet box. "Never have I ever fallen in love with a woman on an airplane. But I did earlier this summer on the way to London. That's when I started to fall in love with you."

My heart swells, thumping hard. "Same for me, with you."

"Never have I ever thought the woman who called me a Marriage Grim Reaper would fall in love with me."

I lean closer, unable to resist him. I press a kiss to his lips. "But I did, and I am."

He flips open the box, and I'm nearly blinded by the ring's beauty.

Just as I was when I picked it out.

"Never have I ever hoped so badly for your yes."

I cup his cheek. "You have it. You've had it for months."

The reality is this: I'm not surprised. We were pretty

much promised to each other in Anguilla, both by each other and again by his daughter.

I shopped for the ring with Lucy and Zach a few weeks ago. She helped me pick it out. He had it sized.

The only thing I didn't know was when.

And I couldn't be happier that *when* is right now.

He slides the ring on my finger, and I whisper, "Once upon a time, a wedding planner thought she despised the divorce attorney."

"But somehow, opposites attracted and enemies became lovers. And so much more."

"Sounds like a good story," I say.

He kisses me. "That's because it's true."

* * *

Early the next year, we marry.

When I say it's a simple ceremony, I mean it. We take our vows in the Raphael Room at the Luxe Hotel—discount rate, thank you very much—and we dance all night with our closest friends and family.

With Paige and Lisa and baby Katherine.

With Charlie and Jessica and their infant son, Callum.

With Zach's sister, Emmy, their mom, and my mom and her new boyfriend.

Our friends from college are here.

Adrien, my stylist and shrink, for all intents and purposes, is my "bridesman" and, naturally, he makes sure the rest of the ladies in the bridal party look fabulous. And I remind him how fabulous he's going to look at his ceremony in a few months when he marries Carlos. I'm planning that one, and I can't wait. The grooms are both gorgeous.

My friend Jason attends, snagging a minute to whisper a secret about how his best-man-for-hire business is changing, and I ooh and ahh and promise not to say a word till the time is right.

My good friend Kristen is here from Florida, with her husband, Cameron.

"Mini golf soon, girl? You owe me a game," she says, hugging me.

"Always mini golf. I'll beat you though."

"I know. You always do."

Sloane is here too, her belly huge since she's ready to pop any day. Her hubby dotes on her the whole time, and Malone even sings a song for our first dance: "It Had to Be You."

After we dance, Charlie taps a champagne glass and returns the favor Zach did him in Anguilla, making a speech with just enough roasting and ribbing. "I'm not as eloquent as this guy, so I'll keep it simple and say this: I saw them coming together from fifty miles away, and I couldn't be happier to be making this toast."

We all raise our champagne glasses, the kids' cups filled with ginger ale, of course.

That's the best part: that they're here celebrating with us.

Our kids.

Yes, they *feel* like mine. And they *are* mine. They wanted me to adopt them, so we filed the paperwork.

But we don't need paperwork.

We were already a family, and I have faith we always will be.

ANOTHER EPILOGUE

Zach

Maybe you *should* believe what you hear about me.

I can be a pretty good guy. A great guy, even.

But I don't always let on. Because sometimes you need a shark on your side.

I can play that role and I still do. I play it for all my clients. I take on the part for my kids when they need me to. Every now and then, I do that job for my wife, though she rarely needs any backup.

But if she does, I'm not afraid to go to battle for her.

Because I have a heart. Only it's not made of iron or ice. It's forged from fire, and it's sharpened by love.

Even though I might dismantle marriages for a living, I do it so those in the bad ones can have another chance.

There's nothing better than a second chance when it comes to love.

I found mine, and I'm not letting it go.

Never will I ever.

The End

Curious about Jason's romance? His story is told in INSTANT GRATIFICATION, available everywhere. You can also find more books in the Always Satisfied series of standalone romances in New York including OVERNIGHT SERVICE, Haven's love story with a hot, dirty-talking hero, available everywhere!

Top three reasons why sleeping with the enemy is a bad idea...

1. She's my fiercest rival.
2. She's also my firey ex.

3. We're going up against each other in a stiff competition to win the hottest new client on the market.

And yet, I'd like to be up against the wall in a stiff competition to get her to call out my name.

Time to double down on my resistance to her tough-as-nails, take-no-prisoners, sexy-as-sin attitude. The same attitude I find irresistible.

That's a big problem, because in this race to nab the client, I run into Haven in the hotel, on the beach, in the guest quarters late at night.

Hate sex would be a terrible idea.

Except, it's the complete opposite, and now we can't keep our hands off each other.

Trouble is, I'm not so sure it's hate I'm feeling anymore.

And that's the biggest reason sleeping with the enemy you're falling for is a bad idea — my job literally depends on never letting her into my heart.

Sign up for my newsletter to receive an alert when sexy new books are available!

ACKNOWLEDGMENTS

Big thanks to Lauren Clarke, Jen McCoy, Helen Williams, Kim Bias, Virginia, Lynn, Karen, Tiffany, Janice, Stephanie and more for their eyes. Love to Helen for the beautiful cover. Thank you to Kelley and Candi and KP. Massive smooches to Laurelin Paige for access to her brain and heart. As always, my readers make everything possible.

ALSO BY LAUREN BLAKELY

FULL PACKAGE, the #1 New York Times Bestselling
romantic comedy!

BIG ROCK, the hit New York Times Bestselling standalone
romantic comedy!

MISTER O, also a New York Times Bestselling standalone
romantic comedy!

WELL HUNG, a New York Times Bestselling standalone
romantic comedy!

JOY RIDE, a USA Today Bestselling standalone romantic
comedy!

HARD WOOD, a USA Today Bestselling standalone romantic
comedy!

THE SEXY ONE, a New York Times Bestselling standalone
romance!

THE HOT ONE, a USA Today Bestselling bestselling
standalone romance!

THE KNOCKED UP PLAN, a multi-week USA Today and
Amazon Charts Bestselling standalone romance!

MOST VALUABLE PLAYBOY, a sexy multi-week USA Today

Bestselling sports romance! And its companion sports romance, MOST LIKELY TO SCORE!

THE V CARD, a USA Today Bestselling sinfully sexy romantic comedy!

WANDERLUST, a USA Today Bestselling contemporary romance!

COME AS YOU ARE, a Wall Street Journal and multi-week USA Today Bestselling contemporary romance!

PART-TIME LOVER, a multi-week USA Today Bestselling contemporary romance!

UNBREAK MY HEART, an emotional second chance USA Today Bestselling contemporary romance!

BEST LAID PLANS, a sexy friends-to-lovers USA Today Bestselling romance!

The Heartbreakers! The USA Today and WSJ Bestselling rock star series of standalone!

The New York Times and USA Today
Bestselling Seductive Nights series including
Night After Night, After This Night,
and *One More Night*

And the two standalone

romance novels in the Joy Delivered Duet, *Nights With Him* and Forbidden Nights, both New York Times and USA Today Bestsellers!

Sweet Sinful Nights, Sinful Desire, Sinful Longing and Sinful Love, the complete New York Times Bestselling high-heat romantic suspense series that spins off from Seductive Nights!

Playing With Her Heart, a

USA Today bestseller, and a sexy Seductive Nights spin-off standalone! (Davis and Jill's romance)

21 Stolen Kisses, the USA Today Bestselling forbidden new adult romance!

Caught Up In Us, a New York Times and

USA Today Bestseller! (Kat and Bryan's romance!)

Pretending He's Mine, a Barnes & Noble and

iBooks Bestseller! (Reeve & Sutton's romance)

My USA Today bestselling

No Regrets series that includes

The Thrill of It

(Meet Harley and Trey)

and its sequel

Every Second With You

My New York Times and USA Today

Bestselling Fighting Fire series that includes

Burn For Me

(Smith and Jamie's romance!)

Melt for Him

(Megan and Becker's romance!)

and *Consumed by You*

(Travis and Cara's romance!)

The Sapphire Affair series...

The Sapphire Affair

The Sapphire Heist

Out of Bounds

A New York Times Bestselling sexy sports romance

The Only One

A second chance love story!

Stud Finder

A sexy, flirty romance!

CONTACT

I love hearing from readers! You can find me on Twitter at LaurenBlakely3, Instagram at LaurenBlakelyBooks, Facebook at LaurenBlakelyBooks, or online at LaurenBlakely.com. You can also email me at laurenblakelybooks@gmail.com